The *Ashwander* Rules

The *Ashwander* Rules

A Novel of the Supreme Court

Neal Rechtman

Columbus, Ohio

The *Ashwander* Rules: A Novel of the Supreme Court

Published by Gatekeeper Press
2167 Stringtown Rd, Suite 109
Columbus, OH 43123-2989
www.GatekeeperPress.com

ISBN: 9781642372786
eISBN: 9781642372779

Printed in the United States of America

"Our country is, after all, not a country of dollars, but of ballots."

—Louis D. Brandeis [LDB]
The Opportunity in the Law, 1905

Prologue

"If the government becomes the lawbreaker, it breeds contempt for law; it invites every man to become a law unto himself; it invites anarchy."

—LDB, dissent in *Olmstead v. United States*, 1928

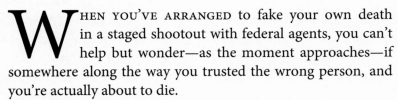

WHEN YOU'VE ARRANGED to fake your own death in a staged shootout with federal agents, you can't help but wonder—as the moment approaches—if somewhere along the way you trusted the wrong person, and you're actually about to die.

Amir Maitre, dual citizen of the United States and Cyprus, guided the Baker's Treat delivery van onto the shoulder of Maryland County Road 31 and stopped in the shadow of an abandoned rail trestle. A pilot by training, he thought in checklists: *gearshift in park, engine off, headlights off, sideview mirrors aligned.* He tapped twice on the door leading to the back of the truck and received the expected knock-knock reply.

The digital clock on the dash blinked 4:50 a.m. He slid open the driver's side window and savored the cool night air. He had ten minutes to reconsider, but it would hardly take that long: there were only three options. He could plead guilty to statutory rape and related charges in Georgia (it was all on video) and spend the next seven years in a place called Reidsville, a maximum security prison reputed to be sweltering during the summer and dangerous for pedophiles year-round. The second option was to plead guilty, surrender his U.S. citizenship and be deported back to Cyprus, where it was equally hot, and where he owed several hundred thousand dollars to various people—at least one of whom would be dangerous to encounter in person. The third choice was the path he was currently on: in exchange for his participation in one last arms deal—a sting that would hopefully draw out a key ISIS operative in the United States—he would be given a new identity and a new life through WITSEC, the federal Witness Protection Program.

And that was that.

Ain't America great? One day you're arrested for having sex with a minor in an Atlanta hotel room. The next day you learn you're on a U.S. Department of Homeland Security watch list. The following day you're flown in a private jet to Washington, D.C., and by the end of the week you're planning your new life as a shift manager in an auto glass distribution center in Eden Prairie, Minnesota.

He had asked if his new home could be somewhere in the North, some place with a lot of snow. This was intentionally brazen—he wanted to see what his handlers' reaction would be. When they didn't balk, and made inquiries and discussed specific relocation options with him, he took it as a sign that, for whatever reason, they really needed him. He imagined a scenario in which they had gone to great lengths to lure out their ISIS target, and all they needed to pull it off was a credible middleman. After almost five years of miscues and delays and no-shows, he was finally—when he least expected it—in the right place at the right time.

Or so it seemed. It was almost too good to be true, which is what made him wonder if it was.

His most serious reservations all centered on this slick ATF agent, Owen Petersee, the man in the back of the van posing as his second, who would soon shoot him in the chest. He was the prime mover of this whole operation. Petersee was the first federal agent to visit him when he was in the custody of the Atlanta police. He had accompanied him on the plane to D.C., removed his handcuffs, and proposed the arms deal/witness protection scheme during the flight. In all his interactions with other agents, Petersee was clearly leading, not following.

Amir also noted that Petersee spent a lot of time in private tablet communication with unknown third parties, and had come to the conclusion that there was some other agenda in play that superseded even this elaborate double-sting. The plan was to sell unarmed surveillance drones to an intermediary, a Qatari man named Khalid al-Jaber, and to then follow al-Jaber to a hoped-for rendezvous with Cadiz, the code name for the ISIS operative who was the ultimate target. As major an operation as this seemed—over seventy agents were deployed in the field, with helicopter support assigned— he was sure it was part of something bigger that he couldn't quite grasp. This made him uneasy. He'd been thinking his role was that of a bishop, or perhaps even a rook, in a chess game of a certain size. Now he was beginning to see he was more likely a pawn on a board much larger than he originally perceived. Instead of having strategic value, he may well be cannon fodder.

Not that he *really* believed he was about to die.

First of all, the idea of faking his death was all his own. The arrangement Petersee proposed during the flight to D.C. was a simple swap: participating in an undercover arms deal in exchange for dropping the sex charge and a new life in witness protection. Amir had agreed to this immediately. By the time they landed, however, the euphoria of his good fortune had faded. He realized that if he just disappeared, the people he owed money to would come after his family in Cyprus—his retired parents, his sister in Larnaca. He needed to find a way to be dead, at least for purposes of perception. This would settle his account and his family would be left alone; such was the esoteric moral math of the Mediterranean Mafia.

He knew not to propose anything to Petersee or his colleagues right away. He had pushed things far enough already. But a week later, after several days of intensive planning for what was dubbed Operation Cadiz Crossing, he saw a way that it might work, and pitched his idea.

Once again the Feds bit, and now he was wearing a $10,000 bulletproof vest designed to spurt fake blood when struck by bullets. Was it possible the vest would fail? Yes. Was it possible Petersee would accidentally miss and hit him in the head? Of course. Was it possible Petersee would intentionally shoot him in the head? He didn't think so, but he had learned long ago there's no way to know what's going on in another man's mind.

If any of the above happened, he reasoned, at least his family wouldn't be threatened or harmed. He was 29 years old and had been nothing but trouble for them for the last half of his life.

Headlights appeared in the side-view mirror. There was no other traffic; this was likely the drop. He sipped from a bottle of water while watching the mirror, the reflected light splintering into shards as an identical Baker's Treat van pulled alongside and shut off its headlights.

Amir put away the water, turned on his interior dome light for five seconds, posed for identification, then turned it off. The driver of the adjacent truck duplicated the signal, shifted into park, and turned off his engine. They both exited their trucks and met at the back.

Khalid al-Jaber was a tallish, dark-complexioned man with a shaved head and goatee who introduced himself in a Gulf-accented Arabic that Amir responded to with native ease. This was Amir's crucial contribution to the whole enterprise: the drones needed to be fronted by someone Al-Jaber would trust, and Amir had all the right credentials.

After the requisite formalities and exchange of eye contact, al-Jaber got down to business. "Our mutual friend tells me you can supply drones," he said, switching to English.

"All avionics," Amir replied. "Components, kits, whole systems. I have brought six Vulture drones tonight. Eighty thousand each; all six for four-fifty."

"I've brought my expert," al-Jaber said. "He can inspect?"

Amir nodded and both men rapped on the rear doors of their vans, which were quickly hoisted up from inside. After a nod from Amir, Petersee set a battery-powered floodlight on the floor of their truck and removed a green tarp fastened over two shelves normally used to stack bakery pallets. Shadows bounced around the inside of the van as he worked.

Al-Jaber's expert eased himself down the metal-rung ladder of the second van and approached his boss nervously. He was young, athletically trim, with a shock of jet-black hair. Under other circumstances he might be thought handsome; now his visible anxiety projected the aura of a computer nerd appearing before an inquisition of corporate suits.

"Vasili," al-Jaber said, "he has six Vultures. Please be good enough to take a look and tell me what you think."

"Vultures req-vire codes," Vasili replied in an accent Amir first pegged as East European, and then identified as somehow familiar. "They can have all ze hardware, all ze modules, but each unit req-vires unique code. Not just for launch but also to power up." Amir was now sure. This Vasili was someone he knew—but there was no time to sort it out.

Amir looked up toward Petersee, who was propping open the first of several coffin-sized, gray fiberglass crates, and signaled his approval with a single nod.

Petersee called down from the truck. "We have the codes," he said in a loud whisper. "You can run a loop test to check each one." He displayed a plain 3-ring binder, and gestured for Vasili to climb up and join him. Amir intervened, boosting himself up into the truck first. "One moment, please," he flashed a time-out "T" to his buyers. "I must discuss something first with my colleague."

Amir and Petersee began a rehearsed, heated exchange in whispered tones, but loud enough to let key words float out. "Not happy . . . don't trust . . . not your call to make . . . *is this a fucking joke?*" Petersee grew agitated and drew Amir further back in the truck into dimmer light. The two traded hostile-sounding undertones for another ten seconds until Amir made a slashing motion with his hand and returned to the edge of the truck. He hopped down to the gravel roadbed and spoke to al-Jaber.

"I'm sorry," Amir said. "I'm not prepared to go forward. If you want to discuss it with our mutual friend you know how to reach him."

"What is the problem?" al-Jaber asked. "You won't tell me yourself?"

"No, but I assure you, I am protecting both of us."

"That's disappointing. He led me to believe you can deliver."

"And maybe I'll deliver to you some other time—but not now. I have my reasons."

"Amir!" Petersee called from the back of the truck, his Texas drawl now hoarse. "Don't pull out, buddy. Come on back.

Listen to me for a minute. There's a way to do this. I have an idea." He extended his arm and offered to help Amir clamber up.

Amir paused. This was it. He had come this far; it was now or never. He thought of his parents, his sister, the absolute mess he'd made out of his own life—a mess that was about to engulf his family if he didn't pull this off.

He clambered back up into the truck. Petersee swiftly drew him into the shadows and shot him twice in the torso with a small .22 caliber pistol. Amir's eyes bulged as he staggered backward and fell against the bare wall of the van.

Petersee squatted briefly over Amir's prone body to inspect his handiwork, then stood up, pocketed the revolver, and returned calmly to the buyers.

Amir remained limp, slumped against the wall, his eyes shut. He felt warm liquid seeping onto his legs and stomach. His heart was pounding. Was he hit? He didn't think so. He felt bruised and pinched in several places, but he didn't think he'd been shot.

With his heart throbbing he strained to hear what was happening outside. He knew what Petersee was scripted to say; he had heard it repeated in at least a half-dozen role-plays they practiced beforehand. After a minute or so he began to hear expected snippets—". . . he would never have done business with you. . . . I have other obligations . . . it was him or me."

Soon Petersee and then al-Jaber and Vasili hoisted themselves up into the truck. Vasili gagged at the sight of Amir's bloody corpse, which Petersee dragged further back into the shadows and covered with the tarp that had been used to hide the cargo.

This maneuver had also been rehearsed as an option, if circumstances allowed. Now, in complete darkness, Amir scratched his nose and shifted his body slightly so the vest wasn't digging into his armpits. He listened intently as Petersee drove home the sale, insisting that he see the cash before revealing any of the launch codes. When that hurdle was overcome, Petersee began reading the codes out loud and Vasili entered them into the keypads mounted on each drone unit.

Suddenly, Amir was hit by a flash of recognition: Vasili was a man he remembered as Bogomil Mladenov, nicknamed Pogo. Amir had met him several years earlier, when Pogo acted as a technical agent for Tula Aerospace, a faux-Russian trading firm that turned out to be a joint ATF/FBI sting operation attempting to sell drones to would-be terrorists. Amir never did business with Pogo or his employer. After a few months everyone in the trade knew who they were, and they closed the operation down.

The implications of Pogo's presence here were myriad. Lying motionless under the tarp, he tried sorting through the possibilities, but couldn't concentrate. He could hear them sliding the fiberglass crates to the rear lip of the truck. In minutes the transfer was complete and the engine of the second truck started up. After it pulled away, someone bounded back into the van and pulled down the overhead door. Amir remained still under the tarp.

"Act Two in Five Minutes," Petersee called out, giving the all-clear signal. "You alive under there?" He pulled the tarp away and beamed a flashlight into Amir's face.

"I think so," Amir said, shifting his legs and body until he was sitting upright against the wall. After he was settled he held his forearm up to block the beam of light. "Do they think I'm dead?" he asked, looking up at Petersee.

"I have no reason to think otherwise. It all went as planned."

"I guess then I should thank you," Amir said.

Petersee held out his palms, deflecting the comment. "I don't want your thanks," he said. "We did business. I got what I wanted, you'll get what you want. Here's where we part ways. Take off the vest. Can you stand up?"

Amir nodded and pushed himself up. Once standing and stabilized, he shed his jacket and began unbuttoning his shirt.

While keeping one eye on Amir, Petersee slid open a smartphone and whispered a voice-dial command. When the connection went through he repeated the all-clear code, "*Act Two in Five Minutes*," then pocketed the phone. He looked directly at Amir. "There's a change in Act Two," he said.

"What's that?" Amir asked as he struggled with the last Velcro straps on the vest.

"Bravo Team is down by one man. Ortiz isn't here. Can you drive?"

"I think so. Look at me. Am I bleeding anywhere?" He dropped the fake-blood-sodden vest to the floor and held up his now red-and-white undershirt.

Petersee ignored him, snatched up the vest, and found the indentations made by the two bullets. "You weren't hit," he said, showing Amir the evidence. "Can you drive?"

"I guess so. What do I need to do?"

"Instead of riding back to the warehouse with Ortiz, we want you to drive the van. Captain DeMolay will follow you in the Explorer. When you get back to the warehouse, Act Two resumes—U.S. Marshals will be waiting there to take you to wherever it is you're going."

"That's it? That's the whole change?" Amir asked.

"Affirmative," Petersee replied. They heard vehicles skidding to a stop outside. Doors opened and closed. Gravel crunched under approaching steps.

"One other thing," Petersee said. "This is private, between us. I have friends in the Marshals Service. I'm going to receive regular reports on your situation. If I ever find out you're fucking a minor, I will have access to your relo information. I will find you and personally cause you to have a fatal accident. You got that?"

Amir nodded just as Captain William DeMolay pulled open the partition door from the driver's cab and joined them. "Everything okay here?"

"Everything's fine," Petersee answered. "He's going to drive the van," gesturing toward Amir, who was re-buttoning his bullet-holed shirt. "Follow him to the warehouse, sign him over to the Marshals, then process the van."

"Understood." DeMolay nodded and handed Petersee a pair of clear plastic bags filled with electronic gear. Petersee opened the first and removed a GPS ankle bracelet. "Put this on," he said, handing it to Amir, who knew the drill. He'd worn one since he got off the plane at Andrews Air Force Base. Petersee opened the second bag and pulled out his own earpiece. He inserted the plastic nib in his ear and dropped the transceiver in his inside coat pocket. "Testing, testing, Alpha Team, this is Alpha Team Leader. Do you read?" He covered his wired ear with one hand to capture the response, and gestured to DeMolay with the other to check the anklet that Amir had just snapped on.

"Act One complete," Petersee said, then turned towards the back of the truck, looking at no one, and resumed his radio conversation. "Request SitRep Act Two."

DeMolay pulled a pocketbook-sized tablet from inside his blazer, launched the tracking app and verified that Amir's GPS was functioning. He signaled a thumbs-up to Petersee.

Petersee turned to face Amir. "Your instructions are to drive directly to the warehouse on the established route with no stops. Captain DeMolay will be following you at no less than one car-length, and he is pre-authorized to shoot-to-kill.

If you deviate from the plan, you're taking your life in your hands."

Amir nodded, trying to look appreciative. Petersee ignored him. "Okay, let's move," he called out, leading DeMolay through the front cab and out the driver's door. Amir, still in the back of the van, retrieved the battery lantern, switched it off, and stowed it with the vest on the shelves where the Vultures had been stacked. He looked around to see if anything else was loose. He left the tarp crumpled on the floor and pulled down the safety latch on the rear door. Then he returned to the front, settled again into the driver's seat, gripped the steering wheel, checked the side-view mirrors, and let out an audible sigh. It was daybreak, and he was alive. He sat for several seconds just listening to his own breathing.

Petersee's car started up and peeled off in a spray of gravel and dust. In the mirror Amir could see DeMolay ten yards back, sitting behind the wheel of the Explorer, waiting for him. He pumped the clutch and brake, started the engine and buckled his seat belt—noticing for the first time the briefcase containing Al-Jaber's payment wedged behind his seat.

He was surprised to find he had no interest in even looking at the cash. Money was now far down his list of priorities. He wanted his family to be safe and he wanted a chance to start over again. He re-engaged the clutch, wrestled with the pole-style stick shift, and drove the truck to the edge of the road. He spent the last few moments of his life looking over his left shoulder, checking to make sure there was no approaching traffic.

DeMolay, now a safe distance behind, entered a code in his tablet, clicked confirm, and the briefcase behind Amir's seat, lined with C-4, detonated with the force of five sticks of dynamite. The explosion shook the ground, and the fireball produced a blinding glare inside the Explorer. Truck parts and debris rained down like hail. Then there was another, smaller explosion. When the smoke cleared all that remained was a skeleton of the truck—just its frame and engine block, engulfed in flames.

When the glare subsided, DeMolay messaged Petersee: "Act One Coda complete."

*   *   *

The following day, ATF Special Agent Owen Petersee, on loan to the U.S. Marshals Service for the past two years, went out for lunch at the Atrium Café of the National Portrait Gallery on G Street, two blocks from his office. He bought a sandwich, chips and a bottled drink, and seated himself at a table adjacent to a bench where a man sat reading a newspaper.

After unwrapping his sandwich and taking a bite, he heard a voice from behind the raised newspaper.

"Congratulations are in order," the voice said. "I hear from Captain DeMolay that we have the drones. Well done."

"Thank you, sir," Petersee said as he opened a tablet and downloaded the current *Washington Post*, the same paper the man next to him was reading in print. "Is the press angle working for you the way you wanted?"

"No results so far, but it's early," the man said, turning a page in his newspaper and giving Petersee a knowing nod during the brief visual interval. "We wanted to announce Cadiz was taken out by federal agents to provoke him into a response. We're monitoring his outlets—we're just waiting for the chatter. Have you completed the WITSEC paperwork for the arms dealer?"

"All set. It looks like any other sealed record."

"Have you posted anything on the forum about our acquisition?

"I was waiting to meet with you."

"Go ahead and put it up. They should know we've made progress."

"You do know there's still a lot of work to be done," Petersee said, sounding a cautionary note.

"You mean converting the drones?"

"Exactly."

"Mladenov's our guy. Do you have reason to think he can't do it?"

"No, I think he can," Petersee replied, "but it's not done yet. It could take some time before we're sure."

"There's no rush." Department of Homeland Security Deputy Secretary Lowell Pendergast folded his newspaper in half and stood up. "Congratulations again," he said, staring upward like a tourist at the diamond-patterned steel mesh that framed the glass roof of the courtyard. "You have the Committee's appreciation." Without any further acknowledgment or eye contact he tucked the paper under his arm and walked toward the F Street exit.

1

"If we would guide by the light of reason, we must let our minds be bold."

—LDB, dissent in *Jay Burns Baking Co. v. Bryan,* 1924

~

NOW THAT HE was about to do the deed, 42-year-old Senator Ezekiel Sherman, a West Virginia Jew inhabiting a Boston Brahmin body, was having second thoughts.

Hesitation was not the senator's usual style, and being an astute observer of all things including himself, he recognized something serious was amiss. As he crossed the marble-floored lobby of the Hart Senate Office Building, staffers in tow, on his way to a press conference that he had scheduled, it suddenly came into sharp focus: *he was about to make a lot of people very unhappy.*

Not that this had ever stopped him in the past. Before his appointment by Governor Arnault to the Senate, "Zeke" Sherman had been the U.S. attorney in the Southern District of West Virginia for four years. It was his full-time job to make people unhappy and he learned to do it well. Of all the people he prosecuted, former Senator Kenneth Falwell, late of Lewisburg, Pennsylvania, might be the unhappiest. Zeke oversaw the senator's very public trial and conviction on bribery and corporate espionage charges, and administered the *coup de grâce* by moving into Falwell's office in the Hart building.

The problem this time was that the people he was about to make unhappy were not corrupt politicians or insider traders. They were friends, relatives, supporters—people he cared about.

He already knew how unhappy Rachel Chen was. Lover and lawyer extraordinaire, his girlfriend of the past three years had also been his indispensable chief of staff and political strategist. But when he confided in her his plan to leave the Senate, it precipitated a hurricane-sized confrontation between them. A few days later, when he told her his decision was final, she had her resignation letter in hand: she had taken a job as the new host of IVC's controversial cable show *Women in Charge*. She also informed him that she was re-opening her apartment in Bethesda, which was closer to IVC's studios, and would be spending some nights there instead of with him in his Cathedral Avenue townhouse.

This scenario was not one he had fully anticipated in his calculus of the consequences of *the deed about to be done*, but it was not the rift with Rachel that was the reason for his hesitation now. If his resignation from the Senate brought their relationship to an end, surely that meant she was more in love with his career than with him. His concern was the realization that his decision may have other unintended and as yet unknown consequences. Since law school, where he was thoroughly intimidated by the intellects of numerous professors, Zeke had developed a keen awareness of his own limitations, and a particular respect for the axiom "you don't know what you don't know."

As they arrived at the elevator bank, he signaled with his eyes to Leslie Graev, his press secretary, that they'd meet upstairs, and headed to the car on the far left marked "Senators

Only." The entourage following him melted away. Among the five staffers, Leslie was the only one who knew what the press conference was about, and he was carrying that knowledge like a pro, maintaining his typical upbeat and humorous banter with his junior colleagues.

Zeke pushed the UP button for the elevator, dropped his briefcase to the floor, and paused to examine his reflection in the polished stainless steel doors.

He still had his square, all-American jaw, deep-set blue eyes, the photogenic smile—all those things that could help get him elected next year if he wanted. But the wear-and-tear from the three years since his appointment was all too apparent, at least to himself. His formerly dark brown hair was now peppered with gray and thinning on top, to the point where he had to keep it cut short or risk looking like he was cultivating a comb-over. The long hours left him physically exhausted and he wondered if he got any REM sleep at all anymore. When he entered the Senate he was physically fit and played tennis and looked younger than his 38 years. Three and a half years later he got almost no exercise and felt like he was 50.

The doors hissed open. Thankfully Senator Nash of Ohio, whom he had noticed out of the corner of his eye, was not running to join him. He entered alone and pushed 11. The doors closed. Thirty seconds to himself—a rare and lucky occurrence.

His mother would not be pleased. He knew this. When he received his appointment to the Senate she told him it was one of the happiest days of her life. Would leaving the Senate make it one of the worst days?

It seemed he had perfected the art of disappointing his mother. She was thrilled when he went to law school, but disapproved of his decision to go into government service. When an academic opportunity opened up at his *alma mater*, Columbia Law, she urged him to take it, get tenure, and have long-term security. He stuck with prosecuting drug lords and stock manipulators. From time to time he had lived under protective custody because of threats to his life. On one occasion, before the trial of a Russian mobster, Zeke received a threat naming his mother. She was furious when two dark-windowed Suburbans screeched into the parking lot of her local synagogue one Friday evening where she was attending Sabbath services and disgorged a handful of polite but armed-to-the-teeth FBI agents. They whisked her away to a safe house in Charleston until Zeke, three days later, made arrangements for her to live in Florida in a location of her choosing for the remainder of the winter. After six weeks on Sanibel Island, on Florida's Gulf coast, she was somewhat mollified.

When he announced that he and Rachel had decided to live together, his mother was frantic. "Live together? Just marry her, for god's sake! Have a family! You're going be forty years old! You have no legacy, you have no children, you've got no idea what you're missing, what is passing you by. What are you waiting for?"

Zeke adored Rachel. She was sexy, smart, and they shared what he considered an open and honest relationship. But she was 36 and wanted to start a family—if not immediately then in some not-too-distant future. Zeke was having trouble making that leap. He was deeply ambivalent about assuming the lifelong, non-cancelable role of father. He was an only child; when he was growing up his father worked as a traveling salesman and played no significant role in his upbringing. He had no reference point, no confidence, and no patience for little children. So at least for now there would be no marriage, no children, and more disappointment for his mother.

The elevator doors opened and Zeke stepped out to find a few journalists and aides milling about in the hallway. They all glanced in his direction to see who it was, then returned to their conversations. His staff hadn't arrived yet. He headed towards a water fountain down the hallway. Another reprieve.

It was true that he enjoyed a lot of support, both from the state Democratic Party and the DNC. Everyone was expecting him to run for his seat, and his departure from the race would leave them scrambling for a candidate. Would an unintended consequence be that the seat flips to the GOP? That was a possibility, but he felt no personal responsibility in the matter— there was no guarantee that he would keep the seat even if he ran. But from a practical perspective the Republicans had few credible candidates, and the local Democratic bench was deep. There would be several young progressives eager to vie for his seat. It was hard to see how Zeke's departure from the Senate could cause irreparable harm to either his party or the state.

His current staff might be upset, but would his resignation trigger some sort of extreme reaction? That seemed improbable. More likely they would, like Rachel, jump ship as soon as possible. The professionals among them knew that Congress is always fluid, forever in motion—senators come and go all the time. The interns and less experienced staff would be caught more off-guard, but would learn an important lesson.

He leaned over to drink from the fountain. The water tasted delicious, and he let the stream run off his lips for several seconds.

Rachel had argued with some passion that he should run if for no reason other than not to deprive the nation of urgently needed leadership. He tried to take this at face value, but after some time came to understand that her idealized view of him as a politician was a kind of reflective narcissism. She saw him as Kennedy-esque, as someone who articulates ideals and offers a vision of a better future. As his chief of staff, she was the one who crafted this image. She decided what issues he would embrace, and edited every speech he gave and statement he issued. He would be the first to admit that his popularity as a politician and whatever effectiveness he had as a senator could largely be credited to Rachel's management of his affairs. So his leaving the Senate was in essence tossing out her political child, and it was this rejection that precipitated the storm between them.

As stark as this observation was, he put it aside. For purposes of the decision to be made, it was irrelevant. Even if he was this dashing politico that the nation sorely needed (he still thought of himself as a lawyer, and more narrowly as a prosecutor), he knew that no individual senator, or even group of senators, could bring about any fundamental change. This was a reality that had been demonstrated to him over and over again the past three years, but it was a reality that Rachel could never grasp: she had to believe in the power and purpose of her creation.

Senator Dottin passed by and Zeke acknowledged her greeting with the requisite nod and smile. His staff arrived and gathered in the elevator lobby, waiting for him. Leslie signaled, pointing in the direction of the press auditorium. Zeke nodded and bent down to the fountain for one last drink.

Rachel, *in absentia*, was still not done with him. She had argued that if he stayed with his career he could become president. At the time he took it as another manifestation of her narcissism: if he was presidential material, Rachel was the one who had spun the cloth. Now, only weeks later, he learned that his name, without his knowledge, had been included in a poll of five potential Democratic presidential candidates. He came out as the front-runner in several survey metrics, and was seen as the one most likely to beat incumbent Republican Burton Grove the following November. What was he to make of that?

Leslie approached, twisting his wristwatch. Zeke raised his eyebrows, inviting him to speak.

"You're still planning on going through with it?" the press secretary asked.

"Why, do I look reluctant?" Zeke replied.

"Well, you're due there now and you're not there. I don't know if it's your reluctance or my wishful thinking. If you're having doubts we can cancel the press conference, or reschedule if need be."

"If I cancel this one I'm not sure they'll come to another one."

"Don't be ridiculous. We'll use the right cover for it. You're not feeling well, a last-minute family matter has come up—whatever. You've got plenty of credibility with the press."

Zeke knew this to be true. In general he had a good rapport with the press, and was particularly effective one-on-one, as an interviewee. On more than one occasion Rachel had referred to him as a *schmooze-meister*. She had studied Yiddish in college for three years, and Zeke was certain she must be the only person on the planet who was quadrilingual in English, Mandarin, Spanish and Yiddish.

"Have you told them yet?" he asked, nodding towards the staff.

"No, Senator, your instructions were not to say anything, and I haven't."

"Well leave it that way for now. I'll join you in a minute. There are a lot of factors to consider."

"If you have doubts, Senator," he said as he retreated, "I urge postponement."

To Zeke, the whole notion of running for president was horrifying. He couldn't bring himself to campaign for a senate seat, much less the presidency. But like a good prosecutor, he tested all assumptions. What if Rachel's assertions of presidential potential, however self-serving on her part and however unappealing to him personally, were accurate? What if a presidential run was a realistic objective? As a pair they had made a great success of his three years in the Senate. He was popular in his own state and had attracted national attention on several occasions. He did agree with Rachel on one thing: if he bailed out now, he'd be abandoning what she described as a thriving political franchise. He understood she used the term as a measure of popularity, but from his cynical perspective he couldn't help but think of each of the one hundred senate seats as a franchise in the legal sense, like a fast food restaurant. In an academic comparison there were distinct similarities: a senate seat might be "independently owned and operated," but was subject to licensing terms set by one of two national political parties.

His plan upon leaving the Senate was to travel the university and law school circuit to promote his new American Majority Party. As he saw it, the two-party system was inherently divisive, and he thought the public would welcome an alternative to the tired Democratic-Republican divide. If he was right about that, and his idea for a new type of political party achieved its maximum potential success, would he accomplish more for the progressive agenda than he could as president of the United States?

And was that the ultimate, objective distillation of the question at hand?

If so, he had his answer.

He rejoined Leslie and the staff, greeting everyone with a collective nod and a practiced blank expression—an invaluable skill he had cultivated as a trial attorney. No one dared ask what was going on. If anyone besides Leslie knew, they were hiding it: just a lot of eager, expectant, hopeful faces. For Zeke, the scene was redolent of naïve optimism, a sentiment for which he had developed a wistful nostalgia.

"Let's proceed, shall we?" He led the way into the press room where some fifteen reporters and photographers were waiting. Leslie, now visibly grim, followed him up to the dais and helped with the microphone and sound check. He made sure there was water in the pitcher, and checked the Senator's appearance one last time, brushing his shoulder briefly. Professionally assisted suicide.

"Members of the press," Zeke began, drawing his notes from his inside coat pocket and unfolding them. "Thank you, as always, for your time. Today I'm announcing that I will not run for reelection to the senate seat to which I was appointed three years ago. I have informed Governor Arnault that I am prepared to finish out the remaining fifteen months of my term, or if he feels it is in the better interests of the state of West Virginia, I will resign as of the end of this session of Congress so that he can have a free hand to appoint someone who will serve the last year of the term and run for reelection as well. In either case, it is time to notify the good citizens of West Virginia that I will not be a candidate in next year's senate race, nor will I run for any other office.

"As honored as I am to have been appointed to this position, the last three years have taught me that I am not a person with a temperament for electoral politics. Even if I am a diligent and honest public servant who can get the job done, there are others of equal or greater qualification who will thrive in the role. The people of West Virginia are entitled not only to honest but also *earnest* representation.

"To my supporters in West Virginia and elsewhere who may be disappointed by this announcement, I urge you to withhold judgment. Upon leaving the Senate I expect to play an active role in public life through the American Majority Party, on the web at www.american-majority.org. This is a new type of political party that doesn't nominate or sponsor candidates. Instead it offers voters an alternative to two-party politics—a way to vote for *what* you want, instead of who you want.*

"The American Majority Party is the equivalent of a new operating system for our democracy, and it will take some time for citizens to understand its full potential. Therefore, while concluding my senate term in an orderly fashion, I plan to use the time that would otherwise have gone to my reelection campaign to promote the American Majority Party. When my senate service comes to an end I expect to devote full-time to this effort.

"As always I thank you for your kind attention. I am prepared to take questions about the American Majority Party, but I note in advance I will have no comment on questions related to my role in the senate or my decision not to run. I have just answered those questions and refer you to the record if you wish to revisit them."

In Zeke's experience the time elapsed between the final words of a press conference and the first reporter's question could usually be measured in nanoseconds. On this occasion there was an awkward pause. Zeke didn't know if they were digesting what he had said, or he had lost them completely. Several seconds elapsed before the first shout of "Senator!" erupted, accompanied by the simultaneous sprouting of arms.

*   *   *

Returning to his office from the press conference, Zeke rushed past a gauntlet of grim faces and glistening cheeks to take refuge

---

* This concept, based on a good government initiative organized by Louis Brandeis in 1903, is demonstrated in real-time at the referenced web site www.american-majority.org.

in his inner sanctum. He was trailed closely by his recently named chief of staff, Armin DeBryin, who closed the double-doors behind them.

Armin was a single man in his mid-forties, Buddha-like in both appearance and temperament, who had followed Zeke to the Senate from the U.S. attorney's office in Charleston. There he had been the District Court's webmaster and head librarian. His job in Zeke's senate office, until Rachel's departure, had been similar: webmaster and social media manager. Armin succeeded her as chief of staff, and Rachel's prediction proved to be accurate: his people skills had not significantly improved. Zeke, however, remained confident that Armin was the right choice. This wasn't a reelection campaign—in Zeke's view, the American Majority Party was more akin to a tech start-up out of Silicon Valley. Different tasks called for different skills.

Zeke shed his suit coat, threw it over a chair, kicked off his loafers and poured himself a glass of water from the pitcher on the bookcase behind his desk. Armin stood patiently, waiting for his cue.

"Well I did it," Zeke said, dropping into his chair. He gestured for Armin to take a seat.

"Was it cathartic in some way?" Armin placed his tablet on the desk, turned it neatly 180 degrees and pushed it forward for Zeke to read. Then he sat down.

"Cathartic?" Zeke stared at the question in mid-air, ignoring the tablet. "I don't know. I can't say I feel a great sense of relief. There's still work to be done; our plate is plenty full." He laced his knuckles together and stretched his hands out, palms forward.

"Speaking of which, here's a list of your calls," Armin said, leaning forward in his chair to push the tablet closer. "I've highlighted the ones I think you should return today. I assume you don't want to burn all of your bridges in one afternoon."

Zeke's mind wandered. The walk through the office had distracted him, leading to speculation about the future of certain people on his staff. Armin had worked out new job descriptions for virtually everyone, but he knew many would leave. He raised his eyebrows, but his expression was inert.

"The vice president, for example," Armin continued. "You might want to consider calling him back. You also might want to return Lady Carteret's call," which was Zeke's derisive name for the Anglophile chairwoman of the West Virginia Democratic Party.

Zeke slumped back in his chair, staring at Armin. He said nothing.

Armin shifted in his seat. "Do I have it wrong? Maybe you do want to piss off the greatest number of people possible? If so, your speech today was a great kick-off effort. Now you can complete the job without lifting a finger. Very neat trick. Very *efficient*, as you like to say."

"Very *funny*," Zeke said, finally sitting up and shifting gears. "No, that is not my goal." He picked up the tablet and glanced at it, swiping at the screen to scroll down. "Your first assumption is the correct one. I don't want to burn all of my bridges." He looked up at Armin with a tightened, mischievous smile. "Some of them, perhaps, but not all. I will be a good soldier and make my calls. In a little while. First, I want to go back out and talk to the staff. I feel cowardly hiding back here in my office. They may also have questions about your reorganization memo."

"That's a good idea," Armin said. "There will also be questions about the American Majority Party. Good practice for your maiden run at the law schools tomorrow."

"Got it. Anything else I need to take care of before we go back out?

"You have two personal calls. One from your mother . . . she knew about your decision, right?"

"Oh, she knew. I'll call her later."

"And another from your cousin, the Israeli law professor whose name I can never pronounce—Matti Rivlin?"

"Moti. Sort of a nickname for Matthew. What did he want?"

"He called only about five minutes ago—said it was important, that he wanted to meet with you tomorrow."

"Really?" Zeke was surprised. His favorite Israeli cousin, out of an inventory of at least a dozen on his mother's side, was a visiting professor at George Washington University Law School. Since his cousin's arrival last year they had gotten together on a few occasions, but nothing had ever been urgent. Perhaps he needed help with a work visa. "Did he say what it was about?"

"No. Gerry spoke to him. She suggested a phone call, but he insisted on seeing you in person. In the meantime, your plan for tomorrow is to be on the stump for AMP. You've got three engagements, starting at Georgetown at 9:30 a.m. Then Mount Vernon at one, and back to James Mason at four-thirty. You're not scheduled to be in the office at all—from Arlington you're heading back to your home for dinner with the chief justice and his wife."

"Good, that's exactly what I want to be doing."

"And your cousin? Do you want me to try and get him on the phone?"

"No, if he wants face time he's got his reasons. Let him know what my itinerary is—if he wants to talk to me tomorrow he'll have to catch up with me somewhere. Georgetown isn't far from his office."

"Okay. We'll fit him in somewhere."

"Anything else?" Zeke poured himself another glass of water, and palmed a few M&M's from the bowl on the credenza.

"Only one thing to make you aware of, for your phone calls later."

"Which is?" He took a long drink.

"I know this isn't what you want to focus on, but I'm just doing my job here. I'm preparing you for what you will encounter. Some people are reading your decision not to run for the Senate as part of a strategy to run for president. You'll be asked about it for sure."

Zeke snorted. "That's preposterous. What is the logical strand that connects those dots?"

"For someone who wants to see it this way, you're positioning yourself as an outsider. Your speech just now was an open indictment of the whole system. For voters who are looking for an outsider, for someone of national stature who sees the system for what it is, you will have strong appeal."

"Anyone who listened to the whole speech also knows that I'm not positioning myself for anything. I could not have been more explicit."

"Senator, in your own words: 'people remember what they want to remember'."

"Right. Thanks for reminding me."

"You should also expect your polling numbers to go up."

"What polling numbers? Not our polling numbers!"

"No, of course not. But no one needs permission to include your name in a poll."

Zeke drilled his chief of staff with a narrow-eyed glare. "Armin, as you correctly point out, people remember what they remember, they poll what they poll. I have no control over it. You, however, know that I am not running for president or anything else."

Armin nodded.

"Please assure me, again, that we are not polling ourselves. For any reason."

"We are not. The polls I'm referring to are outside."

"Armin, what I'm after—you know what I'm after. I'm not running for anything. That's the message I want you and everyone else in the office to project going forward. The notion that I am considering any elected role needs to be laid to rest. Is that clear?"

"It's clear to me, but apparently not to you."

"Okay, I'll take the bait. What isn't clear to me?"

"The message you're sending is an accurate description of your position, but it's having the opposite of your intended effect. The more you insist you're not running, the more appealing you become as a candidate . . . the more some people see it as part of a deliberate strategy to run."

Zeke stared at Armin for several seconds, seemingly in shock. "You have got to be fucking kidding." There was a long pause. "Do you have any suggestions? What is it I should be doing to diminish my appeal as a candidate?"

Armin paused momentarily, weighing options. "Have sex with an intern? Or—this is easy—just do something weird on the Internet."

"Don't tempt me."

"You asked . . ." Armin shrugged.

"Seriously, what should my strategy be here in opposite-land? If not running is running, how do I not run?"

"Sir, I'm a webmaster who has agreed to help you finish out your senate term and provide transition to the AMP. You need to get back with Rachel on this, or someone like her, who can see the whole picture. This is strategy. I am not equipped to answer your question."

*   *   *

"Hi Mom, it's me. Sorry to call so late."

"Good evening, Senator. You're calling from home? You must be exhausted."

"I am. It's been a long day. I'm calling from the car. I'll be home soon."

"You're not driving, are you?"

"No, Mom, I'm not driving. I haven't driven a car for three years. But when I'm done with the Senate I'll be able to drive again. One of the many privileges that will be restored to me after I leave this job."

"You're so . . . so *different,* boychik. I'm always amazed."

"What do you mean?"

"Maybe it's me. I'm very old-fashioned. I thought most people would consider it a blessing to have a car and driver take them everywhere they want to go. For you it's a burden to have a chauffeur."

There was a pause while the car stopped at a traffic light on L Street and Zeke became fixated on a window dresser wrestling with a mannequin in a brightly-lit storefront. "Mom, I have handlers for everything I do and say. Being driven around is just an example. I live in an entourage. Every minute of my day is scripted."

"Dear, I'm so sorry, this is not what I intended for this conversation." His mother sounded contrite.

"Well, you called earlier. I'm returning your call. Was it after my press conference? Did you see my announcement?"

"I watched the whole thing, and I'm very proud that you're standing by your principles. Your father would be too. He would be your biggest defender." His father had been living in a specialized Alzheimer's nursing home for the past eight years.

"How is he, Mom? Have you seen him?"

"I saw him yesterday. He's doing okay, really—physically, I mean. He's well-fed, they keep him clean and close shaven.

"Give him a kiss for me please."

"I always do."

"Mom, I tried in my speech to explain why I've resigned. Did it help you understand any better what I'm trying to do?"

"Son, I just want you to be happy. If you're not happy as a senator I might not understand why—like I don't understand the business with the car—but it's your life dear, not mine. A senate term is six years. That's a long time to be doing something you don't like."

"Good. That's exactly the situation, and I am glad to have your support. It's been a difficult day."

"I'll let you go. Thank you very much for calling me back. I wish I could make things simpler for you."

"I'll be okay. Mom, I got a call from cousin Moti today, Julia's nephew. He wants to meet with me. Do you happen to know why? I haven't had a chance to speak to him yet."

"No, not at all. I hope everything is okay. Should I be concerned?"

"No you should not. You're in touch with Julia, right?"

"All the time. I spoke to her just this morning. Do you want me to ask her?"

"Please don't. I'm meeting him tomorrow morning and I'll find out. I'm guessing it's something related to his stay in the U.S.—an immigration problem maybe. Don't worry about it."

"What, me worry? I never worry."

"Cute, Mom. Very cute. Good night. I'm home now, we're pulling up to the house."

"Good night. Give my love to Rachel."

"I'll try, Mom, I'll give it my best shot."

"I said *my* love, not your love."

"Good night Mom."

*   *   *

Rachel was sitting on a stool at the breakfast bar in the low-lit kitchen, nursing a glass of water and a small mound of vitamins. The screen mounted on the wall was on mute, but he saw it was replaying her show from earlier in the evening. Even at the end of a long workday, with frustration written all over her face and makeup smudges visible at the corners of her brown eyes, Zeke could take one look at her and get aroused. He had discovered in his early twenties that he was attracted to Asian women, and Rachel, the only daughter of a Chinese father and Jewish mother, proved an irresistible combination. When they met at a Democratic Party fundraiser she was senior counsel to the Senate Foreign Relations Committee. A mutual friend supplied Zeke with her phone number, and after two initial rejections she finally agreed to join him at the Kennedy Center for a classical music concert. During the intermission they each had a glass of wine, and the final piece on the program was Rimsky-Korsakov's *Scheherazade*. By the time the violin solo ended in the final movement her view of him had softened considerably. That was three years ago, and they had been living together for the last two.

"Hello," she looked up with a tenuous smile, tucked one leg under the opposite thigh, and turned back to the replay. In her public persona, on television, her jet-black shoulder-length hair was usually in an impeccably coiffed parabola draping her neck. Now it was pinned behind her head with a plastic clamp. Her face was a study in concentration.

"Hi," Zeke said. *Not a kiss-on-the-cheek moment, surely.* He hung his suit jacket on the doorknob and poured himself a glass of water. He gestured towards the screen.

"How'd the show go today? Who'd you have on?"

"Uh, fine. It went fine. This is Elizabeth Ellison—Under Secretary of Defense for Policy." She pointed at the screen. "She's behind the Defense Department's proposal to phase out the Air Force. But somewhere, according to Jim, there's a point where I was asking her a question and dropped a thought, or a word, or something. That's what I'm looking for."

She pressed a button on her remote and the video blurred into fast-forward.

Under a mandate from Congress to identify what the military would look like if defense spending was reduced by 20 percent over 20 years, the Department of Defense had presented, among other proposals, a consolidation of the three branches of the armed forces into two.

"What kinds of questions were you asking her?" Zeke took two long swallows of water and placed his glass on the counter.

"How she came up with the idea, what made her focus on it, and how she persuaded the secretary to move forward. Things like that."

"How did she persuade the secretary?"

"With logic. The Army and the Navy acquire specialized aircraft for their own strategic missions. Many of the Air Force's missions—like long-range bombers and manned aerial combat—have been declining for years. Drones, apparently, are changing everything for the Air Force."

Zeke quickly lost interest in the fate of the United States Air Force; he wanted to get laid. They'd not had a single romantic moment together since Rachel began her new job, and things weren't looking very promising tonight either.

He went to the sink and filled the electric kettle from the tap. Strange how a cup of hot tea would keep many people awake at night, but for him it produced a calming effect. He assembled the ritual paraphernalia: mug, strainer, sugar bowl, teaspoon, a tin of Keemun Black.

"What's the problem there?" Rachel lectured her unseen critic. "That's not a long pause." She stabbed at the remote.

"You're talking about your producer, I assume."

She paused, watching the clip again, this time with the

volume turned up. "Jim. He's one of the associates. I don't think Harrison would have brought this to me. But I will ask him. It would be good for me to know."

Zeke felt it best not to weigh in. The water heating up in the kettle began to grumble.

Rachel clicked off the screen with the remote and rotated on her stool to face Zeke, shifting the folded leg and locking her arms around it. "Sorry about that." She looked at him and smiled.

Zeke was caught off guard. "About?"

"I'm over-focused on this. No need to be. I should have put it away when you came in. Welcome home. How are you?"

"Fine."

"Are we still on for tomorrow night?"

"As far as I know," he replied, measuring loose tea into the strainer. "I've not heard otherwise."

She was referring to a private dinner Zeke had arranged with Chief Justice Anthony Salo-Baron and his wife. Salo-Baron had been his constitutional law professor and mentor in law school. When Zeke arrived in Washington as a senator, he and the chief justice became regular dining partners. At their last meeting the chief justice asked for a dinner invitation on behalf of his wife, a recently retired forensic psychologist and a fan of Rachel's show, *Women in Charge*. Zeke was happy to oblige. As reluctant as Rachel might be to extend social credit at this point in their strained relationship, he knew she wouldn't decline a personal request from the chief justice of the Supreme Court. For her new talking-head career the dinner would be high-octane jet fuel, even if diluted somewhat by the presence of a lame-duck senator from West Virginia.

"Wonderful. It's very exciting. You know he's a hero to me," Rachel said.

"To you, me and a lot of other people. But remember, this

is a private dinner, everything is off the record. Nothing can be reported."

"Of course. Don't worry. Are there any subjects I should steer clear of? Can I ask him about Justice Ross?"

"Oh, he'll want to talk about her, I'm sure. On an ordinary day she's a nightmare to deal with. Now this latest video that's come out makes it all the worse." He was referring to a grainy, 80-second video, now viewed over a million times, of the facial expressions of a woman—looking remarkably like Associate Supreme Court Justice Carla Constance Ross—as she purportedly watches a free video-clip sample on an X-rated website.

"I haven't been able to bring myself to watch the whole thing," Zeke continued. "I find it creepy. Have you seen it?"

"I have. It's got to be her. It's too real."

The video had been posted on WorldLeaks.org by an anonymous hacker who claimed to have taken control of the justice's own webcam and recorded her reaction to a video clip that she apparently watched multiple times. The post contained complete trace information, including the IP addresses of the justice's computer and www.bound4you.com—the site's web traffic having soared in the aftermath.

"I think you can ask him about almost anything as long as it remains off the record. But remember he's not a guest on your show—try not to interview him."

"Zeke, dear, I won't embarrass you. It will be an honor to meet him." She looked at him appreciatively.

Her voice had softened considerably. Something had changed; her mood was different. "Just as a reminder," Zeke said, "his wife Fran will be honored to meet *you*. She's the reason we're having dinner—she loves your show."

"Oh! I just remembered!" Rachel shifted gears. "I'm so sorry! Today was the big day. You announced you're not running.

How'd it go? I saw the press conference, or most of it. I thought it was good. You scored your points."

"Thanks. It was hard. Armin asked if was cathartic—I don't think it was that. I spoke to my mother about it a few minutes ago from the car. She was supportive, which I'm pleased about. Are you over it?"

Rachel sat silently for a long moment, and then glanced up at a clock mounted on the kitchen wall. "Good question. Do you really want to get into this right now?"

"Actually, no. I'd rather skip right to the sex."

"Hah!" Rachel laughed. "Well, if I'm over it, I'm not *that* over it."

"Why not?"

"Because I'm disappointed. As I see it, you've got all this potential and you're just abandoning it because you don't like the work. It's too unpleasant and dirty for you, so you're walking away."

"We've been over this. It's the fundraising. I hate asking people for money all the time. You would rather I stick with something I detest?" As if participating in the conversation, the kettle started to hiss.

"No, I would rather you have a different perspective. There are thousands of coal miners in West Virginia who really hate their jobs, yet they don't have the luxury of quitting. They have other concerns, like putting food on the table and paying rent. They're responsible for their families."

"I feel no responsibility toward the Senate, nor to the people of West Virginia. I am not their only option. Please remember I never wanted to be a senator. This was not a job I asked for."

"Yet it seems to have come your way. Like the coal miner, you've been saddled with an unwanted career. I do feel for you."

That hurt, and Zeke let it show. "You can't find any respect for what I'm doing with the American Majority Party? Have you seen our democracy dashboard recently?"

"Zeke, it's great that you have it working now. But we've talked about this before; we're treading water here. You're asking people to ignore candidate politics and use their vote in a completely different way."

"There are a lot of people right now who are very unhappy with the two-party system. They've just never been offered an option."

"You're talking about changing the voting habits of 120 million people. At best this is a decades-long effort. Yet the opportunity to run for president of the United States, rare as it is, presents itself at your doorstep right now, and you won't even answer the knock."

Zeke paused to grasp at some thread of reasoning in his argument that he was sure had been there, but now was nowhere to be found. "So your relationship really was with my career?"

"That's a conclusion you've drawn. That's nothing I've ever said. What I've said is that I'm disappointed. You say you don't like electoral politics—there's nothing you can do about it, that's just how you feel. Okay, I get it. Now I'm telling you how I feel. I am disappointed—in you, in your decision and your reasoning behind it. Surely I'm as entitled to my feelings as you are to yours. Equal protection of the laws and all that."

"Of course you are. The question is, will you get over it?"

"Time will tell?" This question in response to a question was punctuated perfectly by the boiling kettle, which simultaneously clicked off and fell silent. Zeke emoted a philosophical shrug. The sudden quiet was poetic if nothing else.

Rachel got up from the stool, unfolding her limbs like a stork. "But to answer your more pressing question," she crossed the kitchen and planted a kiss on his cheek, "fooling around tonight is not in the cards. Sorry. I'm exhausted, it's already 10:15, and I need to be out of here at six. I'm headed to bed."

Zeke sighed. "It's okay; I wasn't very optimistic. Can we make a date?"

"We can try for tomorrow night. I don't have to stay in the kitchen for too long—Lizzie can handle it." She flashed her "come get me" eyes and tugged at the top button of his shirt, drawing herself closer to him. "And I'm not due back so early in the morning."

Zeke put his arm around her waist and pulled her in for a real kiss. "That's my down payment," he said after they dropped the embrace. "I'll be in soon. I'm going to have my tea and read just one thing. I have to let Senator Porter know by tomorrow whether or not I'll sign on to his Labor Department bill."

A mere six weeks ago, when Rachel was his chief of staff, any mention of the labor bill would have precipitated complaints, ideas and proposed amendments, no matter the degree of fatigue or time of day or night. Now she shrugged and padded down the hallway into the bedroom, unsnapping her bra behind her as she walked.

Zeke returned to his tea-making, replaying the last few minutes in his mind. Was this progress? She no longer seemed angry, but the disappointment theme was new. He speculated: anger by its nature comes in bursts, and fades quickly. Maybe disappointment was something deeper, more lasting, more *inertial*. He knew how poor he was at reading female cues. It would be best to observe further before drawing conclusions. Tomorrow night's dinner should provide more to work with.

He carried the steaming mug to the kitchen table, retrieved a tablet from his briefcase and sat down to work. After swiping his index finger to sign in, he clicked the "TO DO" icon on the desktop and opened a folder labeled "MUST DO / URGENT." Inside was another folder, "Must Do Tonight 9/7." There were three items: two short e-mail replies, and the multi-page briefing memo about the labor bill. He took a sip of tea. *Well, compared to mining coal, it's not so bad.* He adjusted the screen for a better angle and clicked to open the memo, one section of which turned out to be the justification for a proposed major budget increase for coal mining inspection and enforcement.

2

"Most things worth doing in the world had been declared impossible before they were done."

—LDB, Labor Arbitration Proceedings, 1913

∽

ZEKE'S APPOINTMENTS SECRETARY offered to have the senator's car stop in front of the small attached house on Wyoming Avenue that Moti Rivlin rented for his extended stays in Washington, but Moti had insisted on meeting at the corner of Connecticut and Wyoming. He climbed nimbly into the back of the navy blue sedan.

"*Boker tov*, cousin! Good morning!" Zeke reached out and extended his hand. "You know we could just as easily have driven by your house."

"*Ha-val al ha-benzeen,*" Moti replied dismissively. "Waste of gas. Everyone should make these kinds of adjustments."

Zeke now remembered that his cousin was an ardent environmentalist. He watched as Moti found the ends of his seat belt, buckled them, and returned to the conversation.

"I thank you for the appointment on short notice." He sat back and brushed the empty seat between them with his palm. "I know from the news how busy you've been. Is it true what is reported, that you are considering a run for president?"

"It's all nonsense. Don't believe what you read."

"Too bad. Many people I respect think you would be a good president."

"Hah! I would be an awful president! Your friends needn't worry, however, because I'm not running. I'm leaving the Senate because I don't like electoral politics—campaigning in general and fundraising in particular."

"I'm not here to advise you about your career." Moti held up his hands in quick surrender, grinning his wide smile. "It is a difficult position to be in."

Zeke recognized this broad, delighted grin from twenty years earlier. Upon arriving in Jerusalem for his junior year at Hebrew University, Zeke had made a conscious effort to not disappoint his mother and introduced himself to her half-sister Julia, and by default to Julia's numerous descendants. He discovered them living clan-like in a warren of adjoining flats connected by an ancient courtyard in *Giv'at Sha'ul,* a neighborhood in western Jerusalem. Eventually, amid a parade of exotic personalities, he met his cousin Moti, three years his senior, who had just completed his extended Israeli army service and was entering an undergraduate law program at Hebrew University. This left Zeke in the odd position (as he saw it) of an American showing his Israeli cousin around the *Giv'at Ram* campus, and introducing him to his circle of mostly American friends. Moti latched onto this as an opportunity to improve his English, and to sleep with, by Zeke's count, at least four of his female classmates.

Zeke had watched all of this like a hawk. His cousin, small in frame, was not handsome in any classic or rugged sense that Zeke recognized. His deep-set eyes were accentuated by a long, straight nose, and he kept his hair and beard close-cropped in a way that reminded Zeke vaguely of a raccoon. After some casual inquiries failed to dislodge any trade secrets, he asked Moti directly about his success with women.

"I promise you, this is not anything I do," he had replied, with the same sheepish grin now on display two decades later in the back of the limousine. "These women ask to be with me, they call me and ask me to go out." Zeke remembered concluding at the time that his cousin's success with women must derive from his body language—a confident jaunt that was either a prerequisite for, or a product of, several years of active duty in an Israeli special forces unit.

"The resignation was difficult," Zeke replied, returning to the present. "But I'm satisfied with my decision. I think I'm making the best contribution I can make."

"Stick with the plan," Moti coached. "When you have a plan, stay with it."

"I agree. Thank you for the vote of confidence. Would you like something to drink?" Zeke gestured at the small cooler built into the back of the front seat.

"No thank you," Moti replied, handing Zeke a folded piece of notepaper. "I was hoping we could stop somewhere and have a cup of coffee."

Zeke put on his reading glasses, opened the note and found printed in block letters: "I MUST SPEAK WITH YOU IN A PUBLIC PLACE. URGENT."

Zeke peered at his cousin with perfect composure. During his total of twelve years in the U.S. attorney's office and his three years in the Senate, he had encountered a lot of bombshells. This was a three on a one-to-ten scale.

"I'm sure we're fine where we are, but I'm happy to make a stop and pick up some coffee." He pushed a button on his armrest. "Dennis," he said through the intercom, "please find a place along Connecticut here where we can stop for coffee."

Moti said nothing further, but thanked him with a nod and slight smile.

They rounded Dupont Circle and before the next traffic light the car came to a stop alongside the curb. Moti, closest to the door, tried opening it, but Zeke held up his hand. "When it's locked it means he wants to check things out first." Moments later Dennis came around and opened the door for them. They walked toward a small bakery at the corner of N Street.

"So what's with the cloak and dagger?" Zeke asked. "Do you have reason to think my car is bugged?"

"I'm following very specific instructions," Moti replied. "When I explain you'll understand."

"You've certainly got my attention," Zeke said. He halted in front of the bakery, buttoned his suit coat and folded his arms against the morning chill. In his mind he began guessing what his cousin might want to communicate to him that would be classified. Perhaps a junket to Israel to visit a secret military installation?

"I will be brief. I've agreed, voluntarily, to deliver an unofficial message from the government of Israel that we hope you will share with your friend Chief Justice Salo-Baron. The message is that the chief justice's life is in danger. We believe his personal protection has been compromised. This is an active, imminent threat and we wanted to make sure he received the message."

Zeke stood in the brisk air staring at his cousin, speechless.

Moti continued. "My instructions were to approach you in a public place where there would be no possibility of eavesdropping."

"Moti," Zeke finally said, "I find myself at a loss for words. I don't know where to begin. What evidence do you have? But leaving that aside, why are you coming to me with this? Israeli intelligence is connected at the hip with the CIA, with Homeland Security, with everyone."

"Of course, this is a good question. A few weeks ago Israel concluded that there is a high level leak in the U.S. intelligence community. We are still trying to figure out who we can trust, which means we are sharing nothing with the U.S. right now through regular channels. Because of this situation, and because we believe the chief justice is in immediate danger, we tried to find a way to get a private message to him."

Zeke squinted momentarily, thinking about this last response. As implausible an explanation as it was, it was not entirely outside the realm of possibility. "So, cousin, how do you come to be involved in this?"

"I know that you are personal friends with the chief justice. I also know I can pick up the phone and get through to you."

"That's not what I mean. How does the Israeli government know that you know me?"

"Ach, the crucial question." Moti looked at him with pleading eyes. "You ask all the right questions."

Zeke was incredulous. "Moti, I was a federal prosecutor for over a decade."

"Shall we keep walking?" Moti asked. He then turned and peered through the plate glass window into the bakery. "Or would you prefer to get some coffee?"

"Considering the nature of the conversation why don't we just keep walking," Zeke replied as he signalled his driver, who was standing outside the car, by flashing ten digits—give us ten minutes. Dennis nodded and looked at his watch.

They resumed a slow pace, walking south. Zeke put on his sunglasses to cut down on the morning glare.

Moti, wearing a dark blazer with no tie, turned his collar up and rubbed his hands together. "The most important thing now is for me is to maintain your trust," he said, "so I reveal to you, privately, as my cousin and friend, that I make extra money by writing reports for Israeli intelligence. I'm not a spy, I don't poke around, I don't investigate. I observe, and I write up my observations."

"Hmmm," Zeke was surprised, but not to any extreme degree—more enlightened than shocked. It was not as though he had never heard of such a thing. "So my cousin has a second job. But if you just observe, that still doesn't explain how the Israeli government knew to come to you to get to me."

"One of my areas of expertise, that I write reports about, is the US Supreme Court. When this threat was uncovered and we realized we could not take it through standard channels, I became part of a working group created to find another way to communicate with the chief justice. I volunteered my connection to you. I am hoping to keep my government work private. If it becomes public, my academic career will be over."

Zeke stopped walking and peered over his sunglasses at Moti. "You're taking a big risk to come to me with this information."

"I am risking everything. That is why you should take this seriously. This is not a hunch, it's a real threat." They reached the corner of Jefferson Place, turned around and began walking back up Connecticut. "There are people involved in the chief justice's protection, in the Marshals Service, who have been compromised. They are part of the rogue intelligence operation that has made Israel stop sharing information with the U.S."

"Salo-Baron relies on the Marshals Service for his security when he travels. If they're the threat, what's he supposed to do? Tell them he received an anonymous tip from a Mossad 'observer' that his life is in danger?"

"For now we urge him to do nothing. We advise him to cancel all public engagements and travel only from his home to the Court and back. We are working on putting together a computer file with information that will point to the problem."

"You will provide evidence?"

"Nothing that you would consider legal evidence. We cannot

have anything traced back to us. What we want to do is keep the chief justice safe while we find a way to point the Marshals Service in the right direction, without revealing the source of the information. We also plan to recommend a specific person in your Department of Justice to take this information to. If it gets into the wrong hands, it could be lost, or worse."

Zeke continued walking in silence. He acknowledged Dennis with a nod as they walked northbound past the car. "This is some story," he finally said. "I understand it's off the record. I understand the risk you've taken. I have no need to tell anyone about your freelance work. But for my own understanding, and confidence, who does the chief justice have to thank for this unofficial warning?"

"It has always been a policy of the State of Israel to warn Jews in the diaspora of threats, especially when it comes to large numbers of people or high-profile individuals like the chief justice. The decision to relay this information to him was made by the Knesset's Subcommittee on Counter-Terrorism in the Diaspora."

"I had no idea there was such a thing."

"Will you agree to pass our message along to the chief justice?"

"I have plans to see him this evening, as it happens. Unless you think he should cancel that engagement as well?"

"No, we are hoping that you will use that occasion to give him my message. Is it possible for you to have this conversation with him outside your home—on the deck outside your office, or down in the back yard?" Moti had been a guest at Zeke's home and knew the layout.

"You have reason to think my home is bugged?"

"The Marshals Service is going to come to your home several hours before the chief justice arrives to do a 'B&B'—a sweep for bombs and bugs. We have concerns about the personnel doing that work. I am asking you to protect us all—you, me and the chief justice—by talking about his security situation only where it can't be overheard. That's why we're outside right now."

Zeke thought, *this is getting better; this is a six or a seven now.* "I will accede to your request," he said. "I assure you I'm taking it all very seriously. I will take the chief justice outside and give him your message. I will press him to curtail his schedule, and I'll tell him about your plans to get us additional information. But I can't predict what his reaction will be to receiving assistance or information from a foreign government, even unofficially."

"Our analysis suggests there is a high probability—over 70 percent—that he will ignore the warning. I hope you will use all the influence you have to persuade him this is real. Trust me, I would not be exposing myself this way if the circumstances were not as I have described."

They arrived back at the corner of N Street, and when they turned to walk back Zeke saw Dennis waving at him and pointing to his watch. "Will you join me back in the car?" Zeke asked. "I'm headed to Georgetown Law on New Jersey Avenue."

Moti declined. "No, my mission is complete—at least for today. I'll be in touch again when we have something we can share with you. This should be within 72 hours, but may be longer. In the meantime, urge the chief justice to cancel everything after your dinner tonight."

Zeke stopped near his car, turned to face Moti, and removed his sunglasses. "Thanks, it would seem, are in order. I am very concerned for the chief justice's well-being, as you know." He embraced his cousin briefly and then stood back and locked onto Moti's eyes. "You knew I was planning to have dinner with him tonight, didn't you? That's why you insisted on seeing me today?"

"Yes, we did. Also," he gestured toward Zeke's parked car,

rippling his one long eyebrow and lowering his voice a notch, "you should have your car checked."

Zeke was nonplussed. He stood by the open back door of the car, his mouth half-open. "*L'hitra'ot*," Moti called out. He waved a cheerful good-bye and walked off, headed downtown.

Zeke climbed in the back of his car, feeling uneasy. Dennis closed the door behind him. *Could it really be bugged?* His concern intensified when Dennis started the car, retracted the partition that separated them and made eye contact with Zeke in the rearview mirror. "Sir, you should know you were being watched the whole time you were walking with your friend."

"What do you mean? Who was watching us?"

"At least two people. A tall, dark-skinned man wearing a green parka, with a hood. He was pacing back and forth in front of that store, talking on the phone, but he kept glancing at you. He's gone now. And the blond woman, wearing a beige trench coat, waiting at the bus stop at the corner, with a magazine. See, she's walking away now?" He pointed to guide Zeke's gaze. "The black scarf? She was watching you the entire time. At least four buses came and went."

"A dark sedan with senate license plates pulls over, two men get out to go for a walk. A lot of people in D.C. might recognize me as a senator. Maybe they were just celebrity watchers."

"Sir, you could be right. It's possible. I'm telling you in my professional opinion, as your security manager, that you were being watched. Or perhaps your guest was being watched. But in either case, your conversation was observed."

"Thanks for letting me know, Dennis. I'll bring it up with Armin."

* * *

By the time Zeke arrived at George Mason Law School at four in the afternoon, he realized that campaigning for the

American Majority Party wasn't going to be that different from campaigning for elective office. Local anecdote, stump speech, Q&A; local anecdote, stump speech, Q&A. It was becoming tedious very fast.

This barely formed thought, alive for milliseconds only, triggered a flash recollection of Rachel's remark the previous evening: it's not like he was mining coal. He also wasn't a candidate in an inane, pointless senate election. He was visiting law schools, teaching, doing what he wanted to be doing, on his own terms.

Another synaptic spark and he jumped to his mother's remark about the car and driver. Most people would be thrilled to have a chauffeur. His arrogance was heaving into view, as massive as an ocean liner, now visible even to his blunt, obtuse male mind. He would stow for now any complaints about his new job.

As usual, the women in his life were in charge.

This made Zeke all the less inclined to give in to the attractive (long, silky blond hair, perky smile) and posture-conscious 3L, president of the Such-and-Such Society, who was making a compelling case for him to submit to an application of anti-glare make-up before his presentation. They were standing inside the wing of an amphitheater lecture hall with 200-plus seats rising in multiple tiers. The podium will be brightly lit, she explained. The event was being streamed live on the web, and just a little powder under his eyes would make it easier for him to see the audience and for the audience to see him.

He resisted. He was not trying to be uncooperative, he explained. At both of his last two stops, the Q&A included questions about him running for president. "I'm trying to avoid doing anything that makes me look like a candidate."

Posture Perfect gave up. "I understand. It's your decision.

You'll be squinting a lot. We'll keep our person standing by in case you change your mind."

The house lights went down. Zeke stepped onto the stage. He could see faces in the first two rows, but above them, all he could make out was a gallery of humanoid shadows. And he noticed the glare from the spotlight on the lectern, in addition to the footlights. He stepped back into the wing and smiled at his host. "Okay," he relented, "I see your point. I'll do the make-up."

There was an unseen cue and the make-up technician arrived moments later with his vinyl cape and pouch of powders and brushes. Posture Perfect straightened her skirt and walked onto the stage to introduce the dean. The dean in turn kept his introduction of Zeke brief and included a reminder that the Q&A was limited to questions about his presentation. There was polite applause.

"Thank you for your kind welcome," Zeke began in a casual, soft-spoken cadence. "I always try to start with a point that everyone can agree on." He paused as the room settled down. "Not as easy as it sounds in a room full of would-be lawyers, but what I have in mind is this simple assumption: the Internet has transformed most transactional activities in modern American society.

"I'm thinking of activities like banking, shopping, travel, dating, even mating. Can I get everyone here to agree that the Internet has disrupted and reorganized each and every one of these fields, as well as dozens of others?"

He waited for a brave soul to break the silence. "Any dissenters?" he called out, pausing again. There were no takers. Not a rustle.

"Well, that was easy; *I'm on a roll now.*" He had them, he could tell. He had a trial lawyer's jury radar. "Starting from this unanimously agreed-upon point, I make the observation that the Internet has had no such transformative effect on our elections and our governance. By almost any measure our democracy remains as inefficient as it was before the Internet arrived. There's no on-line voting. At least a third of eligible voters still don't register to vote. If anything, our democracy seems more dysfunctional than ever. Does anyone have a theory to explain why the World Wide Web hasn't transformed our democracy the way it has transformed everything else?"

Hands went up in all rows. Zeke held a palm out over his forehead to block the glare, trying to adjust to the dim upper reaches. Posture Perfect had been right about the make-up. "I'll take three comments, 40-second limit; your first name and hometown please."

The responses were thoughtful and earnest. Zeke acknowledged each one and then segued at the end. "As just demonstrated, there are many reasonable answers to this question. Here's another, perhaps simpler, answer: our democracy hasn't been transformed by the Internet because no one has yet invented the right application."

He then turned briefly to make sure the lectern's computer desktop was projected on the screen behind him, and navigated to the American Majority Party website. "What I'm going to show you now is an on-line voting app that could bring our antiquated democracy into the Internet age.

"The app is called a No Vote Pledge, and here's how it works. Every voter who signs up at www.american-majority.org gets a personalized democracy dashboard like the one displayed behind me. The dashboard offers several issue-specific proposals that voters can pledge their future *candidate* vote to. Take for example the proposition that I have highlighted on the screen:

I'm a registered voter and I promise I won't vote for any candidate for federal office who does not support legislation to legalize and tax marijuana, and regulate its use like alcohol and tobacco.

Of the first three No Vote Pledge campaigns we've activated on our website, this one has attracted the most support so far. This may be because Katzanikas mentioned it on his comedy news program last night, and by 1 a.m. our servers crashed from the flood of traffic. I've been told his audience is majority-stoned at that hour."

Zeke's own audience howled and clapped, but he tamped their reaction down with inverted palms. "As you can see," he continued, "our web site recovered and we managed to take in 180,000 new No Vote Pledges—we call them NVPs—on this one issue since yesterday."

He worked the mouse and highlighted some NVP tallies broken down by state and congressional district. "The object of every NVP campaign, for each issue, is to attract a majority of voters. When a majority is achieved in a given jurisdiction, it sends a clear message to the elected officials representing that area: either comply with your constituents' wishes, or expect to lose your next election."

Zeke looked up from the console and turned his attention to the room. "Is everyone following me so far?"

Hands shot up. Zeke called on a female silhouette in the right-field bleacher seats.

"I'm Paula from Baltimore, Senator. I'm a Democrat. I'm happy with my Democratic representative, but if for some reason she was opposed to legalization of marijuana, I wouldn't want to *not* vote for her. What am I going to do, vote for the Republican? Not vote at all?"

"Thank you Paula," Zeke said, leaning into his microphone. "Your question brings us to the heart of the matter right away. There may be many voters like you who are loyal to their party and its candidates, and don't want to tie their support for a candidate to just one issue.

"My response has two parts. First of all, as genuine as your feelings are towards the Democratic Party, I invite you—as well as voters who identify with the Republican Party—to recognize that the two-party system is the primary cause of our nation's democratic dysfunction.

"Remember that the U.S. constitution says nothing about the two-party system. In fact future president John Adams declared in 1792 that the two-party system was 'to be dreaded as the greatest political evil under our constitution.' The evil he was referring to is the situation we face today, in which partisan politics has invaded and polarized all of our democratic institutions, from Congress to the Supreme Court to the executive branch. Even facts have become subject to partisan interpretation, and fact-based disciplines like journalism and science are under attack.

"Why do we stay with this poisonous, inherently divisive system? Why do we cling to our party allegiances? Because we have no better alternative. We concede that democracy is messy and expensive and we muddle through as best we can.

"Except now there is an alternative. The new Internet voting app I just described—the NVP Campaign—changes everything, by giving voters a *non-partisan basis* for deciding who to vote for. At any time, and as often as you wish, you can visit your Majority Party dashboard and vote for *what* you want—for specific policies that you want your elected representatives, whoever they are, to enact. Of course in November you still need to vote in regular candidate elections, but now your dashboard will identify those candidates you can vote for based on the *issues* you've pledged your vote to.

"Emphasis on *issues*—plural. This is the second part of my response to your question, Paula, about not wanting to tie your future candidate vote to a single issue. Right now, in addition to the marijuana proposition, we have only two other active NVP campaigns. Our Issues Committee, however, is busy crafting additional NVP campaigns that have the potential to attract a majority of voters. Soon you'll be able to vote on even more issues, and to participate in the issue vetting process yourself if you wish.

"To summarize, what I'm suggesting is that we all abandon the two-party system—walk away from both the Republicans and the Democrats. As a member of the American Majority Party you can now safely ignore all candidate ads, party appeals and television talking heads, because on election day your AMP dashboard will show you who's running, and who supports the policies you've pledged your vote to. What party a candidate is affiliated with becomes irrelevant.

"Finally, I think it's possible the American Majority Party will appeal to some of the 90 million Americans who are eligible to vote but haven't registered to do so. Perhaps these citizens may consider joining in our governance if it no longer requires constant exposure to political soap operas and hypocritical grandstanding."

Applause broke out and again he deflected it. He'd gotten carried away; that was a mistake. He sounded like he was running for something. Rachel, if watching the live web stream, would be rolling her eyes.

To maintain momentum he scanned the audience for another raised hand and proceeded to field a half-dozen more questions. How do you prevent fraudulent registrations? Will voters actually follow through on their NVP commitments? What if politicians don't act on their promises? Zeke was primed; he batted back answers with examples, with statistics, with wit. It all felt right. He wondered, was this the catharsis that Armin had been referring to?

3

"The most important political office is that of the private citizen."

—LDB, declining to run for mayor of Boston, 1903

WHEN 20-YEAR OLD Ezekiel Sherman first started attending Anthony Salo-Baron's Introduction to Constitutional Law at Columbia Law School, he quickly became convinced that the professor, then 44, was dressing and grooming himself in deliberate imitation of Albert Einstein, whom he was physically (and perhaps mentally) well-equipped to emulate. His pale eyes, salt and pepper mustache, and Tesla Coil hair were all natural features, so it was easy to complete the effect with a pair of wrinkled trousers and a frayed sweater.

Zeke saw this as intentional theater on the part of Salo-Baron, but when he pointed it out to his classmates they were skeptical. They saw the resemblance, but didn't believe the professor was putting on a show.

"Why would he do something like that?" someone asked. "You think he's trying to impress us? To get on our good side, so that we give him good Scorecard ratings?"

"I think he's having fun with his job," Zeke argued. "This is his way of adding some other dimension to his work."

No one was persuaded. The professor's pronounced New England accent, it was agreed, was the biggest barrier to a successful Einstein impersonation.

Soon afterward, however, in the middle of a lecture, Salo-Baron defined a specific point of law that was the keystone to an entire legal edifice he had just constructed, and then asked in perfect, deadpan German: *"Was lehrt uns das? Was können wir daraus schließen?"*

Zeke was delighted and let out an audible guffaw. He was alone, however; this was not the usual decorum in a class of terrified first year law students who ordinarily sought to remain as still and invisible as possible.

The professor scanned the 100-seat lecture hall. Zeke thought it would be childish to try to avoid him and raised his hand. "Sorry, sir. That was me. It slipped out."

"You found this amusing, Mr. Sherman?" the professor asked.

Zeke, while not entirely confident of his intellectual capacity, had an uncanny sixth sense about people and their personalities and motivations. Among other talents he was an acute listener, and he was sure the professor's tone was one of inquiry, not accusation. He kept his composure.

"I did. I thought it was funny. It completes the whole Einstein image."

"You think Einstein was funny?"

"He was known to have a sense of humor. If he saw your imitation I think he'd get a big kick out of it—or a big bang, maybe, in his case."

Zeke glanced to see if this might generate some type of reaction from his classmates, but most were staring at him, some with their mouths open.

"Why do you say that?" Salon-Baron persisted.

"I've read his biography."

"Which one?"

"Stetham most recently. I thought Isaacson was better."

The Professor seemed pleased. "Do you speak German?"

"No sir. I didn't understand what you said—I just recognized it as German."

The professor turned away from Zeke and addressed the class. "Are there any German speakers here today?"

The class was catatonic. Zeke wondered if the room had not been engulfed in a time warp, where everyone except he and the professor had shifted into hyper-slow motion.

"No? No fluent speakers of German? No LL.M.'s from Heidelberg U?"

Finally a student in the second row raised his hand halfway. "My parents spoke German at home. I lived there—not at home, in Germany—for two years. I took it as a minor in college."

"Your name again is Mr. Hammond, is it not?"

"Hamline, sir." He spelled it out.

"Mr. Hamline, how was my German? Did you understand what I said?"

"Sir, I think so. I'm not sure. Can you repeat?"

"I will ask you to translate for the class. Here it is again." The professor revved his vocal chords for clearance. "*Was lehrt uns das?*" he called out with thespian confidence, flinging his forearm. "*Was können wir daraus schließen?*"

"*Was lehrt uns das,*" Hamline repeated, "*Was lehrt uns . . .* means 'What do we learn from this?' Or better, 'what does this teach us?' And the other phrase again?"

"*Was können wir daraus schließen?*"

"*Was können wir daraus . . .* 'What can we conclude from of this . . . what conclusion can we make from this?'"

"Excellent. Thank you for your assistance. What did you think of my accent?" The professor then blandished a mischievous wink for all to see. "Of course your answer will have no effect on your mid-term grade."

"Sir, I am completely sold on your German. It sounds great to me."

"Well done, Mr. Hamline. Your grade remains unchanged, however you earn a gold star for demonstrating the concept of expediency."

Laughter and applause erupted in all rows. The slow-motion collapsed. Students exhaled and shifted in their seats.

Then, pointing to a hapless, random student in the uppermost row, the professor moved on with the lecture. "Ms. van den Heuvel from Boston, if I recall—what does this teach us? To regain our bearings, what is the key precedent from which most erosion of privacy decisions were derived during this era?"

At the end of the class the professor asked Zeke to remain behind.

"I love to practice my Einstein," he said after the room emptied. "I'm glad to know someone gets it."

"Oh, sir, I think we all get it. There's not more of a reaction because we're trying to stay off your radar. My laughter was spontaneous. I couldn't have done anything to stop it."

The professor invited Zeke to his once-a-month Sunday afternoon salon for 3L's and faculty colleagues, and from there the relationship grew along professional lines. Zeke was sure it was the professor's recommendation that secured for him a clerkship with a senior judge in the 4th Circuit, which led to an offer for an assistant U.S. attorney position in Charleston.

Over the years they kept in touch, celebrating each other's career advances with phone calls, e-mails, and reunions at the occasional professional meeting. When Salo-Baron was nominated to the Supreme Court he provided a list of professional references to the Senate Judiciary Committee. Zeke was on the list, and the Committee invited him to testify on the professor's behalf. Zeke dedicated almost a full week preparing for his appearance, and at show time delivered a compelling performance. Despite conservative opposition the nomination was approved narrowly by the Committee, and in the Senate by a healthy margin.

Several years later, when Zeke landed in Washington as an appointed senator, he called on the chief justice and soon they were dining together almost every week. Initially Zeke was drawn to these meetings by a desire to learn from his mentor how to navigate the pitfalls of public life, but it soon became clear that the chief justice had his own reciprocal motive. He cast Zeke in the role of extrajudicial confidant, someone he could trust to talk to about the raging partisan feud he had inherited upon his arrival at the court.

Sometimes these dinners were in the chief justice's private chambers, but often enough they were in public settings like the Senate dining room, or restaurants on K Street or in Georgetown. On such occasions Zeke wondered if he wasn't misrepresenting himself to the public: anyone observing his intense, hushed table talk with the chief justice might assume they were discussing a finer point of law, or at least something of an intellectual nature. In fact, more often than not, it was about personnel. The four Democratic and four Republican justices were barely on speaking terms, which made it hard to come to a consensus on any matter that was subject to partisan interpretation—which was just about everything. The chief justice's conflict with Justice Ross seemed irreconcilable, if for no reason other than its history. During the professor's confirmation hearings Justice Ross's husband Walter—who had already traded on his wife's judicial career to build a million dollar-a-year lobbying practice for conservative causes—

worked intensively behind the scenes in the Senate to derail the nomination. When that effort failed and the professor was confirmed, Justice Ross herself went on the record. Speaking to a Baptist-affiliated law school in Tennessee, she suggested that the new "Democrat/Atheist Majority" on the high court had as its agenda the total secularization of America, and vowed to oppose it at every turn. In subsequent speeches she assailed her liberal colleagues and at one point even singled out the chief justice for censure. She feared the U.S. Supreme Court was being led by a man who was hostile to all people of faith, and that he was a "danger to the moral fabric of the nation." Although the chief justice was Jewish by birth, and distantly related to a renowned scholar of Jewish history, he grew up in a non-religious environment. He described himself as an open-minded atheist, by which he meant *show me the proof; I'll believe in God when its existence can be demonstrated with empiric evidence.*

On more than one occasion Zeke suggested to the chief justice that he was being "too good a Christian" by always turning the other cheek and not reacting to his colleague's unprecedented bad behavior. But Salo-Baron believed that any response, private or public, would only generate more publicity and controversy. This would be the worst outcome, from his point of view, because it would interfere both with the court's work and its reputation. He chose instead to remain focused on his primary goal, which was to broaden the consensus behind the court's decisions. In this spirit, even though his own thinking on most issues was liberally oriented, he was careful to maintain a neutral stance and show some tolerance toward the conservative bloc's views. For these efforts, and all Zeke's advice, the chief justice managed to bring in only a handful of unanimous decisions each year—a dismal record. This was a source of constant torment to the chief justice, who was not obsessed with, but certainly conscious of, the historian's eye. Zeke took his mentor's burden to heart, and together they spent countless hours discussing various scenarios that would keep the court on a dignified path without compromising the chief justice's core values.

On the occasion of their double date, however, they agreed in advance to refrain from serious court talk. When Zeke greeted the chief justice and his wife Fran at the front door of his Cathedral Avenue townhouse, he found his guests back-lit by a fiery late-summer sunset, at the moment blocked by the hulking National Cathedral up the street.

"Everyone is looking saintly in the glow," Zeke proclaimed. "Please come in and join our work in progress. Rachel is in the kitchen for the moment." He held open the screen door with his left hand and swept his guests in with his right. They were trailed at a respectful distance by several plainclothes deputy marshals. As he closed the door, Zeke noticed more agents outside, and a three-car motorcade parked at the curb.

In the darker foyer it took several moments for Zeke's eyes to adjust. When they did, he was startled. "I can't remember the last time I saw you without a tie!" he exclaimed. The chief justice was wearing unpressed khakis and a navy golf shirt.

"I hope this isn't a dinner party. I thought it was just the four of us."

"Oh, it is just us, and informal is fine; it's just not what I'm used to. It's wonderful!"

"You've met Fran, I'm sure," the chief justice said, presenting his wife. Zeke had met her on several public occasions, but never privately. In the past he always thought of her as petite, but now, closer up, he settled on "compact." Everything about her was condensed, solid. Her dark hair, streaked with silver, was cut short, low-maintenance, all business. Zeke found himself hesitating . . . handshake or kiss?

She filled in the blank, reaching up to plant a kiss on his cheek. "You are, I want you to know, the reason we remain happily married." Mischief gleamed in her eye.

Zeke laughed. "No! How could this be? We almost never discuss personal matters."

"Oh, it's very simple," she said. "I could never talk shop with him the way you do. I would be driven mad. He would be driven mad. It's an impossible situation, and in his position it's hard to trust anyone. If he didn't have you, I don't know who he could talk to—about work, at least." She was dressed casually but—unlike her husband—impeccably, in finely tailored charcoal slacks and a light cashmere-looking pullover. She wore pearls.

"I'm honored to play my role," Zeke replied, "but the professor gets most of the credit." He placed his hand on the chief justice's shoulder. "I can't imagine a more difficult cast of characters to work with."

Rachel emerged from the kitchen and Zeke made the introductions. Fran offered some praise for a recent *Women in Charge* segment about delays in rape kit testing in major cities. Rachel responded with a certain look, a light touch on the forearm, and a few softly spoken words, after which they were fast friends, aglow in mutual admiration.

Their bonding was like a chemical reaction, a dual epoxy mixture, instantaneous and permanent. Zeke had seen this phenomenon repeated on several occasions since Rachel took up her new career. He attributed it to the unspoken tag line of *Women in Charge*, which was *men have been screwing things up long enough; women can do it better*. Rachel's television persona was the most earnest imaginable manifestation of this philosophy, and to a certain class of hyper-intelligent, Beltway-savvy power women—of whom Fran Salo-Baron was a prime example—Rachel was a visionary, if not revolutionary, figure.

The women peeled off into the kitchen in synchronous formation.

Zeke guided the professor down the hallway into his office. "Why don't we take a few minutes before dinner," Zeke said. "I've got one thing I want to bring up while we have a moment alone. Can I get you something to drink?" He opened a cabinet, revealing a wet bar.

"Just water for now," the chief justice replied.

Zeke took two glasses from a shelf above the sink and filled them with tap water. "If you don't mind," he said, handing one glass to the chief justice, "I'd be happy to step outside on the deck for a few minutes. I've been in auditoriums and automobiles all day long."

"By all means," the chief justice replied. "Lead the way."

Zeke unlocked the door and stepped out onto the deck, only to encounter two deputy marshals already there, engaged in an intense discussion.

The taller one broke away and approached Zeke. "Senator Sherman, I'm Special Agent Owen Petersee, in charge of the chief justice's security detail tonight. We try to stay in the background as much as possible, which is why you're finding us here. If you and the chief justice plan to use the deck, we'll remove ourselves."

"That would be appreciated," Zeke said. "We'd like to take a few minutes out here before dinner."

"No problem, Senator. I need to keep someone stationed in the back yard, but I'll instruct her to pull back." Petersee signaled to the agent below and then exited through a separate sliding glass door into the kitchen. It was twilight and summer humidity lingered in the air.

Zeke gestured for the chief justice to sit in one of two cushioned deck chairs that flanked a molded plastic table, and then walked to the edge of the deck to see where the outside agent was posted. She was leaning against the fence lining the service alley—safely out of earshot. .

"Hmm," the chief justice replied, "I detect something serious." He placed his water glass on the table and sat down. "It's not Justice Ross again I hope. God forbid."

"No, this is a little different." Zeke sat down next to him and lowered his voice. "This is all off the record," he said. "I've been approached by a member of my extended family, a highly credentialed Israeli law professor whom I've known for 20 years and have every reason to trust, and he's asked me to pass along to you an unofficial message from the State of Israel."

"Hoo-hah! Every day something new!" The chief justice seemed to bounce in his seat with excitement. "What is this message?" He took a drink of water.

"It concerns your security. Israeli intelligence agencies have come across information suggesting your Marshals Service protection may be compromised, and that your life may be in danger."

There was a long pause. The chief justice was no longer smiling. "Something—many things—don't sound right here. The last I heard Israel and the U.S. had good relations, especially in security matters. Why is this not going through regular channels?"

"I asked the same question. My cousin claims there's a high-level leak somewhere in the American intelligence community that's caused the Israelis to hold back on everything. It's very recent and they haven't figured out yet who they can trust. The threat to you is part of what they think is a rogue intelligence operation of some sort that involves people across different agencies, including the Marshals Service."

"Sounds very far-fetched. You know I receive threats all the time."

"My source knew this would be your reaction, and it's not

my intention to press you any further. But I find my cousin's story very credible, and I urge you to take it seriously. I can't imagine that the Israeli government would have gone to all this trouble if it was just a hunch."

"How did they know to come to you to get to me?" the chief justice asked.

"It's an interesting coincidence of national policy and family ties. Apparently Israel has always had a policy of warning Jews in the diaspora of threats, especially when it involves prominent people, or large numbers of people. I was chosen as the messenger because I'm known to have your ear—this is public information—and because they happened to have a way to contact me privately, through my relative."

"Well, I guess I don't know what to say . . . thanks? Unofficially?" The chief justice grasped the back of his neck with one hand and began a self-massage, a thinking pose that Zeke well recognized. He left the silence alone.

"The real issue here," the chief justice started up again slowly, "is not that I doubt your relative or his information. I see that some effort went into bringing this to my attention, so I will take it at face value. The problem is, what am I supposed to do? It's the Marshals Service that handles my security. If they're the problem, who do I trust? Who am I supposed to talk to about this threat?"

"My cousin, or the people he works for, seem to have anticipated this also. He told me they're putting together a computer file that will lead investigators to the problem, and will give us the name of a trusted contact in DOJ we should bring the information to. He's estimating three days to accomplish this, and urges you to cancel everything on your schedule other than regular work. No public engagements of any kind."

"Hmm." The chief justice paused in thought for some

moments. "So the bottom line is, if I'm going to buy into this, I should hole myself up for the next few days?"

"That's the idea. Don't take any side trips. Don't go to the movies, don't go out to eat . . . nothing except your daily round-trip to the court."

"And all the while I'm to say nothing to anyone about this?"

"I think not. The Israelis chose my cousin to deliver the message because it gives them cover if they need to deny anything. He's told me he will acknowledge that we met, but claim that we spoke only of family and personal matters."

"So I shouldn't say anything to Aaron? Or more importantly, to Fran?"

Aaron Rosen was the chief justice's long-time head clerk and *de facto* chief of staff. "Do you trust Aaron?" Zeke asked.

"He's been with me twelve years. The relationship is strictly professional, but it's very close."

"I'm sure it would be okay, but before you do, I would ask the question: what do you want him to do with the information?"

The chief justice paused, his expression descending into a frown. "I'm not sure."

"Same with Fran. If she knew, you'd want her to do what— leave town? Is she a level-headed person in a situation like this?"

"I would think so. She's been understanding about the security routine. But I agree, there's no point in worrying her."

"Professor," Zeke said, engaging his most confidential baritone, "I'm the first to admit—I'm not sure what's going on here. This is new territory for me. That being said, my counsel to you is to do as the Israelis advise. This story seems way too fantastic to be made up. Be cautious here, conservative. It costs you nothing to go along with this for a few days."

There was a knock on the glass kitchen door, which was then slid open by Lizzie Agnew, Zeke's energetic, 61-year-old cook and house manager. "Sorry to interrupt, Senator. I just wanted you to know dinner is ready."

Zeke signaled for her to join them on the deck as he and the chief justice rose from their seats in tandem.

"Chief Justice Salo-Baron, I'd like you to meet Elizabeth Agnew." The chief justice reached forward to grasp her hand and shook it warmly.

"It's an honor to meet you, sir," Lizzie said, nodding her head briefly, "and to have you and your wife join us for dinner. She was just in the kitchen telling me you've known the senator almost as many years as I have." She beamed at Zeke with a mixture of pride and possessiveness. The daughter of a third-generation coal miner from Marion County, West Virginia, Lizzie had started work as a part-time housekeeper and cook for the Sherman family when Zeke was seven years old. A decade later, with the encouragement of his parents and other housekeeping clients, she opened a small catering business and café in Morgantown that flourished for another 25 years.

"Then you're even luckier than I," the chief justice answered. "I can tell you he's been an indispensable friend to me."

"I don't doubt it for a second," Lizzie said. "I'll leave you gentlemen to your business, but please don't be long. Things will get cold." She turned and reentered the kitchen through the sliding door.

After she left, Zeke explained to the professor that when Lizzie retired from her catering business in Morgantown, his mother came up with the idea that she might want to come to Washington to cook and manage his bachelor household. "When I first offered her the job she resisted; she said she was afraid of big cities. When she finally came for a visit, I walked with her down to Connecticut Avenue, introduced her to some of the shopkeepers, and rode with her on the Metro to Capitol Hill. She's come to love D.C., and does a great job for me here."

They retrieved their glasses and stood once more at the deck's edge, looking out over the back yard. The agent was no longer there. Still maintaining a lowered voice, Zeke reiterated his concern for the professor's safety. "The hardest part is that it's all off the record. We can't act on this ourselves because everyone will want to know where our information came from, and as I've said, the Israelis have arranged it so they can deny everything."

"But you trust this man? You have a prior relationship with him?"

"Yes, I trust him, and yes, I've known him for over twenty years. But I've also just learned that my cousin freelances, so he says, for Mossad, writing reports for them about the Supreme Court among other things. That's how they ended up finding this path to you. I want you to have as complete a picture as possible."

Zeke led the chief justice back through his office and into the dining room, where they encountered Rachel and Fran in an intense discussion about *Norville v. Arizona*, an abortion rights case making its way to the Supreme Court.

"The answer to all our questions has just arrived," Fran Salo-Baron said, extending her hand to her husband and pulling herself up to him. "We were just discussing *Norville*."

"So I gather."

Lizzie arrived with platters of food balanced on both arms, and the two couples took their seats. "Senator, are you sure you don't want me to be serving?" Lizzie offered after everything was arranged on the table.

"Thanks, we're going to rough it, family style, and help ourselves. Everything looks and smells terrific."

As they passed the dishes around and began eating, Fran returned to the abortion case.

"Is it correct to say that if this case is upheld," Fran asked her husband, "it will provide a type of protection for reproductive rights that's different from *Roe v. Wade*?"

"That's the idea," the chief justice replied. "This case doesn't rely on the right to privacy, which is the legal basis for *Roe v. Wade*. *Norville* makes an equal protection argument—laws should apply equally to all persons regardless of gender. The plaintiffs argue the state cannot use its police power to force anyone, man or woman, to submit to a medical procedure, even if the procedure might save the life of another person. This is well established. The state can't force a man to surrender a kidney, for example, to save the life of a stranger, or even a brother. If the same laws apply to women—as they should under equal protection guarantees—the state can't force a woman to bring a pregnancy to term. If it did, it would be the same as seizing control of her body to preserve the interests of a third party."

"That seems simple enough. And a little obvious?" Zeke volunteered. "Why hasn't this approach ever been taken before?"

"The concept here has been around since the 1980's. Ruth Bader Ginsburg wrote about this in a law review article before joining the Court.* Others have written about it as well. I guess it's taken this long for the right test case to come along."

"When you came in," Fran said to her husband, "I was trying to explain to Rachel why *Norville* is so important. Thanks for your help."

"Let's not get ahead of ourselves," the chief justice replied. "It's not even been through conference yet. And Ross has her

---

* Ginsburg's original comments on this issue were delivered in a lecture at New York University Law School on April 6, 1984, and later published as Ruth Bader Ginsburg, *Some Thoughts on Autonomy and Equality in Relation to Roe v. Wade*, 63 N.C. Law Rev. 375 (1985). Cf. also her dissent in *Gonzales v. Carhart*, 550 U.S. 124 (2007).

sights set on *Norville*—she's going to do anything she can do to sway this decision, including going public. Again."

Zeke intervened. "I just want to remind you, professor, we agreed we wouldn't talk too much shop."

"Hmmm, correct you are. We agreed we wouldn't talk about *my* shop. But what about your shop? What's all this about you running for president? Since you resigned from the Senate you've been showing up in polls as a presidential candidate."

"Washington is an amazing place, isn't it? It's like Alice's Wonderland; everything is upside down and backwards. I've announced I'm not running for anything, and they continue to poll me."

"I know your reasons for leaving the Senate," Fran said. "Congress is a broken institution as you say. But what about the presidency? You don't think that's different?"

"The root problem is my dislike of election campaigns," Zeke replied. "I see them as glorified fundraising telethons. Senate, president, it's all the same. Plus, I'm feeling good about what I'm doing. Today was my first day pitching the American Majority Party, and it felt right. I was well received."

"I'm sure you were," Rachel countered, "and it's that same popularity that could put you in the White House if you were so inclined. People respond to you. You're in a unique position. You could have this enormous impact on the political landscape in this country, and yet you insist on walking away from it."

"I'm not walking away. I'm facing it head on. Things aren't working the way they are. We need to try something new, something different."

The chief justice intervened. "I'm reminded of a comment made by Louis Brandeis, the Supreme Court justice from the last century, who many times declined invitations to run for elective office. He said 'the most important political office is that of private citizen.' And he stuck by that position his whole career. He always believed he could accomplish more working on his own, without being constrained by political or party obligations."

"Wait . . ." Zeke put down his knife and fork. "You're saying Brandeis rejected politics as a career because he thought he could be more effective in some other role?"

"Indeed. And of course ultimately he was."

"Why Professor, what an excellent . . . *trivium*. Zeke was suddenly buoyant. "I am so . . . *encouraged*."

There was a temporary pause as glasses were refilled and food passed and commented upon.

"Not to detract from your respective contributions," Fran said, nodding briefly at her husband and Zeke, then turning to Rachel. "I was hoping to hear about your work at *Women in Charge*. Is there something you can tell us about the show that's not public information? How do you find your guests? These are the most fascinating women."

"I give a lot of credit to my producer, who happens to be a man—his name is Harrison Starr. He's like a good shrink; he's got a talent for getting people to articulate what it is that makes them tick. He spends—we spend—a lot of time with prospective guests. Fewer than half the people we interview end up on the show."

"Do you have any big names coming up soon?" Fran asked. "I record every show, so if there's someone I really want to see I'll be able to find it easily."

"I don't know if it's a big name," Rachel replied, "but we're planning on having a guest who you know," she said, turning to the chief justice. "Her name is Kendra Hurtig, she's a retired federal judge. Her topic will be judicial ethics in general and Justice Ross's in particular."

The chief justice dropped his napkin over his plate and

shifted his chair back slightly. "This is very surprising to hear. I have tremendous respect for Judge Hurtig, of course, as a jurist. And I understand she recently retired, but still . . . it's not her style to go public. Does she say why she's taken up this cause?"

"Yes, of course," Rachel replied. "I've met with her twice, and Harrison interviewed her yesterday. As you say she has a very professional orientation. She is troubled—appalled, really—at how Justice Ross has abased the judicial profession. All the public speaking she does, and this napping on the bench—Hurtig's professional sensibilities are offended. She takes it personally." In recent years during oral arguments Justice Ross had made a practice of lowering the back of her chair to an almost flat recline, propping her legs up on a hassock under the bench, and closing her eyes. Lawyers who worked for months to hone their arguments and summarize everything into a succinct half-hour presentation were greeted on their day of reckoning by a napping justice.

"It's rude," the chief justice said with a resigned sigh, "but unethical? That's a stretch."

"And that alone would not sustain a segment on *Women in Charge*. What we've found interesting, what we're exploring from a programmatic point of view, is this whole database of Ross's offenses—her conflicts of interests, her public statements, everything—that Hurtig has compiled. There are close to a hundred entries. She has dates, times, locations; it's all searchable and cross-referenced. She couldn't sit still in retirement, so she started a new career as an investigative reporter."

"And this information somehow translates into a guest appearance on your show?" Zeke asked.

"That's what we're working on now. We see it as a two-part program: Hurtig would first talk about the judicial profession, what its objectives and professional standards are, and provide an overview of the ethical rules and guidelines for federal judges. In the second half she'll compare these standards to Ross's record."

"To what end?" Zeke asked. "What is Hurtig trying to achieve? Is she hoping to embarrass Ross? Provoke her? Get her impeached?"

"Her goal is impeachment. She documents two instances of perjury, and claims they qualify as the requisite high crime or misdemeanor."

Zeke sat motionless, looking stunned. The chief justice turned to his friend with inquiring eyes: "I can't imagine you knew anything about this."

"Of course not. This is the first I'm hearing of it."

"Have I committed an error?" Rachel turned to Zeke, looking distraught. "I thought any topic was okay. I asked you last night if we could talk about Justice Ross."

"I didn't anticipate this particular line of conversation," Zeke replied. "It puts the chief justice in an awkward position."

"I'm so sorry," Rachel said, her voice wavering slightly. "I thought it was all off the record; I didn't realize it would be a problem."

"My dear," Salo-Baron replied, "it is all off the record, thankfully. No harm has been done. But you can see how I cannot in any way be associated with what Judge Hurtig is doing, as appealing an enterprise as it may otherwise seem."

Lizzie tapped the dining room doorpost. "Senator, did you find everything to your liking?"

Fran leaned in toward Rachel. "Saved by the bell," she said in a sideways whisper.

"Lizzie, as always, it was a feast," Zeke said. The spinach dish, with the little nuts—just excellent. What kind of fish was it?"

"It's called black cod, Senator," Lizzie replied. "Rarely

available, so when I saw it at the market I scooped it up. Glad you liked it."

There was verbal agreement all around as Lizzie retrieved dishes and bowls, balancing them on her arms in an impossible cascade. From underneath the table a phone emitted a whistling chirp. "Oh, that's mine, my apologies," Zeke said. He retrieved his phone from his pocket and consulted it. "Well, I suppose I should do as they ask." He looked around. "Will you forgive me? Maybe others would like to get up and stretch before dessert. It apparently can't wait—whatever 'it' is."

Zeke stepped into the hallway and headed to his office, dialing Armin along the way. It connected after one ring.

"Senator, I'm sorry to interrupt. I trust you're enjoying yourself."

"I am," Zeke replied. "What's up?"

"I thought it best to check with you, sir. I got a call from the man you met with this morning, your cousin the law professor, Rivlin. Your phone was off, and my number is the emergency contact on your voicemail."

"Moti? What did he want?" Zeke closed the door to his office and stood by the window overlooking the rear courtyard.

"I tried to get some information, but he said it was a personal matter and extremely urgent. He said it could not wait until tomorrow or even later tonight. I thought it best to check with you. He had your private number, and I know you met with him this morning."

"Okay. I have no idea where this is going but let's find out. Did he leave a number?" He moved towards the small desk in the corner of the room to get a pen.

"He did. If you'd like I can dial it on this phone and conference it through."

"That would be great, but please leave the line once we're connected."

"Of course."

When Moti came on the line, Armin clicked off. "Okay, what's going on?" Zeke asked.

"It's about our conversation this morning. Right now we can only speak for a couple of minutes, but first I want to ask, are you alone? Can you go outside again?"

"I'm in my office now," Zeke replied. "I'll be outside in a few moments." He opened the door to find the deck lights ablaze but the area was otherwise empty. He went to the railing and surveyed the backyard, which was now dark. "Okay, I'm outside, I think I'm alone. What's happened?"

"A live audiovisual feed is being transmitted from inside your house, right now, as we speak. It began when the chief justice arrived, so it must have been initiated by someone on his security detail. But it's not a Marshals Service signal. The threat I referred to this morning . . . it's here now. The chief justice is in immediate danger. Possibly as he leaves your home."

"Moti, where are you? How do you have all this information?"

"Zeke, I know you have questions and I promise to answer them all at another time. I'm nowhere near your house, but right now you must trust me. Please. We have known each other many years."

"What do you mean, when he leaves my home? What do you think is going to happen?"

"Think about your house. It's set back from the street, there are steps down and it's a long walk to the curb. Across the street—a park, a school playground, the church, dozens of places a sniper can hide. It's a vulnerable location."

A massive shot of adrenalin kicked in. Zeke's mind raced along with his pulse. "Moti," he said, whispering, "you have to tell me. How do you know this?"

"Through my second job. Remember? Details later. Trust me, your friend is in immediate danger."

"What is it you want us to do?" Zeke asked.

"Nothing. Stay where you are. We've placed an anonymous call to the US Marshals office in Arlington, warning them of an imminent threat against the chief justice at your location. Because we're not really sure what's going on at the Marshals Service, we played the same recorded warning to 911 and the Secret Service in Washington, D.C."

"What will that do?"

"When they receive a specific threat like this, they should switch to a back-up exit plan. More resources will come in— cars, agents. They may take him out through a back door. If he leaves through the front, they should use umbrellas to create a canopy, and there should be at least one decoy run before the chief justice and his wife leave."

"A what run?"

"Agents posing as the chief justice and his wife will make the trip to the car before they do."

"And I'm to do nothing?"

"Not exactly nothing. You must make sure that no one in your party leaves the house through the front door until the new personnel arrive. You're just sitting down to dessert, so the timing should be good. Otherwise, say nothing, do nothing. Try not to show a reaction to this call when you return to the others. *Hay-vanta*? Do you understand?"

Zeke was in a daze. He nodded to himself, and then in a delayed reaction responded. "Yes, I understand."

"Cousin, I'm going to hang up in 30 seconds. Listen to me. The following is important, you must remember this—*sim-lev!* Pay attention!"

"I'm listening."

"You and I have just spoken for three minutes about my Aunt Julia's problems with her short-term memory. I called to ask if your mother, who speaks to Julia almost every day, had ever said anything to you about Julia not remembering things. My call was urgent because *my* mother is taking Julia to see an Alzheimer's specialist in Rehovot tomorrow morning. If you are ever asked about this phone call, that is what we talked about. I will never acknowledge anything else. *Hayvanta*?"

"Yes. Understood."

"We'll speak again soon, but make no references to anything over the phone. Ever. This was a one-time emergency. We must end this call now. Stay calm." The line clicked off.

"Whew," Zeke said out loud, half-whistling to himself. He put his phone back in his pocket, and leaned backwards against the wood banister. Moti had to be more than an academic "observer" writing reports about the U.S. Supreme Court. He knew about back-up plans and canopies and decoy runs.

Zeke quickly rehearsed in his mind's eye their relationship over the years. There had been nothing prying or inquisitive about Moti's manner. In fact, on reflection, it seemed that whenever Moti raised a topic, it was usually about his work at the law school—interesting cases, articles he had written for various international tax law journals, or the machinations of clever students. Now, however, it made sense why Moti wasn't married and never seemed to be interested in dating. Juggling two jobs—law professor and spy—would be hard enough; adding a marriage in the mix would be a mission impossible.

On the way back to the dining room he encountered two agents in the hallway: one talking on his phone, the other was Petersee, the agent-in-charge, who was smiling at him.

Zeke's bio-alarm went off. Something was not right with this smile; Petersee's eye contact was too direct. Zeke kept his composure and smiled back.

"Senator, sir, is there anything I can do for you?" Petersee called out.

"No, no, thank you," Zeke replied, trying to look distracted.

Back in the dining room brownies and fruit salad were laid out and Lizzie was pouring coffee. Zeke tapped a doorpost as he returned. "Will you forgive me, ladies, if I do another sidebar with the professor?" Zeke made eye contact with the chief justice, signaling for him to follow. "I just need to add one more point to our earlier conversation," he said. "Allow me to bring your coffee?"

The chief justice nodded to Zeke, then turned, smiling, to Rachel and Fran. "I always follow his wise counsel." He plucked a brownie from the table as he stood up, wrapped it in a napkin and followed Zeke through the hallway to his office, and then outside.

"Professor, the only way to say this is fast," Zeke began in a hushed voice as he closed the door behind them. "The call I just took was from my cousin, the law professor I spoke about earlier. He tells me that an assassination attempt is imminent. By imminent he means tonight, upon leaving my home."

The chief justice, who was about to reseat himself in the deck chair, froze where he was. "Repeat, please?"

"You heard me correctly. He urged me to say nothing to anyone, but it didn't seem right to keep this from you."

"Goodness, I should think not. And I presume you believe his information could be accurate?"

"I do. I just can't figure out why he'd be doing this if it wasn't a genuine threat. What would his motivation be?"

"Skip the motivation—what evidence does he have? Aside from the fact that you trust your cousin, is there anything specific about this threat?"

"There is. He's concerned about the distance between my front door and your car. Apparently it's a layout that's vulnerable to sniper fire."

"Oh my god," the chief justice said, dropping himself slowly into the chair, dazed. "That *is* specific." Zeke handed him his coffee.

"There's more," Zeke continued, "Mossad has made an anonymous call to the Marshals Service, warning of a threat against you at this location. My cousin claims this will fix the problem—they will send in additional agents, and perhaps handle your exit differently. We're supposed to sit tight for several minutes until this all happens. Before we hung up he coached me to try and cover up any anxiety or alarm from his phone call."

"You did a good job when you came to get me; I had no idea anything was wrong."

"My point is that his call was scripted, like it had been planned." Zeke sat down next to the chief justice and lowered his voice a notch. "This is espionage," he said. "This involves a foreign government, and I'm very uneasy about it—but the threat feels real to me. My cousin has said a lot of little things that just make it seem too real."

"So we're just supposed to sit here and do nothing? We shouldn't say anything to the agents who are already here?"

"We can't. They'll want to know how we know there's a problem, and my cousin has it all worked out. He's got an alibi for our call—a family medical emergency. He gave me the whole story. He'll deny ever having said anything about a threat. Every move he makes is planned. When I first met him twenty years ago he had just finished several years in the Israeli special forces. A lot of stuff is starting to add up."

"So what do we do, just wait?"

"I think that's best. In a few minutes more personnel should arrive, and that in theory will counter the threat."

The chief justice looked at his watch, then unfolded the napkin with the brownie next to his coffee. "I must say this is not how I envisioned spending this evening," he said. "I'm very worried for Fran. I've never put her in a position like this before."

"How are you putting her in this position?" Zeke asked. "You're going about your business, you're having dinner with friends. Neither of us has any control over these events."

The chief justice pondered this for some moments, sipping coffee.

"Professor," Zeke continued, "nor do we have any control over Judge Hurtig," he said. "Why do you object to her effort to expose Ross to some criticism?

"I don't think it's a good idea to have individual justices indicted, tried and convicted by a television show."

"Even if it forced Ross to tone down her rhetoric a bit? This would be a good thing, yes? To use a naval analogy, we have a loose cannon on deck. She could sink the whole ship if we don't do something to restrain her. At a minimum the court would function better if she were not as openly belligerent. Do you agree?"

"Perhaps. But I read it as a poor precedent, and the exposure might not produce the effect we want. What if it inflames her even more? What if she lowers her own voice but then starts leaking things to the press? She might invite the press in for an interview—to tell her side of the story. Would you agree that there is a substantial risk of unintended consequences?"

"Perhaps." Zeke grinned. He should have known better than to try and corner the professor with logic—it never worked. He pulled his phone from his pocket to check the time. "It's been ten minutes," he said. "Back to our immediate problem . . . my cousin suggests there is someone on your security detail who's been compromised, who's passing information along to the bad guys in real time. Do you know the people who are protecting you tonight?"

"Most of them," the chief justice replied. "There are at least two new faces, though, including the agent-in-charge. Petersee is the name, I think. Polite enough, but all business. Didn't give the more personal intro I'm used to."

"I just got a very strange reading from him myself," Zeke said. "Something was off."

"This is not good. This is deteriorating very fast."

"From the beginning," Zeke said, "my cousin has said the problem is inside the Marshals Service."

"I'm not finding much comfort in that observation." In fact the chief justice felt like he was approaching a panic point. His heart raced and he gulped in air.

"No, but it validates his story." Zeke cocked his ear. "Do you hear car doors slamming? I'm used to the sounds out here on the deck." They both rose from their chairs, and moments later Special Agent Petersee emerged from the kitchen door and approached them.

"Mr. Chief Justice," he said, glancing sideways to acknowledge Zeke as well, "my apologies for interrupting. A credible threat has just been received, so we're going to ask you to make an earlier departure than you originally planned. We want to move you now."

"What kind of threat?" the chief justice asked.

"It was a phone call that mentioned your visit this evening to the senator's home. Which is why I'm also instructed to encourage you, Senator, and your household, to leave with us as well. Promptly."

"You think my home is in danger?"

"We are being cautious. The caller knew the chief justice was visiting. We have no authority to move you, but we are advising you to leave with us."

"To go where?"

"We can bring you to a secure facility for the night, in a

hotel-type accommodation. Or if there's another location you'd like to go to, we can drop you there. You're not part of our protective detail, so if you decide to stay we can't leave anyone here with you for the evening."

"Well I'd like to see that the chief justice and his wife are moved as soon as possible. Let's get that going first. I'll take up your offer with Rachel. My cook Lizzie lives on the top floor. If we go I'd want her to leave also."

"No problem, sir." Petersee said.

Zeke turned to the chief justice. "We'll have to finish up our conversation another time. Let's allow these people to do their job." He stepped back to make a path for the chief justice, who cast a wide-eyed look as he passed by.

By the time Zeke returned to the dining room, a female agent was coaxing Fran into the now-crowded kitchen where the chief justice was being escorted out the back door by two other agents. Zeke began to feel better: the backyard, the service alley—the whole area was sheltered by trees; not nearly as exposed as the front entrance.

Rachel came up to him. "Zeke, what's going on? What's happening?"

"A threat was received, a phone call, and the caller knew the chief justice was here. So they want him to leave right away, and they've suggested we leave also—that we go with them."

"Go where?"

"We can go to a hotel," Zeke replied, "or they've offered to take us to a 'safe location' for the evening. That also means a hotel, but a government-grade hotel."

"We could always go to my place," Rachel said. "It's pretty spare, though—I know there's nothing in the fridge. They think we're in danger even if the chief justice leaves?"

Zeke certainly didn't get the feeling from Moti that the house itself was a target, but Rachel knew nothing about that and he wasn't about to bring it up. "I have no idea what to think, except as a matter of policy I think it's a good idea to do what your bodyguards advise you to do. Let's see if there's anything available at the Wardman Park for us and Lizzie."

"Well," Rachel said, "the night turns to adventure. Let's go for it. I'll grab a few things from upstairs—anything I can get for you?"

Zeke calculated quickly. "Thanks, just a pair of boxers, please. I'll grab my away-bag from the office, it has a toiletry kit"—in which, he was sure, there was a condom. His hopes soared. Blood started to flow.

The kitchen was now empty except for Petersee. Zeke stuck his head in on the way to his office. "We're going to leave for the evening as you suggested. Can you give us a lift down the block to the Wardman Park?"

"That's fine, but we want to move quickly. The chief justice and his wife have already left. Your wife and the housekeeper are upstairs—as soon as they're down, we'll head out."

"She's not my wife."

"Sorry, Senator," Petersee said. "I should have known that, but we're moving fast here."

"No problem. I'm just going to grab something from my office."

"When you have what you need please exit right away." He gestured toward the front door. "Deputies will walk with you to the car. Your companion will be escorted out separately when she comes down, and I will leave through the back door with your housekeeper. Please don't delay."

When Zeke returned from his office he was met by two agents in the foyer who asked him to wait a few moments. Ahead of him, just as Moti had surmised, a decoy was dispatched: two agents with open umbrellas escorting a third agent to the car. A minute later they returned to walk with Zeke.

"Is all this really necessary?" Zeke asked. "The chief justice is already out."

For a moment he was annoyed that he was being ignored, but then realized his handlers were focused on the task at hand—tuned in to their earpieces. He was guided onto the front porch, repositioned under a different umbrella, flanked by two other agents, and then shuttled quickly down the steps to the car. Along the way Umbrella 2, walking behind him, finally responded. "It may not be necessary, Senator," he said, "but if we waited until we knew it was necessary, it would be too late."

The door of the black sedan was held open by a tall, athletic African-American woman who kept sweeping the wider scene with her human radar as Zeke was hustled into the back seat. He pulled out his phone to call the hotel.

Umbrella 2 bent over to address him through the open door. "As soon as your wife joins us, sir, we'll head out."

"She's not my wife." His mother was going to love this. She had resumed questioning him recently, after a hiatus of at least a year, about why he and Rachel were not getting married and having children.

"Sorry sir, my apologies. We've not been briefed; we just arrived on-scene."

Zeke then overheard the female agent's cheerful mocking of her colleague's gaffe. "Don't you know, Marco, his girlfriend's the *Woman in Charge*? She's the lady who has that show on IVC."

"Oh, my sister told me about her. What's her name again?"

Zeke was waiting expectantly to overhear Rachel's name, but suddenly the female agent's voice veered into alarm: "Whoa, Marco, listen to that, that isn't right . . . holy shit!" Then vehemently into her collar microphone: "Code yellow, no drill! I repeat, condition yellow! Evacuate now! All personnel exit now!"

Marco looked back into the car. "Closing up sir, closing the door, watch yourself—" but it remained open long enough for Zeke to hear a high-pitched buzzing sound pass overhead. At first he thought it was the summer cicadas back for one last crescendo, but then a blinding white flash lit up the front of his house, and the force of the explosion slammed the car door shut and knocked both agents to the ground. The car was left bobbing gently next to the curb like a boat in a marina.

Zeke was thrown back, but he remained on the seat and righted himself in time to see a fireball erupt from the bay window of his home and rise 50 feet into the air, illuminating the whole scene in a flickering orange light.

4

"The logic of words should yield to the logic of realities."

—LDB, dissent in *DiSanto v. Pennsylvania*, 1926

ZEKE LIFTED THE heavy visitor's chair to avoid scraping the linoleum floor and repositioned it alongside Rachel's hospital bed. She had open and bandaged cuts on her face and arms, and was tethered to several wires and tubes, but according to the doctors was otherwise okay. She knew her name, what day it was, who the president was, and who he was. She remembered they had been hosting the chief justice for dinner, and that a threat was received. She understood the house had been hit by a rocket-propelled grenade.

The overhead light was off; her eyelids were half open. An automated blood pressure monitor started up, pumping air into a collar on her right arm, beeping to mark its progress.

She turned her head slightly to look at Zeke. "Where is the chief justice? Is he okay? Was he hurt?"

"The chief justice and Frances are fine. I've not spoken to him, but they were escorted out the back a few minutes before the attack. They're okay."

"No one was hurt?" she asked.

"You were hurt."

"No one besides me?"

Zeke paused and worked to control his voice. "Rachel, Lizzie is dead."

She gasped. Reflexively she tried raising her hands to her face, but stopped when she felt the IV line tug at her arm. "What happened?"

"She was coming down the stairs from her room," he said. "The explosion collapsed the stairwell."

"Why am I alive?"

Zeke rose from his chair and sat next to her on her bed. "Because you were in the back bathroom, protected by pipes in the wall." He leaned over and kissed her. "Saved by the shower stall, according to a captain from the D.C. fire department."

"That's right. Now I remember. I was getting my shampoo." She tried wetting her lips with her tongue, then signaled for something to drink. Zeke found a water pitcher on the side table, filled a plastic cup, and held it to her lips. She took several slow sips.

"Was anyone else hurt?" she asked.

Zeke refilled the water cup and left it on the service tray next to her bed. "The agent in charge of the professor's detail was injured. I don't know if you met him—the tallish, balding fellow with the Texas drawl. His name is Petersee. He was in the kitchen, waiting for Lizzie. He's at a different hospital, in stable condition I'm told."

"You're okay?" she asked.

"Unscratched," Zeke replied. "I was already outside, in a Marshals Service car."

"My father knows I'm alright?" she asked.

"I spoke with him. As usual he was polite and unemotional. When I called it was the first he'd heard of it. My mother, on the other hand, saw a flash news report on television and was pretty much hysterical by the time I spoke to her."

"Work. What about work? When can I check in with my office?" She began looking around the bed for her phone.

"Rachel, you almost just died in a rocket attack. Your office knows you're okay. I've spoken with Harrison. Think about it— you're lucky to be alive."

Rachel sat quietly for a moment, then started looking for her phone again, then stopped. She looked at Zeke with an odd, vacant expression. He sat on the edge of her bed and grasped her hand.

Under normal circumstances, when confronted with a problem or obstacle, Rachel would shift into a thinking mode that Zeke could easily read. Her eyes would narrow and her forehead wrinkle; he could almost hear the wheels turning. This was not the case now. Her processor was barely running.

"Harrison called," Zeke continued. "He plans to visit as soon as you're up for it. He's got everything under control at work."

"Good, thank you," she said, sounding satisfied. "Tell him thank you for me." She closed her eyes.

"Of course." Zeke stood up but continued holding her hand. Half a minute passed in silence.

"I'm going to close my eyes for a little while," she finally said.

"Good," Zeke replied. "You need the rest. I'll be right here." He withdrew and lowered himself quietly into the side chair.

He was exhausted and tried closing his eyes, but soon found he was too wired to sleep. He sat up, took out his phone, checked his messages and e-mail, and texted his mother to tell her he had seen Rachel in person and she was fine. He sent an e-mail to the chief justice, asking to meet with him as soon as possible. He received an immediate bounce-back: his message had been received, but the chief justice would not be replying to e-mails or phone calls for at least 48 hours.

He kicked off his shoes, crossed his extended legs, and sank back in his chair again, eyes closed. This time he tried focusing

on his own breathing, counting his inhales, his exhales—a
technique he had learned at a college-era yoga retreat. This
worked until Rachel's blood pressure robot started up again,
wheezing and clicking. He kept his eyes closed and switched his
focus from his breathing to the sounds from the monitor, now
blended with background noise from the hallway. A techno-
fugue, he thought. A medical concerto in the style of PDQ
Bach. On the cusp of sleep, he tried remembering—who was
PDQ Bach? A bearded, jolly genius, like a Santa Claus from
Julliard—what was his real name?

The answer came to him in a dream—Schickele; Professor
Peter Schickele. But he remembered nothing of the question or
the answer when he awoke later.

*   *   *

"Senator," Armin said in a whisper, resting his hand on Zeke's
shoulder. "Senator, it's six in the morning. Sorry to disturb; you
have visitors."

Zeke sat up in his chair and rubbed his eyes. He peered at
Rachel, who was asleep in the same raised-back position, her
face poised with a faint smile. She still had an IV line in one
arm, but all the wires and monitors were gone. "Visitors?" he
repeated, keeping his voice low.

Armin nodded. His stocky frame, blocking the half-open
door, was backlit by the brighter hallway light. "You've spoken
to her?" he asked, gesturing toward Rachel.

"I have," he whispered. "She seems okay. It's incredible . . .
there was this huge fireball, and poof," he flipped his hands
upward. "The whole front of the house disintegrated. I can't
believe she survived."

"I was very sorry to hear about Lizzie. I didn't know her well,
but it was hard not to like her."

Zeke rose quietly from his chair and pulled a privacy curtain around Rachel's bed to block their conversation. "You said visitors. What's up?" He nudged Armin toward the door.

"Well, about a third of your staff is here, and there's a press pool outside waiting for a statement, but the visitors I woke you about are a DHS deputy secretary and the deputy director of the Marshals Service. I didn't ask them, but I assume they're here to brief you on the attack. I've set them up in a doctor's conference room one floor down."

"Thank you." Zeke felt his head was beginning to clear. "Thanks for waking me—maybe now I can actually learn something about what's happened. I gather we've said nothing to the press?"

"No, nothing," Armin replied. "Leslie's on his way in. He's drafting now and will have something for you when he gets here. Also I ran back to the office for a few things and got you this." He handed Zeke a black leather satchel imprinted with a senate seal.

"Thank you," Zeke said. "Good thinking." It was one of the overnight away bags that his staff kept stocked in the office, at home, and in his car. It contained a toiletry kit, a clean shirt, fresh socks and boxers, a throw-away phone, and a plastic sandwich bag with packets of Keemun Black tea and Barbados sugar. "I'll duck in here to wash up," he motioned toward an adjacent bathroom. "Please ask a staffer to sit with Rachel while we're away—someone she knows, like Angela or Gerry—in case she wakes up. And if you can find me a cup of very hot water that would be great. I'll wait out in the corridor if you're not back when I'm done."

*   *   *

During the walk to the conference room Armin reviewed for Zeke the dossiers of the two officials they were about to meet. DHS Deputy Secretary Lowell Pendergast, 62, was a political appointee whose qualifications appeared to be a five-year stint as the president of a division of Boeing, and a prolific talent for bundling campaign contributions. Before Boeing he had been career Air Force for 35 years, retiring as a brigadier general before moving into the private sector. There was a certain logic to this, Zeke explained to Armin. A matrix of military and corporate job titles might easily suggest a brigadier general was equivalent to the CEO of a corporate operating unit with $4 billion in revenue.

The second participant in the meeting was U.S. Marshals Service Deputy Director Anders Winther. He was a decade younger than Pendergast and his entire resume was Marshals Service: twenty years in various district offices and then five years running the Judicial Security Division.

Armin made the introductions. Pendergast ended up looking exactly as Zeke imagined from his *curricula vitae:* a sixty-something, silver-haired banker from Connecticut central casting.

"Senator Sherman," the Deputy Secretary greeted him in sonorous tones, "we are all so grateful that you're okay. I've spoken with the secretary, who as you may know is in Mexico City with the president. Like everyone else, they're horrified, and they both asked me to convey their condolences on the loss of your staff member."

"That's very kind," Zeke replied. "Please thank them for their concern."

"We're already applying all available resources to the investigation, but the president and secretary wanted me to assure you that they're committed to finding the perpetrators, whatever it takes. The president plans to call you later today, when your time zones align."

"Just as important," Zeke said, "or more important—is the chief justice safe?"

Pendergast nodded at Deputy Director Winther, a compact man with a short, meticulous haircut and round wire-rimmed glasses who exuded an utterly humorless aura. *Himmler*, Zeke thought. *With a postage stamp moustache he'd be a spitting image.* He knew this was unfair and of course would never verbalize it. It felt like a compulsion. He couldn't stop with the Nazi business.

"The chief justice is safe," Winther said, his cadence slow, his voice an authoritative bass. "We're going to keep him sequestered for at least 36 hours, until we're confident we understand what happened. We have invited the Secret Service and other agencies to join in the investigation, which is why Deputy Secretary Pendergast is here."

"Can I speak to the chief justice?"

"We could arrange it, certainly, with some lead time. We would have to get you to a secure phone. Absent that, we'll relay any message you wish to convey to him, and he'll receive it. For at least two days we don't want him to make or receive unsecure phone calls. As it is we have too many unanswered questions about the event."

"What have you learned so far?" Zeke asked.

"I'm sure you understand there's a limited amount we can reveal at this point. We're at the very beginning of an intensive investigation. Which I'm afraid is going to involve you, Senator. We have a number of questions for you."

"For me?"

"You and your staff. With all due respect, think of how a prosecutor would run this case. The chief justice's visit to your home was on his private schedule. A finite number of people had access to that information, including you and certain people on your staff. We're going to want to talk to everyone on that list."

"Naturally," Zeke replied. "Forgive me, I hadn't been

thinking of it that way. As you know I lost an employee, and I've been focused on my girlfriend, who was injured. We will all cooperate, of course." He glanced at Armin to confirm his instruction, and quickly began shifting things around in his mind, testing various scenarios and anticipating questions. He needed to avoid saying anything that would lead to his cousin.

"Would you be able to answer some questions now?" Winther asked. "To start we're going to want a list of everyone in your office who knew about your dinner with the chief justice. We'll be looking for their e-mail, appointment and phone records for the past month."

"I beg your pardon?" Zeke's eyes widened.

"How many people in your office knew the chief justice was visiting your home last night?" Winther asked.

"Deputy Director, with—as you say—all due respect, there is a big difference between interviewing my staff and having blanket access to all of their communications. There is such a thing as probable cause, not to mention the separation of powers. Do you have reason to think someone in my office was involved in the attack?" Zeke watched both Pendergast and Winther for their reaction: an obvious visual cue was exchanged.

"Senator," Winther responded, his voice an officious monotone, "you know we can't discuss our investigation."

"Well that's a resounding *yes*," Zeke replied. He turned to his chief of staff. "Armin, plans have changed; we're lawyering up. Try Sally Lebensohn at Paul Weiss. If she's not available, call John Harkin at his firm. Everyone in the office gets counsel. No one says a word without representation, including you." Then, turning back to Pendergast and Winther: "Are we done here? Or do you have an arrest to make?"

"Senator," Pendergast rejoined the conversation, his tone now conciliatory. "A few moments ago you offered cooperation, now you want to hire lawyers. What can we do to get this back on track?"

Zeke locked onto the deputy secretary's faux-sincere gaze for several long seconds, then back to Winther. "Okay, I understand, he's the good cop," Zeke said, gesturing toward Pendergast, "and you're the bad cop. I'm asking politely. Would someone please tell me what's going on here?"

Winther squinted and pushed his glasses up on his nose. "Senator, you can characterize the situation however you'd like. The president wants the perpetrators found. That's our directive. We plan to go wherever we need to go to find them. I was just advising you of the information our investigation will require from you and your office."

"And I'm advising you that I won't comply with any unsubstantiated request for wholesale information," Zeke answered.

"So you don't really want an aggressive investigation?" Winther asked.

Zeke reached his boiling point fast. "I don't want an investigator using tired old tricks to try and put words in my mouth. Do I look like a street perp to you?"

"Senator," Pendergast said, now signaling overtly to Winther to hold back, "may I ask that you assign blame for the deputy director's aggressive tactics to me? I had emphasized to him before our meeting that no special deference should be given to elected officials in criminal investigations."

"Hah! You might include in your future instructions that they shouldn't be treated like idiots either. And for the record, I'm not an elected official."

"Of course," Pendergast said. "I'm sorry for any misunderstanding. A moment ago I asked what we can do to get this on track?"

"What can *we* do?" Zeke shot back. "I can only speak for myself. Last night my home was destroyed in an assassination attempt against my good friend the chief justice. An employee—a family friend of 25 years—was killed. My girlfriend is hospitalized. The chief justice and his wife barely escaped with their lives. Now it seems I'm suspected of being complicit in the attack. What is it you suggest that *I* do, Mr. Deputy Secretary?"

"Nothing, Senator, nothing. Again, I'm very sorry—and speaking for the administration, we're very sorry—for your loss. I apologize for our unnecessary roughness. What if we start by just interviewing the people in your office who knew about the dinner, and we'll take it from there?" Pendergast offered.

Zeke stared him down. At the same time he was watching Winther from the corner of his eye. These were skills he had utilized as a prosecutor, coming back to him now as naturally as riding a bike. He realized he was enjoying it; he felt juices flowing that he hadn't felt in years.

"No," Zeke said. He looked at Armin to make sure he was following. "No questioning the staff, no list of people who knew, no voluntary cooperation of any kind, until you answer one question for me."

"What question is that, Senator?" Pendergast asked.

"I want to know if you have any information suggesting that someone in my office was involved in the attack. You're after me like I'm a suspect. I want to know why."

After another silent cue from Pendergast, Winther responded. "We have no such information," he said.

Zeke looked at Winther directly in the eye. "Please, so I'm sure I've not misunderstood, say that again?"

"I'm telling you we have no specific information about a connection between you, or your office, and the attack."

Zeke had a practiced sixth sense when it came to lie detection: he read it in body language, in eye movements, he felt it in his bones. He knew that stressful or hurried circumstances might jam his radar, but this was not one of those situations. His mind was clear, his view unobstructed. He was 95 percent sure Winther was telling the truth. "Okay," he said. "I'll accept that at face value for now. You were just trying to shake the tree to see if anything was loose?"

Pendergast didn't let Winther respond. "Senator, we've requested the same information from the chief justice," he said.

"With more tact than you approached me, one would hope."

"I'm aware of your relationship with the chief justice," Pendergast said. "I'm sure he'll report we've taken good care of him."

"Well, it's his well-being that I'm most concerned about, so despite your poor treatment of me, I will do everything I can to help you find the attackers, including asking Rachel for a list of people *she* might have mentioned the dinner to."

"Rachel Chen," Winther said, reading from a small tablet he had opened. "Minor injuries, was in the rear of the structure, now hospitalized here, room 826 . . . this is your friend, correct?" Winther asked, peering over his glasses.

"My girlfriend, yes," Zeke answered. "She has her own residence, but she's been living with me for about two years."

"And she had advance knowledge of the chief justice's visit to your home?"

"She did. She was the reason the dinner took place."

"Ah!" Winther said. "Now we're getting somewhere." He started tapping information into his tablet. "Please elaborate, if you don't mind."

"The chief justice's wife, Frances, wanted to meet Rachel, who is a television personality of sorts."

"So I gather. And when was the dinner scheduled?"

"The chief justice and I have a professional relationship. We meet for lunch or dinner—just the two of us—a few times a month. About two weeks ago we agreed to set aside last night as a social occasion, so his wife could meet Rachel."

"About two weeks ago," Winther repeated to himself as he typed. "Do you think you could pinpoint the date you first discussed it with the chief justice? That would establish a timeline."

Zeke stopped to think. "I'm not good with this kind of thing in my mind, but Armin can look it up for you—he's got my calendar." Zeke shifted his attention to Armin: "I'm pretty sure it was when we went to that Greek restaurant in Georgetown that he wanted to try, on M Street. You'll find it in my dailies."

"And that's when last night's dinner was first discussed?" Winther asked, looking up from his tablet.

"Yes. Except we didn't at that point know when it was going to be. I got a couple of dates from Rachel—she travels a lot—and gave those to my scheduling secretary, Gerry Austrian. She put the rest of it together."

Winther tapped for a few more moments and then swiped his tablet closed. "We'll want to speak with Ms. Chen, of course, when she's well enough. But if you are willing to work with her on preparing a list beforehand, that would speed things up. Time is crucial now."

"I'll save you even more time. There's an executive at IVC who produces her show *Women in Charge*. His name is Harrison Starr. You can reach him at their studios in Bethesda. He may know more than Rachel does about who had access to her schedule."

Winther opened up his tablet again and entered the information. When he was finished he looked Zeke in the eye. "Senator, I apologize," Winther said. "I know you are highly regarded at DOJ. I should have been more circumspect. Is there anything else you think we should know?"

"I don't think so. I myself didn't mention the dinner to anyone outside my office. My housekeeper Lizzie knew, but she only found out the night before who our guests were going to be, and now she's dead. Armin here will go over with you who else on my staff had access to my private schedule."

"That's fine, Senator, we've covered a lot of territory already. We can circle back if we have more questions. Anything else? Think back." Winther took off his eyeglasses and examined them in the light.

Zeke leaned against a wall, crossed his arms, and thought for a few moments. "Before dinner I took the chief justice onto our back patio for a drink. When we stepped out we interrupted two security agents who were having a heated discussion about something."

"Could you identify which two agents were having the argument?" Winther asked.

"One of them was the agent-in-charge, Petersee, who came over and introduced himself as soon as we appeared. I didn't get a good look at the other agent, but the chief justice might know—he was with me."

Winther worked his tablet for a few moments. "Did you hear any of what they were saying?" he asked.

"No, but I'm sure it was contentious. Their voices were raised, there was gesturing."

"What are you implying?" Pendergast asked.

Now Zeke and Winther exchanged glances. "Mr. Deputy Secretary," Zeke said, "there is no implication. Your colleague asked if anything stood out, and to me—considering what's happened—an argument between two on-duty federal agents stood out."

"Sir," Winther now addressed Pendergast directly, "Senator Sherman is only confirming something we already know. The chief justice reported this during his debriefing a few hours ago; he identified the second agent."

"Weren't you in College Park a few hours ago?" Pendergast asked. Zeke detected stress in Pendergast's voice—he was not happy about something.

"I read the transcripts," Winther replied. "On the way over. They're in the package we got from AG."

Pendergast had no response. Winther turned to Zeke. "It is standard procedure to review all the personnel involved in an incident—whether they're new to a detail or not. So while your comment is noted, it's not really going to change how we conduct our review. Are you aware that Special Agent Petersee was injured in the attack?"

Zeke nodded. "I was told he's going to be okay."

"His condition is serious but stable," Winther said. "Former Air Force lieutenant colonel, on loan to the Marshals Service from ATF."

"What do you know about the weapon?" Zeke asked. "Where was it fired from? What do you know about the perpetrators?"

Winther looked at Pendergast for a signal, but was left to respond on his own.

"Senator," Winther said, "this investigation is less than twelve hours old. There's a lot of evidence to collect and process. We're on top of it all, but it takes time. We'll have more to share with you after the first 24 hours."

"Good. Are we done here for now?" Zeke asked.

"Yes sir," Winther said, exchanging nods with Pendergast. "I'm assuming our investigation can move forward, with your chief of staff's assistance?"

"Mr. DeBryin," Zeke said, "make it so. Everyone who knew about our dinner should be made available for interviews this afternoon in the office. When you're done here, join me in the hospital cafeteria with Leslie. He just texted me,

I'm meeting him there for breakfast." Zeke walked over to Pendergast, shook his hand, asked that his regards be relayed to the secretary and the president, and then returned to face Winther.

"Senator," Winther said, "Thank you for your cooperation. You'll remember to ask Ms. Chen who she might have mentioned the dinner to?"

"I will, but I want to see how she's doing first. When I left her she was asleep. We've got your card, so we'll call as soon as she's able to talk."

"No need to call. We're going to have agents standing by outside her room, so we can speak with her as soon as possible. The sooner you ask someone about a recent event, the more they remember. I know I don't need to be explaining this to you."

"Is *she* a suspect?" Zeke asked. It suddenly occurred to him that maybe he hadn't framed his original question broadly enough.

Winther again looked at Pendergast; Zeke discerned no communication, but the whole Frick and Frack routine was annoying. There was some agenda in the background they were hiding.

"She is not a suspect, Senator," Winther replied.

This again passed Zeke's lie detector test, but he wasn't satisfied. He'd learned nothing from this meeting.

"Good, I'm glad to hear it," Zeke said. He shook Winther's hand, and headed toward the door. On the way out he said to Armin, "I'm going to make a couple of calls, then I'll be in the cafeteria with Leslie. Meet us there."

He exited the conference room looking at his phone, but moments later reappeared in the doorway. "I'm sorry, one thing I kept meaning to ask," he directed his question at Winther. "What about the phone call that saved the chief justice? The tip, or whatever it was. What progress has been made with that lead?"

Winther looked at him with a blank expression. He didn't even try to get a read from Pendergast.

"Senator," Pendergast answered, "it was an anonymous call from a burn phone."

"And that's the end of it?" Zeke turned to look at the deputy secretary. "That's the end of that lead?"

"Of course not. It just hasn't yielded immediate results. I assure you we have plenty of manpower, pursuing all possible avenues."

Zeke paused. He looked at Winther momentarily, then returned to Pendergast. "Mr. Deputy Secretary, I'd like to remind you that I'm a victim here. I have suffered a severe loss. I'm also an acting United States senator, and while I know that's not very high in your pecking order, I will insist on a modicum of respect in the form of regular updates regarding your investigation. Since you have all the manpower you need, I presume that's not asking too much?"

"Not at all, Senator," Pendergast replied, now in maximum sincerity mode. "Not at all. You'll be kept apprised of all significant developments."

"Thank you," Zeke said. He nodded, smiling appreciatively, and left.

In the hallway he let himself go. The pulse of the hunt coursed through his prosecutor's veins. He had been patient. He had poked, he had prodded, and finally, at the very end, he had caught the deputy secretary in a lie. He was one hundred percent sure. The alarms were clarion-loud; every sensor and filament in his body was tingling.

As Zeke read the situation, the anonymous tip that was received before the attack was a primary focus of the investigation, and Pendergast had no intention of keeping him apprised of anything.

*   *   *

Zeke and Armin returned from the hospital cafeteria to find Rachel sitting up in bed, hovering over a breakfast tray and exchanging hushed exclamations with Gerry Austrian. While they finished up their conversation, Zeke instructed Armin to introduce himself to the two suits they had seen standing in the corridor across from Rachel's room. "For starters," he said, "I want to verify they're the agents Winther was referring to. For all we know there could be other agencies involved. I have no idea what's going on here. I thought the meeting we just had was very strange. What do you think?"

"There was an act of some kind going on between them. I couldn't really tell who was in charge."

"Exactly. The whole thing was erratic, off the charts. Why would they want everyone's communications logs for the last month? What was that all about?"

"Senator, I've no idea. I'm way out of my league here. Remember, I'm a web jockey. I don't know if I'm the best sounding board for you—for this situation."

"Noted. I appreciate your candor, and it may be a valid point. In the meantime, you're all I've got, so I need you to summon all your courage and confront the goons outside." Zeke couldn't resist. Armin took things so seriously.

"Sir?" his eyebrows rose.

"I'm speaking euphemistically, Mr. DeBryin. Just find out what agency the gentlemen outside are from, and what their purpose is here."

"Yes sir. Assuming they're Winther's people, do you want me to say anything about Rachel's condition?"

"No. Just tell them I'll be out in about fifteen minutes to let them know when they can expect to talk to her."

"Okay. And if they're not Winther's people?"

"Try not to look alarmed and report back who they are. I'm hoping that's not the case."

Armin nodded. "After this, do you want me standing by here?"

"No, I want you back at the office to prepare people for this visit from the Marshals Service. Call Sally Lebensohn and explain what's going on. Ask her to come in and spend the afternoon at the office with you if she's available. If she's not, schedule a conference call with her for you and me ASAP."

"Anything else?"

"Yes. I want to know more about this Deputy Secretary Pendergast. This is not to be assigned. I want you to handle this yourself from home. Phone calls, e-mails, web searches— do everything through the VPN on your office laptop. Use trusted sources only. I want to know who his sponsors are in the administration, what his portfolio is at DHS, whatever you can come up with."

"Not the other one also? Winther?"

"One at a time. Pendergast I know I don't trust. I'm not sure about Winther."

Armin nodded and left with Gerry, closing the door behind them. It was only when Zeke returned to Rachel's bedside that he realized how much better she looked. There was a single IV line running to her right wrist, and a few translucent suture strips on her cheek and forehead. Indirect sunlight flooded the room from a row of casement windows high above her bed. Her hair had been brushed. A TV monitor, mounted on a wall bracket, was tuned to a news channel with the volume off. It was showing panoramic aerial footage of the remains of Zeke's townhouse.

She pushed the monitor aside and greeted him with a surprising crispness in her voice. "Thank you," she said. "Thank you for being here."

"Thank *you* for being here," he said, and leaned forward to kiss her briefly on the forehead. As he did he noticed that her phone was resting on the bed, tucked alongside her thigh. "You're feeling better? You sound more alert."

"I am. I just spoke to my father. We might as well have discussed the weather." Leong-Zhu Tsien had raised his only daughter at an emotional distance, with the help of several nurses and caretakers.

"Do you think it's possible he's intimidated by you?" Zeke asked. "By your public success?"

"No, not at all. It's just the way he is. In China, men of his generation were not involved in child-rearing. He's proud of me; that much he can communicate. And I know he loves me, but he has no way to express it."

"Sort of the opposite of my mother, who can't keep it in."

Rachel raised her plastic mug and took a sip. "For hospital coffee it's not bad. So you met with the Marshals Service? Gerry told me. Have they come up with anything? Do they know who's behind the attack?"

"Wait! Hold it . . . you first. I'll tell you about my meeting, but not until I hear what your situation is. Have you seen a doctor this morning?"

"The doctor was here about an hour ago, while you were out. She said I was in good shape. Really, I'm all checked out. No more ringing in the ears. She's waiting for the results of one more scan, to rule out a concussion. If it comes back negative, I can be discharged when I feel like it."

"That's incredible. Fantastic." Zeke beamed at her. "I don't know if you've thought about it yet, but we don't have a place to live. Or at least I don't. You've got your place in Bethesda.

But anyhow, it's something we should talk about if you're up for it."

"Why can't we both stay at my place?"

"Too small, don't you think?"

"I don't know," Rachel said. She put the coffee down. "I'd be happy to be your host for a while. You were very generous to me with your place."

Zeke's antennae went up. Something was different; the hostility was gone. "That's very considerate," he said. "Thank you. And maybe for a few days that's what we'll do. But I'm going to look into other options. Insurance should cover something." He rose from his chair and gave her a quizzical look. "You seem less angry. Has something changed? You do remember I resigned?"

"Yes to all of the above," Rachel replied. "Something has changed. I don't know whether it was the drugs they were giving me, or the oxygen, or my own adrenalin, but last night was very productive for me. Want something from my tray?" She waved her hand over the remains of her breakfast. "The muffin is good; the fruit cup was okay."

"No thanks," Zeke said. "Last night was productive? I was sitting with you right here; you were asleep."

"I was, for some time, I know. I don't know how long. But then I woke up. It was the strangest thing—my eyes popped open and suddenly I was wide awake. I was sitting up just like I am now; the back of the bed was raised. I didn't have my phone or my tablet, I had no way to keep track of time. You were sleeping, I didn't want to disturb you. So I just sat and thought, without distractions, for what seemed like a long time. And for whatever reason, a lot of things became clearer to me. Things crystallized. I don't know how else to describe it."

"This is a cue for me to sit down." Zeke maneuvered the service tray, a small tower on wheels, away from her bed, and made space for himself in the visitor's chair. "Okay, I'm ready. What's clearer? What have you crystallized?"

"A lot of things. A couple of nights ago you asked if I was in love with you or your career. Considering how I reacted to your resignation, it's a fair question. What's clear to me now is the answer—I love *you*. I was disappointed at first, and maybe I still am, because I know how well you'd do if you stayed with your political career. But after the chief justice's comments last night, I understand better why you're on the path you're on. I respect your decision now."

"Remind me what the professor said? I vaguely remember feeling vindicated, having his support."

"He talked about the value of working outside the system, of not being bound by political constituencies."

"Hah! Like I've never made that point before!"

"I know, I know," Rachel said, raising her untethered left hand in defense. "What can I tell you? When you say it, I hear it one way. When Chief Justice Anthony Salo-Baron says it, I hear it differently."

Zeke frowned. "What else is clearer? You said a lot of things."

"I'm only now grasping how the democracy dashboard you're offering might be a game changer. I now get that it can be used not only for specific issues, but in specific districts."

Zeke was a hair's breadth away from exasperation. "Rachel, it's not as though we haven't discussed this before. I've been talking to you about this for months."

"I know, I'm sorry. I know how it looks, like I wasn't listening. And maybe that's partly true, but the reason it's all come together for me is because now I have an application that I need it for."

"What application is that?"

"The impeachment of Justice Ross."

Zeke recoiled, his chair grating on the floor. "How's that again?"

"I see now that we can use your democracy dashboard to target specific congressmen in an impeachment vote. It could be just the leverage we need to produce a majority in the House."

"Whoa, whoa!" Zeke said. "Back up please. First of all, who's the 'we' you're referring to?"

"Judge Hurtig and myself," Rachel said. "I was planning to have her as a guest on the show—remember we talked about it at dinner? But I've been trying to think of other ways to support her, and that's what finally got me to see how the No Vote Pledge feature on your dashboard can be used to apply pressure on specific congressmen on a particular issue."

"I thought you were going to do a program about Ross's ethical lapses. That's very different than a call for impeachment."

"Hurtig is set on impeachment," Rachel replied. "That's her ultimate goal."

"That's not what I remember from last night."

"Well the conversation was cut short at a certain point, if you recall."

"Rachel, are you pursuing this because you think it's something the chief justice would want? If you are, you're wrong. His reaction to the whole business was negative. He's opposed to anything that focuses attention on the court."

"No!" Rachel was emphatic. "This has nothing to do with the chief justice or your relationship with him. Judge Hurtig came to us with this story, which I rate to be of significant public interest. She's a highly credentialed expert who's built a fact-based case."

"You seem very eager to help her."

"The only way Ross could ever be removed is if the effort is led by women."

"Including starting an NVP Campaign calling for her impeachment?"

"I'm going to suggest it to Hurtig. In an impeachment fight in the House, we need fifteen Republican crossovers, assuming all the Democrats are on board. So my plan is to draw up a list of the 20 most vulnerable Republican districts and launch pro-impeachment NVP campaigns in those districts."

Zeke pulled his chair forward a bit, beaming at Rachel with a mixture of admiration and regret. "I'm gratified, of course, to have the latest convert to my cause, but I'm not sure it will work in this situation. You're talking about getting a majority of voters, in heavily Republican districts, to take your side—to demand impeachment. Where is this majority going to come from?"

"From a combination of Democrats and Republican women. We already know, from our own research, that a lot of Republican women totally repudiate Ross. In some districts Democrats plus disaffected Republican women will constitute a majority."

Zeke pushed his chair back and stood up. "The relevant follow-up question is: what kind of influence does your show have with Republican women, but let's not go down that path right now. It's for a later time." He kissed Rachel on her forehead, and then stood holding her hand. "I'm so very pleased to have you on my side. Not to mention *alive*."

"What did you learn from your meeting with the Marshals Service? Who's trying to kill the chief justice?"

"If they have leads they're not telling me about them. For a while they treated me like I was a suspect."

"What? That makes no sense. Do they know you're his friend?"

"They know. But the way they're looking at it, the chief justice's dinner with us was on his private schedule, so they want to account for everyone who knew it was taking place. That means they want to talk to you, to my staff, to anyone we might have told. Can you think of who you might have spoken to about the dinner?"

Rachel wrinkled her nose and gazed for a moment into blank space. "Harrison knew," she said. "And he would know better than I who else in the studio knew."

"That's what I told them. I gave them his name. I hope that's okay."

"That's fine."

"Did you tell anyone else? Any friends? Your father?"

"No, I never spoke to my father about it. I can't think of anyone else. But still, why are they focused on who we talked to? The chief justice must have an enemies list. There must be a dozen-and-one pro-life lunatics out there who believe killing him would be an act of righteousness. You've told me he gets threats all the time."

"I don't understand it either. You asked what I learned from my meeting—the answer is nothing, except that they're hiding something."

"Hiding what?" Rachel asked.

"That's what I've been stewing about," Zeke replied. "They have some other agenda. It's weird, I can't put my finger on it. For some reason I'm the enemy. It feels like a political thing." He went on to describe Messrs. Pendergast and Winther.

"Wow. Okay. So they're keeping you in the dark. And they want to talk to me?"

Zeke nodded. "Are you okay with that?"

"Sure. I've just told you everything I know."

"You're feeling up to it?"

"Do I seem unready somehow?"

"No," Zeke laughed as he stood up. "You seem ready." He leaned over and kissed her on the cheek. Rachel noticed the

TV was showing a picture of them together, a photo from a Senate subcommittee hearing she attended with him years ago. "I remember that," she said, pulling the screen towards her and tilting it for Zeke to see.

"As do I. We're quite the couple. Which reminds me, since it appears you're going to be up and about, can I get you to join me in Morgantown for Lizzie's funeral? My mother will be there. She's feeling guilty because it was her idea for Lizzie to come to D.C. to work for me. It'll be a lot easier for her, not to mention me, if you are with us."

"Of course," Rachel replied. "I feel so badly for her. I could call her also if you think it will help. When's the funeral?"

"The day after tomorrow. I'm pretty sure at noon. Gerry is working on the arrangements."

5

"The bow must be strung and unstrung; work must be measured not merely by time but also by its intensity; there must be time also for the unconscious thinking which comes to the busy man in his play."

—LDB, Letter to William Harrison Dunbar, February 2, 1893

ZEKE'S MOTHER, ADELE Edith Sherman, a second-generation West Virginian, was a beacon of dignity and grace at Lizzie's funeral. Tall, erect, her silver hair starch-coiffed with a blue tint, she chatted afterward with the extended family in soft and sympathetic tones. Rachel, standing with Zeke at the back of the chapel, was impressed.

"She's how old?" Rachel asked.

"Sixty-eight," Zeke replied. "Quite the southern aristocrat, don't you think?"

"She reminds me so much of you, Zeke." Rachel nudged him with her elbow. "Look at her posture, the angled jaw. It's uncanny—she's a natural. This is exactly where you get your stuff."

"Thank you. Try to remember to mention that to her—she'd be thrilled to know you've made that connection."

An elderly couple, friends of Zeke's parents who had known

him since he was a child, came up to say hello. They too commented on how well Zeke's mother looked.

When they left, Rachel resumed. "If you decide to marry me, I'll take really good care of her."

Rachel loved lobbing grenades like this to get Zeke's attention; it was entertainment for her. But he had wised up to it, and was perfectly capable of playing the game. "I know you would," he said in tempo, with a straight face, "and I can see the benefits of combining your control of my life with my mother's. As it is now I have two chains of command I follow. If we got married and you coordinated with Mom, I'd have one less report-to. My life would become simpler."

Rachel yelped with delight.

"There's the governor," Zeke said. "He's next in the receiving line. When he's done I need to pull him aside for a couple of minutes. Would you keep an eye on my Mom? I doubt she'll be left alone—the whole town has turned out. But just in case."

"Of course. Everything okay with Arnault? He's been your biggest fan."

"Everything's fine. He's attending a meeting of 44 governors next week. He's hoping to get a speaking slot to introduce his colleagues to the American Majority Party. I want to encourage him and give him some talking points. Wish me luck," he said, kissing her on the cheek as he made his move.

"Good luck," she called after him, her words wafting in his wake.

*   *   *

An hour later, Zeke, his mother and Rachel were seated in a riverfront restaurant in downtown Morgantown. Zeke's rumination on the relative merits of the lunch buffet versus the à la carte menu was interrupted by his mother.

"You'd think there'd be a religious tradition somewhere,"

she said, folding her menu face down in front of her, "where after you bury a loved one, you'd fast for a period of time. At every funeral I've ever been to there's always a meal at the end of the day. Shouldn't it be a fast? Show some empathy for the dead? I mean Lizzie loved food, food was her *life*, and she's not getting a choice between the à la carte and the buffet."

"Adele, we don't have to have lunch," said Rachel, quickly folding her menu in sympathy. Both women looked at Zeke for his reaction. *Be careful what you wish for*, he thought, recalling his earlier comment about a coordinated command.

"Might I suggest," Zeke said to his mother, "if you want to honor Lizzie this way, that you order something light instead of fasting completely. We're going to be traveling for several hours and it might not be a good idea for you to be dehydrated or light-headed." As he finished speaking he turned and glared at Rachel, adding with his eyes: *are you out of your mind?* Zeke had invited his mother to spend a few days in Washington with them after the funeral, thinking it might be a welcome distraction from the loss of her long-time friend and the dementia of her long-lost husband.

Zeke signaled the waiter and ordered soup and a club sandwich. The women shared a chicken salad platter and a side of sweet potato fries.

"I will volunteer to change the subject," Adele said, forcing some cheer into her voice. "Lizzie is gone, but you are both here, for which I am very grateful. And of course the chief justice and his wife weren't hurt. That would have been a whole other tragedy, I know." She turned to Zeke. "Have you seen him since the attack?"

"No. They whisked him away and have hidden him somewhere. I've asked the Marshals Service to arrange a meeting, but I still don't know when or where."

"When you see him again please give him my regards. And Howard's, of course," she added, still including her husband.

"I certainly will, Mom. He asks about you and Dad from time to time. He remembers meeting you during his confirmation hearings."

The waiter delivered a carafe of coffee to the table. Rachel offered to serve, but Adele waved her away. "Thankfully I can still pour my own," which she proceeded to do with a steady hand. "I feel sorry for the chief justice, having to contend with Justice Ross and all of her antics."

"You're not the only one who feels that way," Rachel added. "I've invited a retired federal judge named Kendra Hurtig to appear on my show. She plans to lead a campaign to impeach Justice Ross."

"My dear," Adele gasped, "what an appealing proposal. But is there any basis for it? For impeachment?"

"Judge Hurtig believes there is. We're hoping to have her scripts finished by late next week, and taping will be the following Thursday or Friday, so look for it the first week of October. I'm usually on at 8 p.m. in the East."

"Of course. I watch it whenever I'm home, and it's set to record when I'm not."

"I'm flattered. That means a lot to me."

Adele pulled a small tablet from her pocketbook and flipped it open. "I'm putting in a reminder for the first of October to check your schedule." She began tapping an entry in her calendar with a stylus.

Zeke took the opportunity to change the subject. "Rachel, I need your advice on something."

"What's that?" she asked.

"I keep getting included in polls for the Democratic nomination, and there's all this speculation that my resignation from the Senate is really a ploy to run for president."

"I saw something about it in the *Wall Street Journal* just yesterday," his mother said, looking up from her calendar task. "An article by that clever columnist, somebody Martino. According to him you're the most electable of the bunch."

"Well thanks very much for piling on, Mom." He turned back to Rachel. "Martino is exhibit A. The straightforward tactic of not running is not working. Should I be doing something differently?" he asked.

"If not running is driving your candidacy," Rachel said, "maybe you should announce you're running, and that will derail it."

"Very funny," Zeke said, "I'm being serious. Throw me a bone here."

Rachel strained to suppress a grin. "Try this . . ."

Zeke interrupted. "I already don't believe you . . . just from your tone."

"No, no, no!" she giggled. I was thinking of playing with you some more, but just thought of something you might want to consider. This is real." She conquered her smile and lowered her voice. "Endorse someone else. It takes the wind out of anyone who's trying to blow in your sails."

"Hmm. I see what you mean."

"Be careful though. Your endorsement will carry a lot of weight. Make sure you don't get into bed with someone you later regret."

"Point taken. What do you think of Alderman."

"You're kidding! Alderman can't win!"

"Okay, who do you recommend?"

"Zeke, you're not going to rope me into this. Hire a consultant. You don't have anyone on staff for this. Try Jerry Warsaw with Case Media, or one of the partners in Allen & Pagano's political practice—they're all good."

Zeke was aghast. "Hire someone to advise me how to *not* run? You can't be serious."

"Of course I am," Rachel replied, her expression blank.

Zeke raised his eyebrows high and held them there. "I have no idea whether to believe you or not."

"She seems serious to me," Adele added, putting her tablet back in her pocketbook. "May I contribute something else on this same subject?" She paused, waiting for Zeke's go-ahead.

He rolled his eyes. *Like I could stop you.* "Of course, Mom."

"I was going through our books last week, trying to pare things down, you know, before I move into the apartment, and I came across an old novel from the 1970's called *The Wanting of Levine.* Have you read it, or heard of it? The author is somebody Halberstam; I can't remember the first name."

"No, I haven't. Why? What's it about?"

"I'm halfway through. It's a satire, very funny. Anyhow, I bring it up because it's about a single Jewish man, like yourself, who becomes a reluctant candidate for president."

"Mom, you understand what this conversation is about? I'm not going to be a candidate for president, not even a reluctant one."

"Yes dear, I know. I brought it up because in the book the main character is in exactly your situation—the more he says no, the more popular he becomes. How many books can there be about a single Jewish man who doesn't want to be president?"

Zeke waved to a waiter and pointed at his empty water glass. "Mom, if you want to send it to me, fine, but I can't promise you I'm going to read it. My plate is very full."

"Of course. I didn't mean to impose. I thought you might be curious. I also thought it might be your book—I have no memory of how it came to us."

"It's not mine. Maybe it was Dad's?"

"Not to worry. I'll finish reading it. If Levine does something clever that I think you'd want to know about, I'll just tell you."

Rachel excused herself for a visit to the ladies' room. The waiter arrived with a pitcher and refilled everyone's water glasses. As soon as he left, Adele reached across the table to grasp Zeke's hand. "Son, I am so relieved you're okay. You did all that dangerous work for so many years. I was so happy when you were done with it—and now this."

"I'm lucky to be here," Zeke said. "Believe me, I count my blessings. Rachel was even luckier."

"So does this bind you together at all, this experience?" his mother asked. "Has it made you closer?"

"I don't know Mom. It's too soon to say." He withdrew his hand. "But I will tell you that we've made arrangements to share another place together, while the house is being rebuilt."

"That's good." She paused, thinking. "But you were already living together, yes?"

"Well, after she left her position in my office and took the TV job, she started spending some nights at her apartment in Bethesda. It was closer to work for her. I told you she was displeased about my senate decision."

"And now?"

"Now we're okay. I think. She says she understands my decision now. And she invited me to move into her place in Bethesda, but it's too small, and without Lizzie there's no cook, no services. So I've rented a suite for us at the Wardman Park for a few months, until my place is ready."

Adele Sherman looked pained. "I don't understand why you're not married. She is such a sweet and intelligent woman. What could you possibly be looking for that you don't have right under your nose? Do you think some goddess is going to emerge from the mist? You're 42 years old."

Zeke decided to forgo the engagement. He looked at his mother with sympathetic eyes, but said nothing.

After some moments, she relented: "I'm sorry, dear. I am too harsh, I am so sorry. I know it's not that simple."

"Mom, let me ask you . . . you know how you want me to be happy, right?"

"Of course."

"Well, in the same way, I want you to be happy, too. So let me ask you: can you be happy without me being married?"

"No."

"No? Why is that?"

"Because I want grandchildren."

"Oh." Zeke felt like he had been cruising along nicely and then—*boom!*—a brick wall. He sat stunned. Her biological logic was hard to refute. He was an only child, so there was no one to pass the buck to. His mother, sensing his hesitation, drove home her offensive: "What am I going to have to do to get grandchildren around here—*rent them?*"

*   *   *

When they returned to Washington, Rachel headed straight to IVC's studios in Bethesda, and Zeke checked his mother into her own room at the Wardman Park. "I'm going to be tied up for a while," he explained. "I might be available for a late dinner, but I have calls to make."

"You are a *mensch* to bring me with you. I will not complicate your life. I'm going to lie down for a while. If you're not available when I go down for dinner I'll take care of myself."

Zeke suddenly realized he was getting a whole evening with nothing scheduled. He couldn't remember the last time that had happened. He carded his way into his and Rachel's suite, unpacked his valise, changed clothes, and called Moti to ask if they could meet. Moti gave him an address on Fifteenth Street NW, saying only that it was a club called the Deep Finesse and that they could meet there at 6:30 p.m. for a quick bite.

Zeke had envisioned a walk-down, cellar-level cabaret, but Moti's directions brought him to the windowless basement of a nine-story office building. The Deep Finesse turned out to be a bridge club. Behind a modest reception area was a large, open room filled with card tables, where a contingent of mostly older players were reading or chatting. Posters advertising bridge cruises and tournaments lined one wall. Moti emerged from a smaller side room and welcomed his cousin.

"I'm afraid I know nothing about bridge," Zeke said. "I hope you weren't expecting me to play."

"No, no," Moti reassured him. "I have a partner already." He glanced at his watch. "The game begins at seven. That gives us a half hour. Come with me." With a hooked finger he led Zeke into an adjacent kitchen where a cold buffet was laid out. They helped themselves to sandwiches, chips and bottled drinks. After exiting the kitchen Moti led Zeke into one of several smaller rooms set up for teaching and private games, and closed the door behind them.

"I'm a regular here," Moti said as he cleared one of the card tables to make room for their plastic plates. "Some people watch television, others read; this is how I relax." With both hands he gestured Zeke to take a seat. "Another advantage to this location—I'll explain later—is that our conversation is safe. No one is listening here."

Zeke took off his suit jacket, hung it over the back of an adjoining chair, and took a seat at the table. "How often do you play?" he asked his cousin. He opened his drink and started into his sandwich.

"I try to alternate weeknights between bridge and the gym—exercise mind, exercise body. Weekends I play bridge online for several hours. The game has an addictive quality once you understand it." He turned and nodded towards a silent monitor hanging from the ceiling at the back of the room. It displayed a bridge hand being played in real time, with a commentator's notes scrolling across the bottom of the screen. "It's less complicated than it looks."

"Right now what's foremost in my mind is thanking you for saving my life, and Rachel's life, not to mention the chief justice and his wife."

"We are very sorry that you lost even this one woman. I read about her in the news." Moti examined his sandwich briefly and started into it.

"I was at the funeral earlier today. It was difficult. My mother was there also—she was closer to Lizzie than I was."

Moti lifted the juice bottle for a long drink. "Where is the chief justice?" he asked. "Do you know?"

"I have no idea. The Marshals Service has sequestered him somewhere. Should I still be concerned about his security?"

"No, I'm sure he's okay. This is not what I meant." Moti twisted shut the cap on his drink bottle. "I ask because it's important that you not discuss me, or my actions at your home, when you talk to him, unless you are sure that you are not being listened to."

Zeke nodded. "How do I know if we're being listened to?"

"Safest is to be outside. With the level of security the chief justice now has, you should assume you are always being monitored in some way when you are indoors. And if you talk about me, or if he talks about me, and it's overheard, I'm finished." He made a slashing gesture across his neck. "My law career, my intelligence work—everything. *Hay-vanta? Fahrshteit?*"

"I understand. I'll be careful."

"When you are sure it's safe to talk, remind the chief justice he must never mention me to anyone. The call we made that saved his life, and yours, and others . . . you can never acknowledge, or even suggest, to anyone, that you know who made this call. Think of it as *quid pro quo*: the price of the call is your silence."

Zeke was solemn. He locked onto Moti's gaze. "I have no problem with the cost of the call. Please put your mind at ease."

"Thank you. I rely on you. Please also remember, the same situation applies when we speak on the phone. Use the phone only to discuss family matters and to set up an in-person meeting—nothing specific on the phone."

Zeke nodded his assent. "You said it's safe to talk here? In your bridge club? What's that all about?"

"This space, this entire building, is owned by an Israeli security consulting firm called CL Associates. The report writing that I do for the Israeli government, that I mentioned to you earlier, is done through a contract with this company."

"Hah! So this is Mossad's cover in Washington, D.C.?"

"In truth, no. To you only, because you've been caught up in these events, it might appear that way, but CL is a legitimate business that's been around for decades. They're the grandfather of all the aviation security firms. They have sales of over a hundred million dollars a year from airline consulting, personal protection services, private investigations, ransom negotiations. They do their own forensics—the entire seventh floor of this building is laboratories. They wouldn't jeopardize all this by doing covert work or anything illegal. Their assistance to Mossad is limited and one hundred percent legitimate."

Zeke thought about this. His cousin resumed eating his sandwich, and Zeke started into his. They sat together chewing quietly.

Moti reopened the bottle and finished off his drink. "It would be useful for both of us, I think, to exchange what information we have learned about the attack. I assume you were interviewed by the Marshals Service or the FBI?"

"I'm afraid I learned nothing except they don't intend to tell me what they know," Zeke replied. He related his encounter with Pendergast and Winther, including the feedback from his biological lie detector.

"Ah hah!" Moti was exuberant at this report. "You may think you've learned nothing, but in fact you've made a big contribution. In the context of other information we have, your report is very revealing."

"How is that?"

"*Vey iz mir.* This is complicated. I'm not sure where to begin—you know nothing. To start, the weapon used in the attack on your house was not a rocket-propelled grenade. If it was, Rachel would likely be dead—the charge would have penetrated deeper into the house. The reason she is alive is that your house was hit by a suicide drone, a stolen observation drone that had been modified to carry an explosive charge."

"Okay," Zeke said, "I stipulate Rachel was very lucky. Who sent the drone?"

"Do you remember from a few months ago a news story about the death of an ISIS operative in the U.S. who was identified by the code name Cadiz?"

"Of course, this was a headline story. The feds set up a sting and sold him shoulder-launched missiles that were rigged to self-destruct if you tried to arm them. As I remember it, he tried to arm one immediately after acquiring them, and they all detonated in his van simultaneously."

"You remember correctly, that is what was reported. What really happened is different. It wasn't Cadiz who died in the explosion, it was an arms dealer from Cyprus. And there were no shoulder-launched missiles. The deal was for a half-dozen Vulture surveillance drones, which ended up in the hands of a Qatari man named Khalid al-Jaber. One of the first signs of a problem in your Department of Homeland Security came several weeks ago when we warned them about this man, and they went ahead and did business with him."

"And why does this Qatari man want to kill the chief justice?"

"He doesn't. He's another arms dealer. He acquired the Vultures for a U.S. terror cell that calls itself the Action Committee. This group, Mossad believes, has targeted the chief justice, and was responsible for the attack on your home."

"Finally I'm getting somewhere. And this Action Committee, what's their story? Who are they, and what do they have against the chief justice?"

"We are just beginning to learn about them. You know the plan that's being discussed to phase out the U.S. Air Force?"

Zeke nodded his assent. "Rachel had a guest on her show recently who spoke about it."

"It appears a certain group of Air Force veterans doesn't approve of the plan—a group that has a history. In the late 1990's a DOD investigation found the Air Force Academy in Colorado had allowed religious references, to Jesus and other Christian themes, to be included in coursework and official activities."

"I vaguely remember something about this," Zeke replied. "I know the Academy has had its problems."

"When this practice was stopped," Moti continued, "a small group of faculty and academy graduates started an underground society to promote Christian values in the Air Force, which they called the Christian Action Committee. Over the years a few influential people from outside the Air Force were invited to join, the mission was expanded to promoting Christian values in American government, and they started to refer to themselves as just the Action Committee. Even though they remained very secretive, we believe their activities were benign before the Secretary of Defense announced this current review of the Air Force. The Committee's founders then convinced their peers that they needed to take action before—in Air Force terms—a point of no return was reached. They set up a dark web forum to work out the details of obtaining these six Vulture drones, and to plan future operations."

"Who are these people?" Zeke asked.

"So far we've been able to identify 13 of 22 active participants in the online forum. The majority are high-ranking Air Force officers—mostly retired but two active duty. There are two private-sector participants, billionaire types, who we assume contribute financially. We know that someone in Justice Ross's home is a regular participant. This could be either Justice Ross or her husband Walter, or both."

"Whoa! Moti, you must realize how far-fetched this sounds." Zeke suddenly didn't know whether to believe his cousin or not; it was becoming too fantastic.

Moti ignored his cousin's remark. "There are also several government officials, including—now is the interesting part—a man you met this afternoon: Deputy Secretary Pendergast."

"What? How is that possible?"

"Why do you find this so hard to believe? Didn't you just finish telling me how strange you thought your meeting with him was? If you assume Pendergast is part of the Action Committee, the meeting will make more sense. Think about his questions, about his behavior—it will add up."

Zeke pushed his chair back from the card table, crossed his arms, and sat staring at an abstract point in space. The progress of his recollection registered as a series of puzzled frowns.

Moti stood up and carried the remnants of their dinner to a corner trash can. When he returned he remained standing. "I know this is a lot to take in at once, but you should have a complete picture. We now believe they were trying to kill Rachel Chen, your girlfriend, in addition to the chief justice. It was a double shot."

"This is absurd," Zeke blurted out. "I've got to say you're losing me. This is moving beyond believable. Where's your proof?"

Moti pulled a small tablet from an inside jacket pocket, placed it on the card table in front of him, and began tapping commands. After a few clicks and beeps an audio file began to play; he slid the device toward his cousin. Zeke, straining to listen, quickly recognized the soundtrack from his dining room on the evening of the attack. He didn't understand every word, but under the circumstances it was of eerily good quality.

After half a minute Moti reached over, clicked pause, and pulled the tablet back to himself. "Here's a transcript. It's easier to understand," he said as he navigated on the tablet, "when you see it in writing." He retrieved a document, expanded it, and pushed the tablet back to Zeke. "It has the timeline in the left margin. You're looking at it starting at 20:21 hours, which is when Rachel first mentions Judge Hurtig and the Ross ethics investigation. If you read through, you'll see how an already-paranoid person like Justice Ross might easily feel threatened by that conversation."

Zeke went through the motions of reading, but the words didn't register; he was still thinking about the recording. "Okay," he said, "this is now personal. Our privacy was invaded. I want to know how you got this audio."

"In general I'd like to steer you away from this kind of question. I will answer now, because I want to establish your trust, but it is a benefit for us both to not discuss certain things, yes?" Moti awaited Zeke's confirmation with a singular raised eyebrow and expectant eyes.

Zeke nodded. "Sure. This one time, though, I'd like to know. It will, as you say, build trust."

"The bugs and transmitter were activated in your home by Owen Petersee, the agent-in-charge, when he arrived with the chief justice. But the equipment he used was acquired from our Qatari friend Al-Jaber, who bought it from undercover Mossad operatives as part of a different arms sale in Doha last year. They assumed their transmission was highly encrypted, which it was, but Mossad has its own key. So we got everything."

"Petersee! I knew something was wrong there! Not at first, but after dinner he gave a look that I knew was off."

"He and another agent, Vincent Dellacorte, were the Action Committee's inside assets."

Zeke sat back up in his chair, thinking. "Petersee was having words with another agent when the chief justice and I first came out on the deck—we surprised them."

"Is it starting to add up?" Moti asked. "I understand how fantastic it sounds, but do you think I could invent these things?

"Wow, I have to say I don't know what to think. My head is spinning."

Don't become sidetracked," Moti cautioned him. "Even if you remain skeptical, please put it aside for now. The important thing to take away from this is that your girlfriend Rachel and Chief Justice Salo-Baron, as well as Judge Hurtig, are all on an Action Committee hit list. For various reasons we think the chief justice, after the attempt on his life, is no longer in immediate danger. Since the attack he has a higher level of security—something more like presidential protection— and it's highly unlikely his situation will be compromised again from the inside. But Rachel and Judge Hurtig should be warned; protective measures need to be put into place. And it needs to be done in a way that doesn't lead back to me."

Zeke stared at his cousin, concentrating hard. "Okay," he said slowly, "I think I understand. But if you're pointing this out, you have already thought it through. So I assume you also have a solution."

Moti nodded. "I do have a recommendation for you, a suggestion about how to arrange security for your girlfriend and Judge Hurtig."

"Good! I was counting on you." His comment was only half-sarcastic. If he didn't have exactly a drowning feeling, he was treading in deep and unknown waters. Better to learn as much as he could now, from someone who apparently had better information than he did.

"The situation with Rachel should be easy to address," Moti said. "Before the attack at your home she received many threats. You may know this. Did she ever talk to you about it?"

"I suppose this is one of those occasions where I shouldn't ask how you know what you know?"

"It would save time."

"Okay, maybe we'll get back to it. Yes, she did discuss it with me. Her producers were aware of the threats; they kept a file on them. I don't know if they ever called the police. Rachel never seemed too concerned, so I wasn't."

"Good. Picture this: she's told you about these threats at work, and now she's had this close call with the attack at your house. She's now a very public figure. It would be a reasonable thing—out of concern for her safety and your own peace of mind—to suggest to Rachel that she ask her employer to provide some basic security measures."

"That's going to keep her safe from this Action Committee and its drones?"

"I am sure you've heard this before," Moti said. "No one, not even the president, can be protected from every attack. Drones don't make it any easier. But doing basic things, like changing your routines and traveling with a bodyguard, can reduce the risks. And in Rachel's situation, her employer, this IVC Network, has its own security department. If they do a proper threat assessment, they will conclude they need to go outside. When they do, CL Associates will bid for the work with a proposal that no one else will be able to match."

"The Israeli security firm? The building we're in?" Zeke looked up and around.

"Exactly. And if they get the contract, she will get far more protection than the modest coverage they pay for."

"Wow," Zeke said, in a monotone. "Really. You've got all this worked out in advance, do you?" His cousin had everything so organized and pre-planned, he suddenly wondered if there might be a bigger picture somewhere that he was not seeing. He got up from his chair to stretch his legs.

"Not me personally, of course," Moti said, sounding defensive. "But yes, Mossad does. We do a lot of planning." Moti stood up also and took a military at-ease stance, legs apart, arms crossed. "In the arrangement we propose with CL Associates, their personnel would provide Rachel's security, but behind the scenes Mossad will supply intelligence and logistics as needed. This will be crucial to protecting her, for example, from another drone attack."

"And you have reason to believe they'll get this contract?"

"There's no guarantee, but CL's business development can be very aggressive. IVC would be a new client for them, with a lot of future potential, so they can offer a highly discounted rate for their first engagement and it will seem reasonable."

Zeke stood with his hands stuffed in his pockets, thinking. He had to keep open the possibility that he and the chief justice were being used by the Israelis for some larger purpose. He speculated about what such a larger agenda might be: a diversion to draw the chief justice away from something else? Was it cover for some other espionage operation the Israelis were running, and this was their way of disguising it? He felt like he needed more RAM; he wasn't processing things, he wasn't getting the whole picture. At the end of any conjecture, however, he still needed to account for the fact that his cousin had made a call that saved his own life, the chief justice's, Rachel's—everyone except poor Lizzie. Moti's fantastical explanation of events was still a more believable scenario than anything else he had heard, or could come up with himself.

Moti took a few steps to a water cooler that was plugged into an outlet in the corner of the room. He filled two small cups, stopped for a few moments to watch the bridge hand being played out on the overhead monitor, and then returned to the table. He handed Zeke one of the cups and they both took their seats again.

"So you're saying all I have to do is tell Rachel I'm concerned for her safety, and suggest that she ask her boss for a bodyguard?" Zeke sipped from his cup.

"In these or other words, yes. Without saying anything to her, or to anyone, about me or the information I'm sharing with you."

"Of course," Zeke acknowledged. "What else do I need to know?"

"For Judge Hurtig," Moti said, "our tactic will be similar to the one we used at your house. We will arrange for some anonymous threats to be made against her, and the Marshal's Service will be called in. If they don't act, you can be our backup plan."

"How is that?"

Moti took a drink of water. "If for some reason the Marshal's Service doesn't respond as we expect them to, you as a senator could contact them on Justice Hurtig's behalf. You might hear through Rachel, for example, or some other source, that she's receiving threats, and you're calling to find out why she's not being given protection."

"I'm not sure a call from me will carry that much weight.

I might accomplish more if I ask the chief justice to intervene on her behalf."

"*Yofi!*" Moti said. "Wonderful. Excellent. This would be completely in character for you and perhaps more effective. Only if necessary, though," he said, lowering his voice. "It's more likely the Marshals will respond right away, in which case you do nothing."

Zeke nodded and took a sip of water, then sat back in his chair and crossed his arms, thinking, trying to absorb it all. "I understand the silence thing, the *quid pro quo*—that's fine. I can talk to Rachel about her security as you suggested. I understand Judge Hurtig's situation. Is there anything else I should know?"

Moti thought for a moment but was sidetracked by his phone, which was vibrating in his pocket. "Pardon me, I should look at this." He swiped open his phone, tapped it a few times, read something, and texted a brief reply. "Where were we?" he asked.

"I had asked you if there's anything else I should know," Zeke replied.

"Well, just now I learned that agent Petersee is dead."

"Jesus!" Zeke's eyes widened reflexively. He ran his hand through his hair. "He died from his injuries? I was told he was in stable condition."

"He was, but at some point after the attack failed, the Committee made a decision to cut their losses—to cut bait. This is correct usage, this expression, yes?"

Zeke nodded. At this point he was numb.

"Petersee was a liability," Moti continued, "because he knew everything, and because they had no way to control what he might say while he was in the hospital."

"You're saying he was murdered?"

"There's no proof, but he didn't die from his wounds. He was a loose end."

"This is bad, this is very bad." Zeke's heart rate shot up. He stood up quickly, nearly tipping over his chair behind him. "How can you be so sure Rachel is safe? It doesn't sound like it to me."

"In truth, we are very confident that our information is accurate. Remember, we continue to monitor their communications. The Committee is going to remain quiet for a period of time. That's why they did what they did with Petersee . . . to make sure things stay quiet."

"You will let me know if this changes?" Zeke asked.

"Of course, certainly," Moti said. "We should stay in touch. When you next hear from Pendergast, for example, it would be good to for us to compare notes again. But nothing over the phone. When we need to talk, I suggest we return here." He rose from the table and collected their water cups. "It's nearby for both of us, and it's private. It also works as a cover for our time together: I'm teaching you to play bridge."

Zeke stood up. "Whew, I'm not sure that's a good idea. I'm dizzy as it is."

Moti smiled. "Not to worry. There will be no test. For our purposes the cover works if you just learn a little about how the game is played by others; you don't have to learn it yourself." He redistributed bidding boxes to the four corners of the table, readying it for the next class. "You may not know that many competitive bridge players think of the game as a turn-on; it has a sensual quality to it."

Zeke laughed. "Sensual? I've never heard bridge described that way."

"It's a point of view; you need to look at it through a certain lens. For example, bidding in bridge is an exchange of coded signals with your partner about what you like and don't like. When you discover you have compatible hands and can take a lot of tricks, it's like chemistry in sex. It's risky, it's exciting, you want to take it as far as you possibly can, and timing is everything. When you play a hand well and take all your tricks, it makes your partner very happy."

Zeke howled. "Okay, cousin, you've convinced me. I'll give it a shot. When we meet again you can teach me to play bridge. It's not like I'm getting laid a lot as it is."

6

*"Most things worth doing in the world had been declared
impossible before they were done."*

—LDB, Labor Arbitration Proceedings, 1913

❧

THE FOLLOWING MONDAY morning Zeke returned to his
office for the first time since the attack and found the
entrance to the Hart Building besieged by a roped-off
trapezoid of shouting reporters, photographers and "Sherman
for President" groupies chanting and waving placards.

Armin and Leslie Graev met the senator's car curbside along
with two other staffers, who acted as shields as they hustled past
the gauntlet. Leslie remained behind as chum for the press.

"I asked Rachel for her advice," Zeke informed Armin when
they arrived inside the glass-walled lobby and the cacophony
had receded. "About the presidential draft."

"Good," Armin replied. "As you can see, the issue hasn't
gone away on its own. What did she have to say?" They were
waved past the security checkpoint and headed toward the
elevators; the two aides fell in line behind like ducklings.

"She blew me off. Said I should hire Allen & Pagano or
somebody like that from the outside. Or—this I thought was
good—find another candidate to endorse."

"Ah, well, that's a possibility," Armin said. "Hmm. That makes sense."

"Except picking the right person isn't that easy, and she won't help me there either."

"Not my area of expertise, as you know," Armin said, reaching to press the up button. "Maybe you'd like to get Dexter's opinion?" Dexter Zipf was Zeke's senior domestic policy advisor and the only member of his staff who'd been asked by Armin to work full-time at the American Majority Party, in the key role of issues director.

"That's good—excellent idea. He's got the general pulse of the presidential race. Let's get it on my schedule as soon as possible."

"Do you want him to prepare anything in advance—a short list, maybe?"

Zeke was considering this when the elevator arrived. They stepped aside to allow people to exit, and their entourage of four then rode silently to the ninth floor.

The rest of his staff had gathered in the reception area of his office suite, and broke out in applause upon his arrival. He spoke briefly about how grateful he was to be there, about the random, arbitrary nature of the universe, and about how important it was that the chief justice was not harmed. As appreciative as he was of his own good fortune, out of respect for Lizzie he did not want to join in anything that might look like a celebration.

This struck a chord, and the buzz in the room dissipated into silence.

He reminded everyone there was important work to be done, and while he remained in office he intended to exceed the expectations of the people of West Virginia.

Armin followed Zeke into his office and outlined his day for him. First was a call with a pool of West Virginia-based reporters and journalists. Next, an in-person visit from Senator Porter about the Labor Department bill. The weekly conference call with the minority leader was at 10 o'clock, and at 10:45 he needed to head to the Capitol to attend a meeting of the Mine Safety and Health Administration Subcommittee. Back to the office by noon; and lunch upstairs with the Democratic Caucus at 12:15. When he got back from that it would be after two, and he'd spend the rest of the afternoon in a conference room with the new Majority Party staff, reviewing their job descriptions and answering questions.

Zeke followed along at half-attention, occupied as he was with a mental replay of his brunch with Rachel and his mother Sunday morning, when he had casually suggested that Rachel ask at work about getting a bodyguard. Including his mother in the conversation proved to be a stroke of genius; once she weighed in, Rachel almost had no choice. She promised to talk to Harrison about it first thing Monday morning, which would be just about now.

"Finally," he heard Armin say, "the Marshals Service called." This refocused Zeke's attention. "Your meeting with the chief justice has been arranged. They'll pick you up here, downstairs, at 5:15 this afternoon."

"Good," Zeke said. "I'll feel better when I see him in person."

"No doubt. Anything else, Senator?"

"Yes. A little bit off the beaten path here. Follow me into the bathroom please."

"Sir? I beg your pardon?"

Zeke laughed. "It's not what it seems. Don't sue me yet. Stand by for a second." He swiveled in his chair, hit the power button on the television behind his desk and turned up the volume. He then headed into his private bathroom, turned on the shower full-force and reappeared in the doorway. "Armin, join me here for a minute."

Armin approached him slowly, his eyes wide. "Sir, what is going on?"

Zeke lowered his voice to a near-whisper. "We need to have a conversation that can't be overheard. Keep your voice low."

"Overheard? Overheard by who?" Armin's expression melted from anxiety into confusion.

"Armin, come closer, I'm not going to bite. I have a task for you. I want to get our offices and cars checked for bugs. Of the eavesdropping variety."

"You think the office is bugged?"

"I don't know for sure, but that's why we're having this conversation here."

"Who do you want me to call for this? The Capitol Police? Or maybe the Federal Protective Service?"

"I want you to contact this man," he handed Armin a folded note, "from a burn phone, outside the office. Use only that phone to communicate with him. When his work is done, dispose of the phone afterward."

"What do I say to him?"

"He'll be expecting your call. Follow his lead. All you'll need to do is arrange for his people to have access to the office late at night, in your presence only. They'll provide a cover story. The same thing with my car; it can be done when Dennis is off."

Armin stared at the note for a moment and mouthed the name.

"It's pronounced Deecop Inagi," Zeke whispered. "He's a former FBI agent I knew from Charleston who moved on to become deputy chief of operations for the D.C. Police. His nickname Deecop is from that job. He runs his own consulting business now. Have the bill come to me personally. No one else in the office is to know."

"Okay." Armin pocketed the note. "I understand. It's all off the record. Anything else?"

"No, that's it. My schedule's on the tablet?"

"The usual place, click on the home icon. Do you want us to get the press call going?"

"No, I have a personal thing I'm going to take care of first. Give me five minutes."

Armin exited, closing the door behind him. Zeke walked across his office and retrieved a burner phone from an away bag stored in a coat closet. He returned to the bathroom doorway, the shower still running, and dialed Deecop's private number. After a round of warm greetings, Zeke cupped a hand over the phone to shield his voice. "I need you to sweep my office and car for bugs. You're going to get a call from my chief of staff, his name is Armin DeBryin. He'll arrange access for you. It needs to be done off the record and after hours. Can you take care of this for me?"

"Of course, Senator, no problem. I will expect his call."

"It's actually a little more complicated. I need you to handle two other matters as part of the same engagement, but without separate line items. I need a generic bill for professional services."

"Also not a problem. What is the additional work?"

"There's a deputy secretary of Homeland Security—the name is Lowell Pendergast. I want to learn more about him. Is it possible to follow someone like this? I don't know if he travels with his own security or not."

"What is it you want to know? I think it would be hard to tap his communications, if that's what you have in mind."

"No, I'm more interested in finding out where he goes after work—where his non-official travels take him. In particular I'm trying to find out if he ever crosses paths with Carla Constance Ross, the supreme court justice. In general, I'd like to get a picture of where he goes and who he intersects with."

"We should be able to track his physical movements; maybe

learn more if we're lucky. This could take a couple of days to organize."

"That's okay, there's no urgency. Now the second item."

"Yes sir."

"I want you to do some research that won't be traced back to me. I'm trying to learn about a group called the Christian Action Committee, a secret society that originated at the Air Force Academy in the early 2000s. Its members might be current or retired Air Force Academy graduates or instructors. Apparently there was some type of religious proselytizing going on there, and this group came together when the practice was investigated and stopped."

"What kind of research? Do you want me to ask some Academy graduates? I know at least a half-dozen."

"No, not that. I mean online research—research that I don't want originating from my own office or home. If you had a 100 percent trustworthy source in Justice or the FBI you could make an in-person inquiry there, but I don't want anyone related to the Air Force to know I'm asking this question."

"Understood. How do you want to communicate in the future?"

"My chief of staff, Armin, will be calling you from a burn phone that will be our contact point for this matter. When you want to meet, call that phone and Armin will set it up. We can't meet in my office. I'm living now at the Wardman Park Hotel off Connecticut Avenue. They have a 24-hour business center."

"I know the place. This is fine. When I heard about the attack on your home I was very upset; I kept checking the news sites until they confirmed you were okay. Does your assignment tonight relate to these events?"

"It does. Deputy Secretary Pendergast seems to be leading the investigation of the attack."

"You're not satisfied with their progress?" Inagi asked.

"Something like that. For legal purposes, if you're ever required to disclose why I hired you, the reason is that Pendergast was not keeping me informed about the investigation and I wanted to know why."

"Understood. I will contact your chief of staff when I have something to report."

"Thanks for your discretion as always," Zeke said.

"Thanks for thinking of me, Senator."

*   *   *

After finishing his call with the minority leader, Zeke started to pack his briefcase for the walk up to the Hill. Armin tapped on his door and stuck his head in.

"You're going to want to know about this."

Zeke, standing up behind his desk, waved him in. "Know about what?"

"I'd say you might want to sit down, except I know you've got to leave. It looks like the film producer Z.K. Dawson has given AmericaOne, the progressive Super PAC, a $20 million donation earmarked to draft you into the presidential race."

Zeke stopped his shuffling of papers. "You have got to be kidding."

Armin handed him a tablet, where the story was in first position on the daily Election Law Blog.

"What do these people want?" Zeke huffed. "Why doesn't 'no' mean no?"

The intercom on his phone beeped. His appointments secretary, Gerry Austrian, came through on the speaker. "Your mother is on line two, and Rachel's holding on three. Their calls came in at the same time."

"Hah! What a surprise!" Just by mentioning it one time, in jest, he'd made it happen. They were working as a team. "I'll speak to Rachel now. Please remember to ask my mother if it's an emergency. If it's not, tell her I'll call her after I return from the Hill."

He punched through to Rachel. "Congratulations," she said, her tone taunting. "I know you must be excited by this latest development in your campaign to not run for president."

"Seriously, Rachel, I'm asking as a personal favor—just tell me who I should be looking to endorse. You don't have to explain why. Give me a short list."

"Zeke, I told you, I'm not going to get involved. I actually called about something else, but right before I called I saw the news come up about Z.K. Dawson. I'm sorry I said anything."

"Okay, okay. What's up?"

"I'm calling to thank you, actually, for your concern about my safety. I mentioned it to Harrison this morning, and I just found out I'll have security starting tonight. A driver, a bulletproof car, and a bodyguard."

Zeke was flustered. They had acted quickly, which was good—but what if it was too fast for Moti's plan? "That's great," he said. "I'm glad they're taking it seriously, but it makes me wonder if I should be concerned. Is there a threat of some kind?"

"No, not at all. It turns out to be about money. I'm insured for a lot of bucks—the bondsmen got involved. You know how this business works."

"No, I don't, but it's good enough for me. I feel much better already. It's all in place?"

"They're using an Israeli firm called CL Associates. Their rep and some suits from IVC corporate will be here this afternoon to go over everything. I just met the team leader, a woman named Eva. She stopped by to introduce herself and get a tour of the studios. All-business type; former Israeli army officer."

"That's great. I'm very relieved. Thank you for taking care of that."

"Gotta run," she said. "Might be on the road tonight. I'll let you know."

Zeke hung up. "Whoa!" he said out loud. Rachel was now being driven around and "protected" by Mossad operatives whose ultimate agenda was unknown. Was Rachel being helped, exploited, or framed? He had no idea.

* * *

Returning from his meeting on Capitol Hill, Zeke found a book had been left on his desk chair with a note inserted in it. He looked at the title on the spine: *The Wanting of Levine*— Michael Halberstam.

Still standing behind his desk, he pressed the intercom. "Gerry, please try to get my mom on the line. Try her cell phone, she's here in D.C. somewhere." He took off his suit jacket, hung it in on the valet rack against the back wall, and retrieved his reading glasses from the inside pocket. By the time he finished cleaning them his mother was connected on the speakerphone.

"Mom, I hope you don't have high hopes that I'll be reading the *Wanting Levine* book. Do you remember at lunch, after the funeral, you mentioned it to me, and I said I wouldn't have time to read it?"

"I do remember, dear. It was only three days ago. Do you think my memory is that bad?"

"No, but the book is here on my desk now. Did you have it delivered to me?"

"*Nu*, son, I'm looking at the book. I packed it in my suitcase. I have it with me here in my beautiful hotel room, which by the way is far more than I need. A simple room with a bed would be fine. You're spending way too much money."

"So who," Zeke asked out loud as he removed the letter inserted in the book, "has sent me the exact same book you recommended? That's some coincidence." He extracted the note, which turned out to be two pages folded together, both typewritten. The first was a letter from one Nora Kalish, a constituent from Wheeling. He paraphrased for his mother as he scanned it: "She's been a fan of the book for years, thought I'd see interesting parallels to my own situation, *et cetera*, just like you told me at lunch, Mom. She continues on, urges me to run for president—hah!—and then says she's available for marriage and/or employment!" The second page was her not unimpressive resume.

"You've got much better already," his mother replied.

Zeke feigned real consideration. "I don't know, Mom, you're not seeing the whole picture here. I'm looking at her CV. This woman's Jewish, she's got a Master's degree, she was a Rhodes Scholar . . ."

"You're making this up."

"And she sent me a copy of the same book you're reading. How clever is that?"

"Never mind. You're playing with me. That's not why I called you anyhow."

"No, that's why I called you. I thought you sent me the book, but now that I understand you didn't, you're off the hook. Why did you call?"

"Do you remember my friend from many years ago, Rose Bernofsky?"

"Yes."

"Her son, Samuel, who you've actually met but wouldn't remember, he was two years ahead of you in high school . . ."

Zeke started to look around on his desk for things to do while the story wended. He found his tablet and swiped it on.

". . . he's an editor at the *New York Times*. He's been with them for years now, he's very senior . . ."

Zeke tapped in his login and password and clicked the e-mail app.

"... and now he's in charge of their Sunday *Magazine*. Did you know they're running a feature story about Rachel next weekend?"

"I knew they were working on an article—they wanted to interview me for it. I declined, of course. But I didn't know they were planning it for so soon."

Well according to Rose, the attack at your home made it a bigger story, so they're not only running it sooner, they're moving it to the cover."

Zeke paused for several moments. "Mom, has anyone asked you to influence me about this article? To persuade me to comment for it?"

"Absolutely not! Son, I'm offended you would think such a thing. Hah! If anyone ever suggested it, they would be rejected immediately." Zeke envisioned his mother lifting her chin dismissively, in the style of FDR.

Zeke knew from past experience this was true: his mother had never once asked him for any Washington favors on behalf of herself or her family or friends. No tours, no tickets, no special consideration of any kind. "So you called just to tell me about this article?"

"Boychik, I just called to tell you the *New York Times* is featuring your girlfriend on the front cover of their Sunday *Magazine*, with a stunning photo, apparently. I thought you might be as excited as I am. I thought you would be pleased for her, and proud."

"I am, Mom. You know I'm very proud of her."

"Well, when Rose called to tell me about it, I felt like I was getting inside information, so for me it's exciting. I guess if you knew about it already, it's not such a big deal."

"It's wonderful that you called, Mom. I'll pass the information along to Rachel; I know she'll be pleased you got the scoop. But I need to go to my next meeting, and I'm tied up this evening. Have you made dinner plans? I'm not sure what Rachel's doing."

"Son, don't worry about me, I'm staying in a luxury hotel with everything I need at my fingertips, thank you very much. Maybe I'll see you for breakfast."

*   *   *

"Welcome to my experiment in open source democracy," Zeke announced, by way of introduction, at the first official staff meeting of the American Majority Party. He stood behind a lectern at the head of a horseshoe conference table, addressing eight people, five of whom he already knew—personnel from his senate office who had been invited by Armin to work part-time in the AMP start-up. The three new faces were full-time hires Armin had deemed essential—a webmaster, a chief technology officer, and a social media manager. He had interviewed them all and seen their resumes before they were hired, but of course now could remember only one of their names.

"As you know our goal here is to persuade America's 200 million registered voters to walk away from two-party politics. We want them to vote first for *what* they want, and then afterwards for who they want. I have complete awareness—as should you, by now—of how daunting this mission is, and the long odds we face." He paused and surveyed the room, trying for eye contact with everyone. "We are the proverbial man on a bicycle attacking a herd of elephants. But this is why I'm here. If this is not why you're here, now is the time to speak up, or ask questions, or do whatever it is you need to do. Everyone in this room needs to be aligned with this objective."

He paused again. There was rapt silence. Even the geeks had put aside their tablets and were listening at full attention.

"Good. I am grateful to have you here, and I hope you're as excited as I am about what we're doing. I do have a few points

I want to make sure we cover, and then each of you is going to review your job description for everyone else, to make sure we're all on the same page. I didn't intend this to be a formal presentation, so please join in if anyone has a question or comment."

One of the newcomers, a young man with a beard sitting at the far end of the table, raised his hand. "Please," Zeke said, "remind me . . . your name is . . . ?"

"Robert Marcus, Senator. I'm the webmaster."

"Forgive me, Robert. I remember our interview, but I meet a lot of people and I have trouble remembering names. What's on your mind?"

"I understand the ultimate goal," Robert said, "and I'm excited to be part of the effort. But getting all 200 million users on board could take some time. There must be other goals we can aim for. What needs to happen in order for us to say yes, we're sure this is working?"

"Thank you, Robert, your question fits perfectly into my own agenda for this meeting, which is to propose some short-term goals. The most important one, I think, is to achieve our first success with an NVP campaign at the federal level. We're looking for Congress to pass legislation in direct response to pressure applied through one of our NVP campaigns."

"What's an example," Robert asked, "of an issue that might work for us?" he asked. "What's something we could make our mark with?"

"I'm not sure," Zeke replied. "I'm not trying avoid your question; I really don't know. My gut says it's something that's not even on our radar right now."

"I've been giving this a lot of thought," Dexter Zipf said, "for all of a week." Dexter was by far the most experienced political operative in the room. "It occurs to me that the next mass murder with an automatic weapon, whenever it happens, might generate a lot of interest in an NVP campaign about gun control."

Zeke acted horrified. "Mr. Zipf, I never took you for being so *mercenary*. Surely you don't want such a thing to happen?"

"Sorry, Senator, not at all. I'm just analyzing, in the abstract. We need to be ready to seize opportunities when they arise, no matter how calculating it may seem. Do you really think there's not going to be another mass shooting in the U.S. in the next few weeks?"

"I hope not, but if there is, and we 'seize the opportunity' as you say, I still don't see this as our signature issue, if for no reason other than I don't think our first vanquished foe will be the NRA. You could sneak a plastic gun into the gallery of the House of Representatives and murder three Congressmen, and they will still not pass meaningful gun control legislation."

"Wow!" said Becky Falcone, the AMP's part-time press liaison. "That's a great hypothetical for the Sunday morning talk shows. When the gun issue does come to the front burner again, we might want to consider taking that scenario public."

"This is why it's good to think about these things in advance," Dexter added. "Even if it's not our signature issue, this is all still great material." He turned to Becky. "I agree with you," he said. "What would happen if someone shot up Congress is a great question to ask, in some version, in a public face-off with NRA-owned congressmen."

"This may be good stuff," Zeke said, "when I'm wearing my senate hat. But it's off-topic right now. I'm still on Robert's question of what short-term goals we can aim for. Winning our first NVP campaign is one—whatever it turns out to be. It's not going to be gun control or something complicated like tax reform, but it will make itself known at the proper time.

"Moving on to additional short-term goals . . . as you know, during election season our democracy dashboard will generate revenue from ad sales to candidate campaigns at the local, state and federal levels. We have enough money to carry us through next December, but the plan calls for significant revenue from ad sales. Robert, you and Farida have done great work bringing us this far, thank you very much." Zeke led a brief round of applause, and acknowledged Farida Rao, their chief technology officer. "Can our ad platform be tested and ready in time?

"The short answer is yes," Farida replied. "The longer answer is yes, but without many of the bells and whistles in the spec. We will have an MVP, which in our world means a Minimum Viable Product, in time for the next election cycle."

"Excellent," Zeke said. "That is the second short-term objective. Having our own source of funding is the key to our independence, not to mention survival.

"There is a third and final short-term objective I would propose, which is to recruit a minimum of ten million unregistered voters to our cause. This is a small number relative to the registered electorate, but it may be enough to shift the balance of power away from Republicans or Democrats in gerrymandered districts.

He turned back to his webmaster. "Robert, have I answered your question about short-term goals?"

Robert offered a casual salute. "Yes sir."

"Good. I will make one further observation before we move on to your presentations. Despite the long-odds nature of our effort, I have reason to be optimistic. The public seems so fed up with the status quo and may welcome an alternative. We still have a massive educational effort in front of us, but our students appear to be well motivated.

*   *   *

For his evening meeting with the chief justice, Zeke was picked up at the Hart Building by three plainclothes deputy marshals and driven to Union Station in an unmarked SUV. Along the way he was given a Detroit Tigers baseball cap, and when they arrived at the station two other agents exited the car with him at the same time wearing identical caps. All three got into identical unmarked sedans; Zeke was driven around for ten minutes, then deposited back downtown at the Willard Hotel and taken to a third floor meeting room, where his identity was re-verified and he was asked to walk through a weapons scanner. Then, still accompanied by two agents, he was guided onto a service elevator that had its floor indicator taped over. When the door opened, it was directly into a suite where the chief justice was sitting at an almost-cleared dinner table, reading from a tablet. Another agent stood in the doorway of an adjoining bedroom, and a chambermaid was at work in the kitchen area.

"My friend!" The chief justice stood up immediately and welcomed Zeke with a bear hug.

"Professor, I can't tell you how relieved I am, we all are, everyone is, that you're okay." Zeke stepped back to look his friend in the eye. "It is so good to see you in person. The way they restricted access to you worried me even more. But you look well. How is Fran?"

"Very rattled. Very distraught about Lizzie. She had the option of staying here with me or taking a trip to visit one of our kids. I encouraged her to go. She arrived in Dedham yesterday."

"That's best, for sure."

"We were both so charmed by your cook, just in that one evening."

"She'd been a family friend for over twenty years. My mother was devastated."

"I'm very sorry."

They stood for a moment in silence. The chief justice invited Zeke to join him in the suite's living room, which had been converted into a makeshift office. "Would you like something to eat or drink? I just finished dinner, but it's the Willard—the room service is first-rate."

"Thank you, I'm set." Zeke said. "I wonder, since we've both just eaten, if there isn't a place we can go for a walk? Can you go outside, or do they have you locked down here?" After checking to be sure no one was looking, Zeke pulled a folded note from his jacket pocket and passed it quickly to the chief justice.

PLEASE: DO NOT MENTION THE WARNING FROM MY COUSIN OR ANYTHING RELATED. ASSUME WE ARE BEING LISTENED TO.

The chief justice pressed his lips together, reread the note, and then transferred his gaze to Zeke. "I'm sorry, what did you ask?"

"Can you go for a walk somewhere, or do you have to stay inside?"

"Ah, yes. I'm not sure." He returned the note to Zeke, who tucked it back in his pocket. "I haven't asked, but it's not an unreasonable request. I've only been here since last night. They've had me in three different places since the attack. I'll ask."

Ten minutes later they were walking along a lighted garden path on a rooftop patio adjacent to the hotel's unoccupied presidential suite. The evening temperature had dropped to the mid-50s and there was a fine mist left in the air from an earlier rain shower. Zeke turned up his suit coat collar against the chill. The chief justice was wearing a bulletproof trench coat and his trademark beret.

Two agents trailed them by twenty feet, and there were others scattered around the roof, but Zeke concluded it was the best they could do for privacy.

"We're probably okay now," Zeke began, keeping his voice low. "I apologize for acting so paranoid. I promised my cousin I would try to protect him from exposure. He did after all just save all of our lives."

"For which Fran and I are eternally grateful. I would thank him in person if it was possible."

"He would react modestly and claim it was a group effort."

"Meaning I should be thanking Mossad?" the chief justice asked. He exhaled into cupped hands and then rubbed them together.

"It goes higher up than that. I was told this whole effort has been authorized by the Knesset. The Israeli parliament has a Subcommittee on Counter-Terrorism in the Diaspora."

"I've never been much of a Zionist, but this whole thing has given me plenty to think about. We're alive—Fran and I are both alive—because there were institutions in Israel that could warn us. I must say I'm impressed."

"I had the same reaction, Professor. If I may, allow me to bring you up to date with the latest information from these institutions. I met with my cousin again last night." Zeke related everything Moti had reported to him: the Air Force origins of the Action Committee; Justice Ross's possible involvement in it; Pendergast and his role in the investigation; and the theory that Rachel had been targeted along with the chief justice after the Ross impeachment campaign was discussed.

The chief justice stopped their stroll and tugged at Zeke's coat sleeve. "You understand how hard it is to believe all this? Where's your proof?"

"I became convinced when he played the soundtrack from my dining room on the night of the attack. But whatever proof there is, from a legal point of view it's not evidence we can act on. If asked, my cousin will deny ever having a conversation with me about any of this."

The chief justice shrugged his shoulders. "Seems very far-fetched to me."

"I'm the first to agree. The problem is that the story he's spinning—no matter how improbable—offers a better explanation of events than I've seen from any other source. If you have a better theory let me know what it is."

The chief justice considered this.

"Also," Zeke continued, "I ask myself, why would he invent a conspiracy story like this? What would be his motivation? I know my cousin as a highly regarded law professor. He's putting a 20-year career in serious jeopardy. Why would he do that?"

"I don't want to sound ungrateful, but this is a foreign government we're dealing with. You're asking me—we're trusting a foreign intelligence agent to keep us safe. I'm struggling with this—it runs counter to my basic instincts."

"That's fine, struggle away. Just remember you wouldn't be struggling, with instincts or anything else, if you had not already relied on information from this same foreign agent. Your *instinct* would be *extinct*."

"Point taken. So, if we continue to rely on his information, what does he say to do now?"

Zeke repeated Moti's assertions that the professor and his wife were safe for the time being. The Action Committee was lying low, and with his higher level of protection he was no longer vulnerable from the inside. "He promised to notify me if anything changes," Zeke said.

"I'm certainly going to be looking at Justice Ross differently from now on," the professor said. "Your cousin says it could be her husband who's involved; is there any way to find out if it's him and not her?"

"Professor, even if we can establish that it's Walter Ross and not his wife who's involved with this Action Committee, do you think they don't talk to one another about what they're doing? Our past experience—during your confirmation hearings, for example—would suggest that they coordinate pretty closely."

"Hmm." The chief adjusted his beret and shifted his weight from one leg to the other. "You know better than anyone that I've tried every possible path to connect with her. I understand how profound our differences are. I'm just having trouble seeing her as a violent person, as someone who would be involved in a murder plot."

"Well I can tell you in my experience as a U.S. attorney, some of the mildest mannered people turn out to be killers, especially if they don't have to pull the trigger themselves."

They turned around and began walking slowly back toward the hotel suite. "While we're talking about Justice Ross," Zeke continued, "I should bring you up to date on Judge Hurtig's activities, which are receiving full support from Rachel. Their goal is impeachment—they're going to make a push to get her removed. This is just information, I'm not advocating anything."

"Listen, between you and me and that lamppost, I wish Judge Hurtig luck; I would like nothing more than to come to work one morning and not have Ross to cope with. The only reason I'm opposed to their effort is I don't think it can succeed, and while it's underway it will shine a harsh and unwelcome spotlight on the court. That's not what we need right now."

"Understood. And agreed. I just want you to be informed."

The chief justice didn't respond. They walked in silence for several moments.

"I'll offer a new subject," Zeke said. My mother, who's connected somehow through her Hadassah grapevine to an editor at the *New York Times*, tells me that Rachel's going to be the Magazine's cover story next Sunday."

"You must be very proud!"

"I am, and I'm very pleased for her. But I try to look at it from a different angle."

"Meaning . . . ?"

"I try to put our relationship aside and look at it objectively. I understand all the media attention because she's made *Women in Charge* a huge success in a few short months. But that's a five-paragraph story. They're running a feature article, so I have to wonder if they're going to delve into what's really happening here, which as I see it is a far more interesting phenomenon than a hit TV show."

"What phenomenon is that?" the chief justice asked.

"I'm convinced that many of the issues that Rachel has focused on in her show—such as reducing defense spending and corporate welfare—these issues are now on the front burner in Congress and the press because the women who are her audience have become much more forceful in their relationships with the men in their lives, and have pushed them on these issues. She's teaching America's women how to recognize what they want, and how to get it. You may laugh; I have no data, but I'll swear to you this is what's really happening."

"Oh, I can give you data—or at least a datum. I'm a perfect example. As you know, Fran is a fan of *Women in Charge*, and so via my wife I have been fully informed about the issues you just mentioned."

"I imagine that's the point—or at least *a* point—of the *Times* story," Zeke said.

"Zeke," the professor queried, "might I venture to ask a personal question?"

"Of course."

"Do you and Rachel plan to get married?"

"Aha!" Zeke's voice spiked. "So you're in league with my mother? She's been in touch with you on this subject?"

The chief justice broke out laughing. "No, of course not." He stopped and faced Zeke. "To what league do you refer?"

"I'm seeing conspiracies everywhere. My mother has recently been pressing me on this same subject."

"I apologize if I've overstepped my bounds. My inquiry is completely independent of your mother, I assure you."

"Professor, no apology is needed. I'm flattered that you've asked. Do you really want to be burdened with my personal situation? You have plenty on your plate."

"*Unsinn!*" the professor exclaimed, trotting out his Einstein impersonation. "*Nonsense!* You've been an indispensable friend to me for years, and now you go and save my life! How much more personal does it get? I want to reciprocate—I want to do something to help *you*."

"That's very kind." Zeke became flushed. "I don't want to impose, but I would be grateful for any advice you have to offer. The situation, for me at least, is complicated. Maybe you can help simplify it." They reached the sliding glass door to the presidential suite; an agent standing on the inside pulled it open for them. "Let me organize my thoughts," Zeke said as they were ushered into the hallway. "To be continued downstairs."

Back in the chief justice's suite, they shed their jackets and ordered a pot of hot tea from room service, along with Amaretto and toast for Zeke and a double shot of Kahlua for the professor. They settled into two oversized armchairs separated by a lamp table. The nearest agent was standing at the elevator, a good twenty feet away. Zeke lowered his voice, shifting his body in his chair to face his friend. "There are certain things in my life right now that seem out of control—a very uneasy feeling for me. And I'm not referring to the attack on my house, although that's made it worse. But anyhow, if you're willing to listen and throw in your two cents, I'd be more than grateful."

"Well I'm not trained for this, but I went to college. Let me give it a shot. What's your situation?"

In whispered tones, Zeke poured out his anxieties about marriage—how he adored Rachel and was very attracted to her, but in his mind getting married ultimately meant having children, and he was far from sure he was ready for that.

He compared having children to moving to another planet—a totally different universe with longer, almost infinite days, and continuous, lifelong worries of a heretofore unknown intensity. "Where is it written," he asked, "that you must spam out genetic copies of yourself? It might be a deeply ingrained evolutionary trait, but it is not a universal law." He argued that modern humans are creatures of cognitive reasoning—he more than most—and that they needn't be compelled by instinct to reproduce.

"If Rachel isn't pressuring you about children," the Professor asked, "why the concern? Some people get married and don't have children. Rachel seems like a very career-oriented woman; maybe that's the path you'll both take, and there won't be children."

"Oh, Rachel will want to have a child. I know her; she wants to do it all, she wants to have it all. Her career wouldn't be complete if she didn't have kids."

"You might talk to her about it."

"I might, but it's moot. Because the other woman in my life, my mother, is outspoken on this subject. I'm an only child, and she tells me bluntly that she wants grandchildren." He went on to explain she had threatened to *rent* grandchildren—whatever that meant.

The professor burst out laughing; Zeke was half in tears. He was relieved when the elevator arrived and a waiter emerged bearing their room service order on a wheeled trolley.

After everything was laid out and they were alone again,

Zeke shifted to his career. His carefully planned exit from the Senate had backfired. He seemed unable to convince anyone he wasn't running for president, and now there was an official campaign draft committee with a $20 million bank account. He asked the chief justice if he had heard about it.

"I saw it online this morning."

"What do you think?"

"About the draft? The money being raised? I don't think anything. The last I heard from you, which was just the other night at dinner, you were very clear. You didn't want to campaign, you don't like fundraising—you wanted nothing to do with any of it. You were devoted to your new effort. So unless that's changed, what's to think about?"

Zeke shrugged. "More disappointment for the women?"

"These are strong women. They'll get over their disappointment."

"I guess more to the point, am I doing the right thing?"

"Ach!" The chief justice sat up straight in his chair and nodded his head gently. "Now you ask an interesting question. Doing the right thing for whom? For you?"

"For me primarily, but also for the people who are close to me, Rachel, and my mother. And you. What do you think is the right thing to do?"

"Well this is now different. Now you are asking me to be counsel to the situation. That would have me consider the interests of all the stakeholders in the matter, not just yours."

"That's it! You've said it exactly. I would be so grateful to have that perspective; my own is too selfish."

"By definition one's own perspective is selfish, at least to some degree," the chief justice said.

"Perhaps."

"My point being, don't berate yourself for being selfish. It's a natural point of view, and essential for self-preservation. But since you've asked, I'm happy to advise you on behalf of all interested parties. Give me a few minutes to process all this. I'm sure I'll have questions . . . we'll talk some more. Let's enjoy our drinks. There's a lot to work with here."

* * *

It was 11:30 p.m. when Zeke arrived back at the Wardman Park. He ran into Rachel in the hotel lobby on her way out, complete with entourage: a segment producer, personal assistant, and bodyguard.

"Congratulations on the *Times* article," he said, kissing her on the cheek. "Did you know it's now a cover story?"

"Yes, I know, I know." She was in a rush, her brown eyes active and alert. "Harrison saw some advance copy, which he didn't share with me, but his assistant said he was thrilled. They've had a photographer with me all week."

"Well I'm pleased to see you've got some security now."

"It was so thoughtful of you to think about it. The first word out of my mouth and Harrison ran with it. Which is what I have to do now. Sorry."

"Where are you headed?"

"Cambridge, Mass. A pharmaceutical whistle-blower. We're going to do our on-site first thing in the morning so we can be back in the studio by noon. We're meeting a film crew at Reagan in half an hour."

"When will I see you again?"

"Tomorrow night? I think. I'll text you." She blew him a kiss as she was towed away by her handlers.

"I'm making a reservation for tomorrow night," he called out. "We've got to talk; it's important. We're having dinner tomorrow night!"

"Okay," she waved back.

Zeke let himself into their suite. Alone at last, and blessedly quiet. Exhausted, he shed his jacket and headed to the bedroom. He looked at the bedside clock: 11:45 p.m. Having Rachel away was actually better . . . it gave him time to rethink the professor's plan. Once he was sure he was committed to it, he would figure out the best way to approach her.

7

"The insight that women have shown into problems which men did not and perhaps could not understand has convinced me not only that women should have the ballot, but that we need them to have it."

—LDB on Women's Suffrage, *Boston Herald*, 1911

THE FOLLOWING EVENING Zeke arranged to have a candlelit, room service dinner brought up to their suite before Rachel returned from work at 8:30.

"What's the occasion?" she asked as she stowed her briefcase and took off her coat.

"No occasion. I rarely see you nowadays. You work very hard. This is something nice I wanted to do for you."

"That's very sweet," she said. Finally unburdened, she approached him for a kiss. "But I don't believe you. What's on your mind?"

Zeke's game plan was set. He pushed on. "Would you like some wine?" He offered her a glass already filled with chilled Riesling, her favorite. The dining nook had been transformed with a white tablecloth, crystal stemware and an array of covered dishes and open appetizers.

"Ooh," she exclaimed, looking it over. "So, what's going on

here? I like it!" She touched her wineglass to his. They both took a sip.

"I'll get to it. But I'm trying for an atmosphere here, so I need you to work with me."

Rachel's facial expressions had a way of signaling everything to Zeke, and he could tell she was with him so far. She took another sip of wine, placed the glass on the table and wrapped her arms around his waist. "You have my undivided attention," she said, looking him in the eye.

"Wonderful." He kissed her, long and sweet, balancing his wine glass in one hand behind her back.

"The first thing I want to do," he said, "is spend some normal time with you. I want to have dinner, hear about your day at work, how the trip to Boston went. I want you to ask me about the chief justice—I saw him for the first time since the attack. Stuff like that."

"Okay," she said.

He broke away to retrieve her wine glass. They toasted again.

"To the future," Zeke said.

"Tease!" Rachel replied. "To the future."

*　*　*

After dinner, over tiramisu and port, Zeke made his proposal. Rachel quickly arrived at an expression he had never seen before—a tilted head, a warm smile, her eyes electrified. Zeke read it as a combination of *how adorable* and *are you out of your fucking mind?*

"Let me make sure I understand," she said. "You're asking me to marry you, and also to run for president in your place, with your endorsement, but without you joining the campaign?"

"That's it exactly."

"And it's all one package? If I don't run for president, the marriage is off?"

"No of course not—I just thought it would be more romantic to combine the two. How many women get proposed to this way?"

Rachel was speechless, which pleased Zeke to no end. She sat with her satin-finish hair illuminated in the candlelight and a stunned, appreciative smile on her face.

Zeke grasped the momentum and continued. "What am I going to do, take you out to a nice dinner and pop the question in public? I'm giving you something unique here—this is a marriage proposal you'll be proud to tell your children about." He wiggled his eyebrows, Groucho style, and reached his hand across the table to grasp hers.

Rachel still didn't respond, but Zeke could now see her mind was starting to work, the wheels were starting to turn.

He was prepared. "Shall we consider things one at a time, then?" he asked, locking onto her gaze. "Will you marry me?"

"I will," she said, collapsing in laughter. "Yes, I will marry you."

"Good," Zeke said, squeezing her hand. "Now, next, will you run for president for me? Or, more to the point, if you ran for president, between my endorsement and your *Women in Charge* audience, do you think you could win? If I didn't think you could win, I would never ask you to do it."

"Zeke, I'm overwhelmed by the idea. I can't respond; I need to think about it."

"Okay, think about it out loud with me. You're a political strategist; you know how to analyze this. What's your read on it?"

Rachel engaged slowly. "In the abstract," she said, "if you ask the question 'what is the probability that an Asian-American woman will win the U.S. presidency anytime in the next half century,' the answer is going to be a very small number . . . no doubt less than ten percent. But that's a generalization; the dynamics of each election cycle are unique." She paused for a moment. "The correct starting place, in building a model, I think, is to look at the people whose support we already have. I have my audience, and you've got the base that's supporting the presidential draft."

"I was thinking the right way to announce you're running would be on *Women in Charge*—your current audience will be your biggest base of support. I could be your guest on the show, to endorse you."

"Maybe we'd announce we're getting married at the same time? Hmm. I like that idea—it would complement your proposal to me so nicely."

"It would be *symmetrical*," Zeke said. "I've been trying to think of a way to keep our private life private, but we both know that's not going to happen; and the media boost here would be significant. I've already decided I'm willing to do whatever needs to be done to help you win, short of actually campaigning. That's where I draw the line. If I was going to do that, I'd run myself."

"Okay, so after my audience and your anti-establishment Democrats, who else do we attract?" Rachel asked. "Another block would be Asian-Americans—it's a significant group, but not so important in swing states."

"You speak Spanish," Zeke said. "And you're from an immigrant background—crucial in a state like Florida. You could beat the president in Florida, I would think. Not that it would be easy, but it seems possible."

"You are correct. The question to focus on is how I would do in swing states—Florida in particular, but also Pennsylvania, Ohio, Michigan and Colorado. It would require a detailed analysis—but it's far from impossible."

Zeke noticed Rachel was now looking at him oddly—still

with a smile, but adding a question mark expression. "Ezekiel, dear," she asked, shifting her tone. "Whose idea was this?"

"What idea?"

"Me running for president."

This derailed Zeke for a moment, but the right path came to him naturally. He hadn't an ounce of intellectual vanity. "That part of it was the professor's idea," he said. "Marrying you was exclusively mine."

"Whose idea was it to put the two together?"

"Both of ours. We spent several hours together last night— it's the first time in all these years he's ever offered to advise me about anything. I've always been his counselor. But let me tell you, for someone who claims not to be a politician, he sure thinks like one."

"That's an understatement," Rachel said. "This is genius, really, if you think about it . . . this is political theater. We'll produce far more recognition as a couple than we ever could pursuing separate careers. This will be like nuclear fission or fusion or whatever they call it—the result will be greater than the sum of its parts."

"And, for what it's worth, the professor thinks you can win."

Rachel raised her glass again. "To the professor!"

Zeke tapped his glass against hers and took a sip. Rachel drained her glass.

"There's another party to this party," Zeke continued, "who may not turn out to be as cheerful as we all are. That's my mother."

"What do you mean? Your mother wants us to get married. She'll be thrilled!"

"She'll be happy about that, but what she's really after are grandchildren."

"Okay, we can try for children. If you want to, that is."

"Well I'm thinking you'll run for president, and win, and there won't be time for children."

"Why wouldn't there be time for children?" Rachel asked, teasing. "At most it takes about a half-hour at inception. Then maybe another 72 hours for labor and childbirth. So far I'm at seventy-two and a half hours . . . what else is there?"

Zeke collapsed in laughter, his cheeks glistening. "You're not taking me seriously, are you? I want you to run for president, and I really think you can win."

"Do you think we couldn't have children if I was president?" Rachel asked.

"I'm not sure it would be a good idea."

"Well, I'm not going to worry about it. That heart is way before the course." Rachel had a tendency to spoonerize when she was tipsy. She smiled at Zeke and blew him a kiss. "You know what I mean."

"I do. And you are right, my mom will be happy we're getting married. I'm just saying she's got her own agenda."

"Don't we all?" Rachel asked.

"We most definitely do," Zeke agreed. "Except now, it seems, you and I are going to combine our agendas—or at least coordinate them in certain ways."

"In *many* ways," Rachel said as she pushed her chair back, stood up and extended her arm to Zeke. "It seems to me these agreements call for something more than a handshake."

8

"America has believed that in differentiation, not in uniformity, lies the path of progress. It acted on this belief; it has advanced human happiness, and it has prospered."

—LDB, Independence Day Address, Boston, 1915.

ACHEL TOOK A contractual leave of absence from *Women in Charge*, trying to protect her position as best as possible if her rookie presidential campaign didn't gain traction. The network, IVC, and the show's producers were in a win-win situation and happy to cooperate. They were losing a host who had boosted the program's audience exponentially in less than half a year, but would continue to benefit from her visibility as a presidential candidate. If she didn't win, she would return to *Women in Charge* with an even bigger audience.

Rachel met privately with Harrison Starr and IVC's chief operating officer to discuss the basic terms of her departure. They agreed she would be replaced by a series of daily or weekly guest hosts until the sooner of Rachel's exit from the race, or her election as president. The details were worked out by a platoon of lawyers, executives and political consultants during a marathon 12-hour meeting in a Crystal City law firm.

Three days later, in her final appearance on *Women in Charge*, Rachel formally announced her intention to run for the Democratic nomination. The idea of having Zeke appear alongside her in person was quickly scrapped, the biggest obstacle being that no man had ever been invited to appear as a first-chair guest on the program, and it wasn't clear how violating this tradition would be received by the audience. In addition, everyone agreed it was vital that Rachel's announcement appear self-generated—grounded in her own ideas and ambitions, and not the product of other people's machinations.

So in a carefully scripted presentation she addressed head-on the prospect that many voters, especially men, might view her as a radical feminist, or as a single-issue candidate. She spoke of a keen awareness of the different roles played by the government and the media, and—alluding to her three-year stint as Zeke's chief of staff—claimed experience and success in both worlds. She swore allegiance to good government for all citizens, and asked to be judged based on her proposed policies and positions on key issues, which she proceeded to outline in detail. Many were issues she had advocated in previous episodes of *Women in Charge,* such as the gradual elimination of federal flood insurance subsidies and support for the Department of Defense's 20-year budget reduction plan.

Rachel then cited endorsements from a half-dozen major public figures—men and women—whose support she and Zeke had quietly lined up over the previous 48 hours. Finally she segued to a live satellite connection with Senator Ezekiel Sherman, who for technical reasons ended up speaking from the same press room and lectern in the Hart building where weeks earlier he had announced his decision to leave the Senate.

Zeke's statement was crafted primarily to win over skeptical white males. He began with a full-frontal disclosure: he and Rachel Chen had been romantically involved for more than three years, and were recently engaged to be married. That was their private life, however, and did nothing to change the fact that professionally he had been Rachel's direct supervisor for the three years she was chief of staff in his senate office. In that capacity he believed he was both qualified and obligated to provide the public with a reference, an employer's assessment of her executive abilities and track record.

He rated her as a highly effective and efficient manager. He praised her personnel and team leadership skills, as well as her political acumen, crediting her with several of the signature achievements of his senate career. He reminded the audience that before managing his office, Rachel had been chief counsel to the Senate Foreign Relations Committee for over twelve years and was fluent in Spanish and Mandarin.

"When I survey the Democratic presidential field," he concluded, "I find that Rachel Chen not only has the best résumé for the job, I also see her as more likely than anyone else to attract the majority constituencies we need to win in swing states. Rachel Chen is a candidate who can *win*."

"That is my best professional opinion. Speaking from a personal point of view. . . ." He tilted his head and nodded at the camera almost imperceptibly, like he was giving advice to his buddies in the locker room. "Take my word for it: this is a woman who knows how to get things done."

* * *

The strategy worked. Not only did Zeke's endorsement of his fiancée for the Democratic nomination completely deflate the draft efforts that had been started on his behalf, it also had the happy effect of priming Rachel's fundraising effort with an initial big infusion of cash. Z.K. Dawson withdrew his $20 million contribution from the AmericaOne Super PAC, but gave half that amount directly to Rachel's campaign and offered the other half as matching funds. This made it much easier for other big donors to get on board, and Rachel's confidence soared. "We're out of the box!" she confided to Zeke with hushed excitement two days after her announcement. "We'll be able to make a run for it!"

"As long as you're referring to the royal 'we' I'm happy for us," Zeke replied. He wanted to make sure there was no misunderstanding: the only campaigning he would be doing would be for the American Majority Party. His plan was to lecture at law schools and universities within a day's drive from Washington, D.C.

"Not to worry," she said. "I'm excited for both of us. You should be doing your thing." Rachel had initially chided him over his refusal to help with the campaign, but over time she came around to his point of view. He was demonstrating an independence of the sexes that was an underlying theme of *Women in Charge*, and a theme she wanted to maintain in her presidential campaign. It also conformed to the general spirit of the chief justice's strategy: they should each assume the roles they were best suited for and devote their energies to those roles.

*   *   *

Kendra Hurtig, at 72, still had an athletic bounce in her walk and bristled with good cheer and intelligence. Upon retiring from her 23-year perch on the U.S. Court of Appeals she let her hair grow down past her shoulders, and gave up her owlish spectacles in favor of blue-tinted contacts. A few of her close friends who knew she wasn't married assumed her cosmetic changes were intended to attract a mate in retirement. In reality Hurtig was shopping for a third career: before becoming a judge she had been a law school professor and dean. Of solid

Scandinavian stock, she thought of herself as middle-aged; her mother had died at the age of 103.

When Rachel's resignation from *Women in Charge* delayed all new production for the show, including the segment Hurtig had been planning about Justice Ross, the retired judge was not content to have it stalled. She contacted Rachel first, to obtain her support, and then together they approached Harrison Starr about adding Hurtig to the show's lineup of regular co-hosts. The program about judicial ethics and Justice Ross would be her pilot; she would host the whole 44-minute show herself. Hurtig made a compelling pitch: plenty of confidence and authority in her voice, but not overly eager.

Starr and his co-producers were doubtful. Hurtig had no television or media experience, and it was not clear how well she would deal with the multitasking demands of the job and its sometimes confusing technology. Also, there were very few on-air personalities her age, and certainly no rookies. But she came with powerful backing, and Harrison ordered a screen test. With only two practice runs and minimal coaching she turned in a highly creditable performance, and the program's development was resumed. Assistant producers were assigned and writers got to work. A month after Rachel's last appearance on the show, Kendra Hurtig brought her case against Justice Carla Constance Ross to the audience of *Women in Charge*.

In addition to calling her out on dozens of ethically questionable extrajudicial statements and actions, Hurtig cited Ross's rock-bottom ranking in something she called the Ashwander Index. This was a rating system of Hurtig's own invention that evaluated a Supreme Court justice's written opinions for violations of the so-called Ashwander Rules, a set of seven principles of judicial restraint laid out by Justice

Louis Brandeis in his 1936 concurrence in *Ashwander v. TVA*.*
Brandeis had been passionate and outspoken in his belief that
the court should always presume the validity of any legislative
act until "its violation of the Constitution is proved beyond all
reasonable doubt." His inclusion of these guidelines in the text
of an opinion was his attempt to give definition and clarity to
this principle.

Hurtig's indexing scheme involved recruiting teams of law
students to review the opinions of every US Supreme Court
justice since 1936, and to assess one point for each egregious
violation of an Ashwander rule manifested in the logic or
language of an opinion. As subjective as this analysis was,
she constructed a strict review methodology with detailed
evidentiary standards, and points were never assessed until at
least two teams of law students, working independently, arrived
at the same conclusion after applying the same standards. The
total number of violations divided by the total number of
opinions written yielded a lifetime Ashwander Index value
for each justice. This was converted with a statistical flourish

---

* 297 US 288, 345 (1936)
   1. The court will not determine the constitutionality of legislation in
      non-adversarial proceedings.
   2. The court will not anticipate a question of constitutional law.
   3. The court will not formulate a rule of constitutional law which is
      broader than needed.
   4. The court will not rule on constitutionality where there is another
      ground for deciding the case.
   5. The court will not determine a statute's constitutionality unless a
      party has been injured by it.
   6. The court will not invalidate a statute at the request of parties who
      have taken advantage of its benefits.
   7. The court will always consider whether any reasonable interpretation
      of a statute allows it to avoid the constitutional issues.

into a zero-to-ten scale, with zero being no violations and ten a theoretical maximum of seven violations per opinion.

In a matter of weeks there were over 1,500 law students at work on this project, the entire effort being coordinated through a secure, dedicated website. It took ten weeks to review and compile a complete index for all 77 post-*Ashwander* justices, the overwhelming majority of which received ratings of between 0.5 and 1.0. Brandeis himself came out in the middle of this range, at 0.73. There were five outliers with scores ranging up to 2.0, and then there was Justice Ross with a 3.3.

None of these details bogged down Hurtig's presentation. The show's writers packaged it all in non-technical language and used graphics to illustrate the disparity in the results. The conclusion was sharply defined for the audience: Justice Ross was not fit for the Supreme Court. She was ethically challenged, she was an extreme judicial activist, and—the crown jewel—she perjured herself during her confirmation testimony when she stated under oath that she had never received any compensation from the Christian Heritage Foundation other than standard directors' fees and expenses. Hurtig, who had developed a compelling on-camera persona, stood alongside a poster-sized blow-up of several annual 1099 tax forms, showing payments from Christian Heritage Foundation to a group called the Marriage Defense Council, and corresponding 1099's showing payments of identical amounts from the Marriage Defense Council to Justice Ross's husband Walter. Hurtig urged the Senate Judiciary Committee to hold hearings on the matter, and appealed to her audience to demand impeachment by joining a No Vote Pledge campaign at www.impeachRoss.org.

She concluded with the organization's tag line: *If the Supreme Court can elect a president, the people can remove a Supreme Court Justice.*"

9

"Experience should teach us to be most on our guard to protect liberty when the Government's purposes are beneficent. Men born to freedom are naturally alert to repel invasion of their liberty by evil-minded rulers."

—LDB, Dissent in *Olmstead v. United States*, 1928

T HE MORNING AFTER the show aired, Harrison Starr took one look at the overnight ratings and called Judge Hurtig to offer her a regular weekly guest-host slot on *Women in Charge.* They met for lunch in IVC's executive dining room to finalize the details, and then toured the studios together— with Harrison making brief introductions to various writers and producers along the way. Afterwards they returned to his office where he replayed several sequences from the previous night's program and narrated a mixture of praise and gentle critique. She responded with modesty and a keen desire to learn the finer points of her new trade.

After finishing up at IVC, Judge Hurtig called on Zeke at his office in the Hart Building to discuss the No Vote Pledge campaign she had launched in support of Ross's impeachment. He was the father of this invention, and she wanted his advice about the best way to use it for her specific issue.

Zeke greeted her warmly in the reception area and then ushered her back to the conference room that still had a handwritten "AMP Headquarters" sign taped to the door, along with a usage log. He signed them in and pulled out adjacent chairs, gesturing for her to take a seat.

"They've offered me Fridays!" she blurted out, beaming like the Dutch boy who saved Haarlem. "A minimum of four shows, starting next month, with a monthly option to renew. When you speak to Rachel, please tell her how grateful I am. She encouraged me and lobbied for me. None of this would be happening if it weren't for her."

"I'm happy to pass along your comments, but don't sell yourself short. I've learned, by secondhand observation of Rachel, what Harrison Starr's production standards are. Believe me, if he's working with you, you've got your own stuff."

"You're very kind." She finally sat down in the chair Zeke had pulled out for her, and he followed suit.

"How can I help you?" Zeke asked.

"I was hoping for your advice about our NVP campaign. Rachel has explained to me how it can be localized—how it can be used to target individual congressmen. We've pretty much settled on the twenty or so Republican districts that we're going after. Any other ideas you have would be more than welcome."

His first suggestion was that Hurtig dedicate a consistent, five-minute time slot every Friday to the impeachment effort, and use it to review the real-time No Vote Pledge tallies in each of the Republican-controlled districts that had been targeted. On a legal pad he sketched out a graphic for the show: a chart, like the scoreboards displayed at the bottom of the screen on sports telecasts, except each row of the chart would have a Republican congressman's name, state and district. There would be three columns of data reported for each congressman: the current

NVP total for the district, the percentage increase in votes over the previous week, and the estimated number of pledges still needed to attain a majority. The idea was to set quantifiable goals in discreet geographic areas, where additional resources could be concentrated without incurring the cost of a national campaign.

"What do you mean by 'additional resources'?" she asked.

"It could be money," Zeke replied. "I don't know how your fundraising's going, but if you have bucks available for advertising, you can run local radio and web campaigns in your twenty congressional districts at a small cost—a tiny fraction of what a national campaign requires."

"Right. This is the localization. I see." Judge Hurtig removed a tablet from her briefcase and began taking notes. "It's too soon to say what our financial resources will be. What else besides advertising can we do?"

"Treat each of these districts as though you're running for office there. Do research, find influential individuals and institutions—clergy, newspapers, chambers of commerce—and try to align them with your cause. You are, after all, doing the same thing candidates do when there's an election: you're hustling for votes. Only in this case you're soliciting No Votes. It's off season—there are campaign consultants available at a steep discount. An experienced campaign manager would know exactly what to do."

"This is all so valuable," she said, squinting at her tablet and tapping away. She looked up at Zeke. "Anything else?"

"I can be an additional resource," he replied. "I can book speaking engagements at law schools in or near your targeted districts, and add to my stump speech an appeal to local law students to go door-to-door and drum up the No Vote. One of our technical geniuses has created a mobile app for collecting No Vote Pledges on a wireless tablet."

"That sounds very useful. Is it an app we can also use on our own—for just our issue?"

"I'm not sure. I will introduce you by email to Farida Rao, our technology guru, who's in a better position to respond. In the meantime I just remembered a question I've been saving up for you."

"What's that?" Hurtig asked.

"Law students," Zeke replied. "You had all these law students working on your Ashwander indexing project. How many were there, and how did you find them?"

"Well over a thousand. I had been a law professor for fifteen years, and I've maintained relationships with many former colleagues. They're all tied together by various blogs and e-bulletins, and my topic was of genuine interest to many of them. The constitutional law crowd, in particular, is fascinated by the whole thing. And, as you know, each law professor has a captive audience of dozens of law students. They can offer extra credit as an incentive . . . there are all kinds of ways to motivate law students."

"I need a thousand law students. Can you help me get them?"

"Sure. What do you need them for?"

"We need to find a way, the Majority Party needs to find a way, to validate its data. We can claim a million registered voters have pledged their vote in one of our NVP campaigns, but are they all really registered voters? How many are duplicates? How many are phony or computer generated? I'm looking for a labor force that can compare randomly selected records in the AMP database to public voter rolls in a quantity sufficient to establish the integrity of our information."

"When do you need them?"

"As soon as possible."

"I don't see why we can't perform a little CPR and breathe

new life into the same system we set up to build the Ashwander database. We had a website that registered teams, kept track of work assignments and results—I must say it was well organized. Even if the same student pool isn't interested or available, I'm happy to share the technology with you, as well as my network of law professors."

"Judge!" Zeke was beaming with gratitude. "I don't know how I can ever thank you enough. Do you see how big a problem this is, that you have just apparently solved by waving a wand?"

"We do have a lot in common, it seems," Hurtig replied.

"We should arrange to meet socially sometime, when Rachel is around. I will tell Rachel about your coup at IVC, but why don't you call her yourself?"

"She's busy campaigning, I don't want to take up her time. She'll find out soon enough, from you or otherwise. IVC's announcing it tomorrow."

Zeke's intercom buzzed. "Senator," Armin's voice came through the two-way speaker. "Deputy Secretary Pendergast is here to see you. Unscheduled. Can you pick up the phone?"

"Please stand by," Zeke called out, "I'm just saying goodbye to Judge Hurtig." He walked her to the door and shook her hand. "Obviously we'll remain in touch," he said in a lowered voice. They exchanged nods.

After she left he returned to his desk and picked up his phone. "Our friend Pendergast returns," Zeke said. "What's his story?"

"He's got half a dozen Secret Service agents with him," Armin said, his voice quavering. "They look armed. They've pretty much taken over the reception area."

"Armin, why are they here? Did you ask?"

"No sir, I didn't. When they first told me he was here I assumed it was to brief you about the attack—but then when

I greeted him in person and saw all the agents, I didn't know what to think. Could they be here to serve a warrant?" Armin wondered.

"If that's what they were here for they would have executed it already. I have no idea what this is all about. Judge Hurtig just left; bring him back to my office, and stay with us."

Zeke greeted Pendergast with a stiff handshake and ushered him in, but remained standing with his guest in front of his desk. Armin quietly closed the door behind them.

"Mr. Deputy Secretary, I hope you've come with news about the attack at my home."

"Unfortunately, Senator, I have nothing to share with you beyond what's been reported in the press. You've done this yourself; you understand the more people who know the details of a crime, the more variables you have to deal with."

"I'm not surprised. When you promised to keep me informed I wasn't very optimistic."

"Why is that?" Pendergast's silver mane twitched.

"I have a biological lie detector. It's a skill I developed as a prosecutor. If someone's addressing me personally, I can tell if they're hedging the truth." Zeke locked onto Pendergast's eyes and bore down on him with a pleasant smile.

Pendergast laughed. "That's quite something. Thanks for letting me know. Am I lying to you now? I'm not authorized to release any non-public details of the investigation, to you or anyone else."

"If you're not authorized to do that, why are you here?"

"To offer you Secret Service protection."

"Why would I want Secret Service protection? Is there a threat I should be aware of?"

"No, there's no threat. You're engaged to be married to a presidential candidate who has just qualified for Secret Service protection. If you were already married you would be covered automatically, by law. As it is the secretary has discretion to assign coverage to other parties and he thought the right thing to do was to offer you protection now."

"I'll pass, thanks. Anything else?" Zeke looked at his watch.

Pendergast was caught off-guard. "Are you sure? This is as much about Ms. Chen's protection as it is yours."

"How's that?" Zeke asked.

"The department's mandate," Pendergast replied, "is the safety and security of presidential candidates. Someone could coerce Ms. Chen, they could force her to curtail or alter her political activity by threatening her immediate family. Even if you're not yet technically family, the secretary concluded that a threat against you would have the same effect on the candidate, and he'd prefer not to take any chances."

"I'll still pass. As you know Ms. Chen and I keep completely different schedules. I'm not involved with her campaign, I don't want to be part of her entourage, and I don't trust you or the Secret Service . . . or the U.S. Marshals, for that matter."

"Senator!" Pendergast was slack-jawed. "What are you saying? Why are you saying this?"

"I don't trust you because you lied about keeping me apprised of your investigation. I don't trust the Secret Service because they work for you. And I don't trust the Marshals Service because if they hadn't received a tip from some untraceable third party we'd all be dead now—me, Rachel, the chief justice, his wife."

Pendergast was speechless. Zeke drilled him with his stare—he could see his prey struggling.

Finally Pendergast replied, speaking slowly, measuring each word. "Senator, I want to advise you . . . I think you're confusing two issues. I understand your frustration about not knowing what's happening with the investigation. The Marshals Service is taking the lead, and for their reasons—whatever they are—

they don't want you or anyone else to have access to inside information. That's a separate matter entirely from your future wife's presidential run and her personal safety, as well as your own."

"Mr. Deputy Secretary, if you have no new information for me, I'd like to resume my schedule." Zeke took a step back to clear a path to the door for Pendergast to leave. Armin moved to open it.

Pendergast stalled. "Have you followed the details we have released? We know the phone was of Chinese manufacture, and we know its signal originated in New York City."

"All cell phones are manufactured in China, and New York City has 15,000 cell towers. What is the significance of these details?"

Pendergast hesitated, then changed course. "I just wanted you to know it's all being properly followed up," he said. "You had used the word untraceable. It's not as if we abandoned anything. The anonymous call is an active lead that's being pursued from several directions."

"The press is also reporting the weapon used in the attack was a rocket propelled grenade," Zeke said.

"Do you have reason to think it was something else?"

"Let me ask you directly, Mr. Deputy Secretary," Zeke said as he locked eyes with Pendergast. "Was it a rocket-propelled grenade that struck my home?"

Pendergast wavered, and then quickly realized he had already paused too long. "We've had to maintain that as a cover story, for other reasons, unrelated to this case."

"Thank you for not lying."

"How do you know it wasn't an RPG?"

"I spoke to a fire department investigator at the scene. He showed me what he guessed were the remains of a small airframe."

"Well, then you know it was a drone. A Chinese-made, kamikaze drone."

"Why are you lying to me now?"

"I'm not lying to you. It was a drone that delivered a plastic explosive charge."

"Well something you just said wasn't true. My detector's buzzing loud and clear."

"I can't help you; I'm telling you what I know, and I've already exceeded my authority."

"It's the Chinese thing . . . you're bringing the Chinese into everything. Why are you trying to pin this on the Chinese?"

"I have nothing further to offer, Senator. I will leave you to your busy schedule."

"This is all political. This is the administration stoking fears about Rachel's ethnicity and therefore her loyalty. Thanks for bringing this to my attention; I have several pundit friends who may want to pick up on it."

"Goodbye, Senator."

Zeke stared at Pendergast for several seconds, then stepped back to clear a path. Armin opened the door only partially, forcing the deputy secretary to slither out.

After he left, Armin asked Zeke if he wanted a call put through to Rachel.

"No," Zeke replied. "No need to interrupt her. Where is she?"

"Right now she's in Las Vegas, at a convention of realtors."

"I'm expecting to speak to her tonight at eleven o'clock, as always. I'll talk to her about it then."

"Will that be all?"

"Not quite—two things. First, don't be intimidated by the Secret Service or any other men in black. They're not omniscient and they're not infallible. They all turn their heads and cough when the good doctor tells them to."

"Yes sir."

"Second, do we still have our Majority Party staff meeting on the schedule?" Zeke asked.

Armin nodded. "It's at 4:30."

"Okay, I want to add the following item to the agenda: could our first successful NVP campaign be the impeachment of Justice Ross?"

"Understood," Armin replied. "I'll write it up and send it to Dexter."

"Also, before the meeting, everyone should watch Hurtig's presentation from last night. Her pitch for no votes at the end, especially."

"That's it?"

"Done for now, thanks." Zeke smiled and gave him a parting wave.

After he closed the door, Zeke dialed Moti on his cell phone and asked if they could meet that evening. "I've got family matters we should talk about," he said.

"Meet me at the Deep Finesse at 6:30," Moti answered. "I'll be in the same room as last time."

*   *   *

"Cousin, I'm here for my lesson," Zeke announced, tapping on the open door of the card room where Moti was already seated with a sandwich and a drink. He waved Zeke in.

"Excuse me for not getting up," he said, smiling at Zeke briefly and then returning his attention to the ceiling-mounted monitor where a bridge hand was being played. Cards from each of the four hands were being moved, one at a time, by an unseen master, to the center of the screen.

"This is live," he narrated, "from a tournament in Bermuda. I know one of the players—a friend from Israel—and I just want to watch his play on this deal. You remember where the food is, yes?" He waved towards the kitchen. "Please help yourself."

"I've had dinner, but I'll pick something up," Zeke said.

By the time he returned with a bottled drink and a paper cupful of M&M's, Moti had abandoned the bridge tournament, which was still silently playing on the monitor. He was now tapping into his tablet with a furrowed intensity and motioned for Zeke to sit.

"Thank you for meeting here again," Moti said after swiping his tablet and dropping it into his jacket pocket. "We could meet in a restaurant if you want, but only once or twice. After that our cover would become fuzzy, as you Americans say."

"Not this American. I have no idea what you're talking about."

"Sorry, this is from my Mossad work. What I mean is that it's safer if we don't meet in public too often."

"No, now you've got to tell me. I want to know what a fuzzy cover is."

Moti grinned. "Okay, I will explain. We could meet in a restaurant or other public place, and our cover is that we're cousins—we're discussing family matters. That would be fine. But if we did that more than twice, let's say, an observer might ask: how often would a U.S. senator want to talk about family with his Israeli cousin? And, if they are discussing anything else, what might that be? Our family cover story becomes fuzzy—less credible."

"Okay. Understood. Meeting here is fine for me."

"I'll e-mail you a link to a learn-to-play bridge website. Just register there and log on once or twice, to create a record. You don't really have to learn to play, but if you go through a tutorial or two that will complete the cover properly."

"I'll look for your e-mail. I wanted to meet because Pendergast showed up at my office today, unannounced. He offered me Secret Service protection, as the fiancée of a presidential candidate. I refused the offer, but want your opinion. I can always go back to him and say I changed my mind."

"Why did you say no?"

"It's unnecessary. There's no threat and, as it is, as a senator, I'm already driven around by a former army ranger in a bullet-proof car."

"That's a naive view. Now that your fiancée is running for president, the risk factors are very different. There may be no threat to you right now, today, but there are a lot of dangerous people out there. When they discover they can't reach her directly, they might look for another route . . . or is it *route*?" he asked, now pronouncing it *root*.

"I think either, or *eye-ther*, is okay," Zeke replied.

Moti half-closed one eye and analyzed this. After a few moments he began laughing. "I've always liked this about you, the word games you play. This was good!"

"According to you," Zeke said, "Pendergast is part of a conspiracy that's trying to kill the chief justice and Rachel and Judge Hurtig. Why will it make us safer to have this known enemy right in our midst?"

"First of all there's a limit to what Pendergast can do by himself, or with the few people he has working with him. The Secret Service is a big organization. Their management is first-rate, they rotate personnel all the time, and he's a deputy secretary—way above the operational level."

"Hah! According to you, he's responsible for the attack on my house!"

"What the Action Committee arranged, to insert two men into the chief justice's security detail, was an extreme long-shot. It happened only because of a series of unlikely events. We are confident they will not try anything again from the inside. It only exposes them to more risk, and in this last operation it cost them one of their own people. If they make another attempt we think it will be with another drone attack, or perhaps they may hire a contractor—an assassin."

"This isn't making me feel any better," Zeke replied.

"Pendergast already has access to Rachel's protection profile, which includes both of your private schedules. So if your goal is to keep him out of your business, it's too late for that. There's an American expression . . . keep your friends close, but your enemies closer?"

"That's Sun-Tzu, I think," Zeke said.

"I know it from *The Godfather*," Moti countered. "In either case it says what I'm trying to say. Pendergast doesn't know that *we* know who he is. If he's with us and his guard is down, maybe he will reveal something. It also gives us a way to feed him misinformation if the need arises."

"So you think I should accept his offer of Secret Service protection? I hate the whole routine, the code names, the radios, the extra cars. It's an environmental crime—surely you'd agree with that."

"Cousin, you're engaged to a woman who's running for president of the United States. You need to get used to the routine. It's not going to go away."

Zeke relented. He lifted his shoulders in a philosophical shrug, and then tossed down several M&M's from the cup. He twisted open his bottled tea and took a long draft.

"For the next two weeks," Moti volunteered, "the risk is not very high if you do nothing. You could wait to see how her campaign does; if she stays in the race past that, you're going to want to rethink your position. You could easily become a target."

"I'll talk to Rachel about it tonight. If she agrees with you I'll call him back tomorrow and get it started."

"Rachel still doesn't know about me, correct?"

"She knows nothing. I have kept you out of the picture with everyone. I did have a private, outdoor conversation with the chief justice where I explained to him your need for complete silence. He understands and agrees. And again he conveys his thanks."

"Have you checked your car for bugs?"

"We hired a private consultant to go over everything: cars, offices, computers—they found nothing."

"What consultant? Who did you use?"

"A small firm, Inagi Associates. I trust the principal; I've known him for many years."

"Hmmm," Moti said, running through his mental files. "I don't know them. Does he do his own work?"

"He had techs who did the actual sweeps. But I trust Inagi. I've worked with him before."

"This is now a puzzle. We believe our information is correct. We'll keep working on it from our side."

"Did Mossad have people watching us the morning I picked you up in my car and we went for a walk?" Zeke asked.

"Several," Moti replied.

"Well that's a relief. My driver said he observed two people watching us as we walked on Connecticut Avenue. Those were your agents?"

"Yes."

"Why were they there?"

"They weren't there to watch us; they were there to observe if other people were watching us."

"Were there?"

"No."

"Is Mossad following me now?"

"No."

"Is Mossad following Pendergast?"

"Yes."

"You follow him after hours, evenings, weekends?"

"Twenty-four seven."

"You do?"

"He is a primary focus of our operation. He is central to everything."

"What have you learned?"

"Nothing significant yet. After hours Pendergast spends time in the DHS gym, and then heads home to his wife and dogs. No children. Weeknights they tend not to eat in restaurants or go out for entertainment. We know they both spend a fair amount of time online when they're at home. Most Sundays they go to church, and his wife spends time during the week with other women from this church. He and his wife are both pilots. He's commercially rated, and sometimes they fly down to Vero Beach for the weekend in a Cessna Mustang he keeps at a small airport in Leesburg, near Dulles."

"Have you followed him in Florida?" Zeke asked.

"We have. They own a condominium in a gated community, Orchid Isle, and have an active social life there."

"That's where he did his fundraising for the Grove campaign. There's a lot of money along the coast there that's not picked up by the bundlers of Palm Beach."

"So far our surveillance has revealed nothing of interest in his personal schedule, either in Florida or the Washington area. The only thing we have found worth noting is that someone else, in addition to us, is following him. It has been going on for about two weeks."

"That would be me."

"We thought it was possible. This makes things more complicated. We could trip over each other. Do you agree there's no need to duplicate our efforts? If you will leave the surveillance to us we will share with you what we learn."

"That's fine with me," Zeke said. "I'll take care of it tomorrow." He was somewhat relieved. The surveillance of Pendergast had been costing over a thousand dollars a day, and so far Inagi had reported nothing different than what Moti just told him.

"Good. I will relay this to our field team."

"Are you following Justice Ross also?" Zeke asked.

"We did for a short while, but not anymore. Ross is followed by *paparazzi* and reporters almost all the time. They stake out her house; they follow her car. She assumes she's being watched, so we think we are unlikely to observe anything of value. Far more interesting has been our surveillance of her husband Walter."

"You have Walter Ross under surveillance?"

"For about a month now. As you know, he's a lobbyist and spends most of his 12-hour workdays on Capitol Hill and in meetings with clients. He is in great demand."

"Tell me something I don't know," Zeke said.

"We've become interested in a Friday night poker game that Walter Ross attends. It seems to rotate among the players' homes. So far we've learned the identity of four of the regular players in addition to Ross—who hasn't yet hosted the game at his house. There is one active duty Air Force captain, two are retired Air Force officers—one colonel and one brigadier-general. The fourth is Parker Lorenz, a private equity fund manager whose firm invests heavily in defense and aerospace companies. There are two we haven't been able to identify because they arrive together in an Air Force pool vehicle that comes from, and returns to, Andrews Air Force Base."

"Ah. That is something I definitely did not know," Zeke said.

"We're now working to try and connect the people we've identified in this game to the Action Committee's web forum. This is not easy to do, because everything that's posted there is auto-erased after ten seconds. Even the session data self-destructs, and new sessions are hosted at different, randomly generated domains."

"Not easy sounds like an understatement." It occurred to Zeke that Mossad was putting enormous resources into play. They were keeping tabs on Pendergast and Walter Ross, following a half-dozen poker players around the Beltway once a week, and hacking into dark websites. This was just the top of the list.

"It's possible it's just a poker game," Moti said, "but it could also be the physical connection that we've been looking for. I will let you know when we've learned more." Moti pulled his phone from his pocket, checked the time, then rested it on the table. "We still have a few minutes. May I change the subject and ask you a personal question?"

"Sure. What's on you mind?"

"This is not related to our business—I'm just curious. How did Rachel end up running for president? The last I heard you were being asked to run, and then I find out you're engaged to be married and your fiancée is running, not you. How did this happen? Was this your idea?"

"Hah! The question of the hour. No, it was not my idea," Zeke replied. "I'm not half that clever."

"Ahhh," Moti nodded, drawing his conclusion. "It was her idea—she offered to run?"

"No, actually," Zeke said, lowering his voice. "Allow me to share with you a confidence. This is something you can't tell anyone, the way I can't tell anyone about your second job. The original suggestion—that Rachel run for president—came from our mutual friend Chief Justice Salo-Baron. No one can know about this. I will deny having said it, to use your words. It's that kind of secret."

Moti beamed a wide smile. "My business is secrets; one more is not a burden." He glanced at his phone again. "I've got five minutes. If you have time I'll give you an introduction to bridge."

"I have the time," Zeke replied, "but how much can you learn about bridge in five minutes?"

"The mechanics of the game are simple," Moti said as he opened his tablet. He navigated to a bridge tutorial and brought it up on the monitor. "Each bridge deal is a competition between two pairs of players, one pair sitting in the North-South position at a square card table, the other pair sitting East-West. The object is to take the greatest number of tricks possible. A trick consists of one card contributed sequentially by each of the four players. The player who plays the highest card in the suit led wins the trick for his or her team, and then plays the first card of the next trick. In a standard 52-card deck this produces a total of thirteeen tricks."

He demonstrated the play of two tricks on the monitor, narrating the cards played and declaring the winner of each trick when it was complete.

"That's how bridge is played," Moti continued. "There's much more to it, of course, but the object is always to take the greatest number of tricks. There are techniques you can use to maximize how many tricks you take. These moves have sexy names like finesses, squeezes, and end-plays, so if you know how to finesse, and can recognize when a squeeze will work, you will take more tricks."

He demonstrated a finesse, using his tablet to play the cards on the monitor. "This is called a simple finesse, where you bypass an opponent's high card by playing a lower card from the dummy. There are also backward finesses, two-way finesses, ruffing finesses, and a half-dozen others."

"I've heard the term 'slam' used in bridge—which seems to fit into the same category. What is a slam?"

"There are small slams and grand slams. A small slam means

you take twelve of the available thirteen tricks. A grand slam is when you take all thirteen. I have to go now, but you can find out more about this online. What I just showed you is the core of any bridge game: you're trying to take as many tricks as possible." Moti closed his tablet and the deal on the monitor disappeared.

Zeke pushed his chair back, stood up and retrieved his overcoat from a nearby chair. "Thanks again for everything."

"Please contact me if anything develops that you think would be useful for us to know. I will call you if any of our information changes."

10

"We must make our choice. We may have democracy, or we may have wealth concentrated in the hands of a few, but we can't have both."

—LDB, Campaigning for Woodrow Wilson, 1912

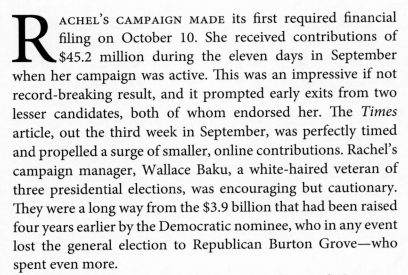

R ACHEL'S CAMPAIGN MADE its first required financial filing on October 10. She received contributions of $45.2 million during the eleven days in September when her campaign was active. This was an impressive if not record-breaking result, and it prompted early exits from two lesser candidates, both of whom endorsed her. The *Times* article, out the third week in September, was perfectly timed and propelled a surge of smaller, online contributions. Rachel's campaign manager, Wallace Baku, a white-haired veteran of three presidential elections, was encouraging but cautionary. They were a long way from the $3.9 billion that had been raised four years earlier by the Democratic nominee, who in any event lost the general election to Republican Burton Grove—who spent even more.

Senator Dalton Daniels of North Carolina and Governor Harold McShan of Illinois remained in the race. They were seasoned veterans who had waited patiently in the wings for their turn, and were now out campaigning at full-tilt–– incredulous at being upstaged by a half-Chinese lawyer and feminist talk show host. Rachel emerged as a front-runner in several blue states—New York, Massachusetts, California— but it was far too early to assume she would garner enough delegates overall. She spent the majority of her time in Colorado, Florida, Michigan, Ohio and Pennsylvania where she attracted enthusiastic crowds, but her progress in the polls in these states was limited. In rural and middle America, the land between the coasts, Rachel was a tough act to sell.

For the most part Zeke and Rachel maintained separate professional lives. Governor Arnault had asked Zeke to serve out his full term in the Senate, so he continued to spend most of his time in D.C. and West Virginia, while Rachel bounded about the country on her campaign plane. On those few occasions when they did appear in public together—once in Philadelphia and a few times in the Washington, D.C. area— Zeke found to his surprise that he didn't mind the campaigning so much. Because he wasn't the candidate he could observe, and from that detached perspective he found it fascinating. He might be unhappy as a senator, but as a future first husband he was perfectly at ease.

In late October Zeke traveled with Rachel's campaign once, to California, at her special request. She wanted to properly introduce him to her father, a retired professor of Asian languages at UC Berkeley who now lived in an apartment near the campus. Properly, she explained, meant Zeke asking her father's permission to marry his daughter. Zeke had always been respectful of Rachel's Chinese heritage and had no problem imagining such a conversation.

Berkeley was also Rachel's hometown. She had spent most of her adolescent years in public schools in the company of hundreds of Asian-American peers, many of them—like her—the children of university academics. Zeke planned to accompany them to her father's *emeritus* office at the university, and then to lunch with several of her high school and college friends. In the afternoon she was scheduled to deliver a major policy address at the university on the subject of higher education and student loans, and Zeke had arranged to speak at Boalt Hall, the law school at Berkeley.

The preceding evening they were sitting in the kitchenette of a hotel suite off Interstate 580 in Oakland, she with her vitamins, he with his tea and toast. Zeke pointed out on his tablet the headline of an article written by an influential Bay Area blogger about Rachel's campaign stop in Berkeley: *Tiger Mom for President.*

It was only a matter of time. They weren't even married yet, much less parents, but the *Tiger Mom* label was too compelling for some editor to resist. An entire story crafted to fit a headline: *what kind of mother would Rachel be if she won the presidency and had children?*

"Do you think of me as a Tiger Mom?" Rachel asked Zeke as she read the article.

It was getting late. Zeke had finished his tea and was fading fast. "No," he replied, "I just think of you as a tiger. Grrrr." He stood up, kissed her on the cheek, retrieved her empty glass, and moved all the dishware into the sink.

"Please be serious," she pleaded. "This is a real image liability." She followed Zeke to the sink and wrapped her arms around his waist from behind.

He turned around to face her, completed the embrace, and then whispered into her ear, "I am being serious. I think you're letting this headline writer get inside your head."

*   *   *

Rachel met with her senior campaign staff—Wallace and three other advisers—twice a day, once early in the morning, and then again late at night, sometimes after midnight. She called this her campaign cabinet, and the meetings were chaired by Wallace, who invited Zeke to join on the rare occasions he traveled with them.

According to Rachel, her cabinet was responsible for her front-runner status; she couldn't praise her campaign staff enough. Zeke saw it differently. When it came to management style in general and running her presidential campaign in particular, Rachel was, in fact, the quintessential Tiger Mom. The cabinet did serve a valuable sounding board function, but it was under her total control. All of the impressive gains she had made, in endorsements, in fundraising, in the subtle steering of her candidacy away from gender dynamics and into mainstream issues like defense spending and tax policy, Zeke attributed to Rachel's own political acumen and personnel skills.

He was therefore not surprised when the following evening the cabinet, meeting in a windowless ground-floor banquet room in the same Oakland hotel, agreed to take several steps to address the Tiger Mom issue. To wit, Rachel would tamp down her "always in charge" persona, and the media handlers would channel more images of her listening to people, asking questions, and seeking counsel from advisers—especially men. Rachel decided to skip appearances at the Asian-American Bar and other venues where she might be surrounded by Tiger Moms.

When Wallace made a comparison to what he termed the Maggie Thatcher factor, Zeke took that as a cue that the discussion was going to continue for a while. He closed his tablet, collected his water bottle and briefcase and glanced around the room to bid his good nights. He blew a kiss to Rachel.

"Before you go," she called out, and apologized to Wallace for interrupting. "We need to ask you one thing. We need your expert opinion on another matter."

"What's that?" Zeke asked.

"When I met with my Dad today he gave me the identification documents he has for my mother. He doesn't have her original birth certificate, and apparently the county's original vital records for her were destroyed in 1989 in a flood. Could this pose a problem for us? In terms of my citizenship?"

Zeke was already half tuned out. He shook his head to reboot. "What are you saying? There's no birth certificate for your mother? What do you have?"

"It looks like the earliest record he's been able to come up with is a substitute death certificate." Rachel never knew her mother; she had died in a hospital in Guam, a day after giving birth to Rachel on a Cathay Pacific flight from Hong Kong to Los Angeles.

"Geez." Zeke put down his briefcase and tucked his tablet in a side-pocket. "The quick answer is, yes, this could pose a problem—for you, for us. A big problem."

"If she traveled to Asia, she must have had a U.S. passport, right?" Wallace asked. "There's no record of her passport?"

"Not so far," Rachel answered.

"If you can come up with a passport, or a record of a passport having been issued, that should do the trick," Wallace said. "You can't get a passport without a birth certificate."

"Even if you found she had been issued a passport," Zeke intervened, "believe me, if someone wanted to make an issue out of this, they could." He turned to Rachel. "Was your father a U.S. citizen when you were born?" Zeke asked.

"He had a green card," Rachel answered, "but no, he wasn't a citizen when I was born. He was naturalized about five years later."

"Well then, your citizenship is tied to your mother, and if we can't prove your mother was born in the U.S., the fact that you were born on an airplane is going to come into focus in a much bigger way than it should."

"My birth certificate says that I was born in Guam."

"That's great, except it's common knowledge that you were born on an airplane over the Pacific Ocean. It's in your Wikipedia entry. More to the point, what's been done to try and obtain your mother's birth certificate?"

"Dad's tried to get a replacement, but he's not gotten very far. He was unable to make it clear to the vital records people why they need to do the research and come up with an identity for this woman who's been dead for almost forty years."

"Rachel," Wallace offered, as always the voice of calm and reason, "we all know that your mother was a U.S. citizen, and eventually we'll get some type of documentation to that effect. This is something we'll be able to work through."

Zeke was cautious. "For the record," he said, "this is a big liability. If we can't come up with solid documentation that your mother was born in the U.S., anyone who doesn't want you running for president will be able to use this to challenge your candidacy. This is headed straight to the courts."

*   *   *

Associate Justice Carla Constance Ross turned on the computer in her husband's home office and caught a reflected glimpse of herself in the chrome base of the monitor as she sat down. She had to go on a diet again; she knew that, and she would.

A twirling beach ball icon appeared on the screen.

In her first year of law school, late at night after a long group study session, a fellow student had posited that every human being could be classified with one of three head types: you were either a muffin-head, a bird-head or a horse-head. In the ensuing analytical melee, Ross was universally deemed to be a muffin head. Several of her peers with round features also earned that classification, but she had a naturally prominent jowl that over the years had morphed into a series of striated chins. The weight problem frustrated her to no end: she would go on a diet, lose twenty pounds and then gain it back in a fraction of the time it took to take it off. She did the best she could to compensate by dressing carefully and being attentive to her hair and make-up, but she also knew she could lose fifty pounds and still never gain people's respect or attention by virtue of her looks. This was not her arena and she chose not to compete in it.

She shifted her focus to her strengths, which were perfectly suited to a career in the judiciary. First and foremost was a legal intellect of encyclopedic dimension, aided by an uncanny ability to remember the details of virtually every case she ever read. On more than one occasion in her Anchorage courtroom, upon hearing only introductory statements from plaintiffs' and defendants' counsel, she would search her massive mental library and spontaneously retrieve a citation bearing directly on the matter at hand that both sides had either missed or disregarded. Lawyers in the district of Alaska quickly learned not to appear in her court unless thoroughly prepared.

Ross also saw herself as a consummate politician—an oxymoron for a federal judge, but she viewed it as an essential skill for anyone seeking advancement in a hierarchical organization. She had a special talent—as she saw it—for interpreting people's personalities and motivations, and she used that knowledge to manage her relationships. The tools she employed included well-timed flattery, razor-sharp humor, and unabashed name-dropping from an impressive contact list. She knew precisely the series of conversations she had engineered—with a lieutenant governor, a law school dean, and a U.S. Court of Appeals judge—that led to her initial promotion to the 9th Circuit Court of Appeals in San Francisco. After that, a whole new network needed to be built to put her on track to a Supreme Court nomination, but she knew where to start and what to do. After several years the pieces were in place and she was lucky enough to get two shots at a nomination: the court was hit, in quick succession, by one justice's retirement and another's sudden death. When the time came, she knew exactly what to say to the president, and then to the men's club that was the Senate Judiciary Committee. She spent countless hours preparing for these encounters—reading the dossiers of the people involved, writing out proposed answers to anticipated controversial questions, and in the end engaging in role-play rehearsals. When it was all over, looking back, she saw her success as largely of her own making.

The beach ball disappeared and the desktop began to populate with various icons and folders. An invisible processor clicked and whirred from beneath the desk.

More than anything else, Carla Constance Ross was determined to be her own person, to make her own mark, to *not* conform to common notions of whom she should be or whose act she should follow. She was not to be compared with others; others would be compared to her.

She was not the caretaker of any previous justice's legacy, least of all that of her immediate predecessor, Eleanor Sorko, whose defense of affirmative action she found so untenable. Nor was she beholden to the dogmas and sacred cows of the liberal law school establishment, of which she was once a member in good standing. Most of her ex-colleagues from the world of academia—some of whom testified at her confirmation hearings, presumably in the belief that she would continue to safeguard their sacred cows—had by now denounced her. Several signed public statements in support of HR 226, the House resolution calling for Ross's impeachment.

When she encountered them in person, some would froth with accusations of intellectual infidelity, while others would simply veer away and avoid contact.

These situations made her uncomfortable, but she didn't allow herself to be derailed by the criticism. It was so interesting, the transformation in thinking that takes place when one exits the laboratory and theoretical world that is the ivory tower, and enters the world of *realpolitik* and actual power. This shift in orientation allowed her—*forced* her—to see a much different picture, a much broader picture that could not be seen by her ex-colleagues. They were rational people, many of them reputed to be very intelligent, but if they weren't seeing the whole picture, how could they be expected to comprehend her actions?

From her perspective on the bench, it was clear to Justice Ross that the Supreme Court should not be using its jurisprudence to engineer sociological outcomes of any flavor, whether liberal or conservative. The court was ill-equipped as an institution to anticipate, monitor, measure, or undo the consequences of the social tinkering that it was constantly called upon to endorse or reject. For that reason she argued against granting *certiorari* to the overwhelming majority of such cases that were filed with the court seeking judicial review.

Ross saw the role of the court as an evolving one. In its first hundred years the court overturned only a handful of laws on constitutional grounds. Then came the era of social engineering, which see-sawed back and forth, first between *Lochner* and the New Deal, then between Earl Warren and Rehnquist/Roberts, like a pendulum moving in slow motion. Ross believed the court should embrace a completely new "re-balancing" framework in which its role would be defined by its status as one of the three governing institutions in the nation's tripartite system of checks and balances.

In her view the other two branches, the executive branch and Congress, had over the past century been leading the government and the country in a steady retreat from the Judeo-Christian values and states' rights principles that she saw as the core of the American democratic experiment. Madison and Monroe would be aghast if they knew their nation had acquiesced to a standing army that consumed over a third of the nation's wealth. What would Jefferson have to say about the effect of federal entitlement programs on personal responsibility and entrepreneurship? In Ross's view, the Federal Reserve Act of 1913 was proof positive that the executive and legislative branches had run off the rails. How was it possible, in any version of the democracy envisioned by the framers, that a quasi-governmental organization could have the authority to print dollars backed by the United States Treasury whenever it wished, in whatever quantity it desired, without direct accountability to the Treasury or any other branch of government? Even Alexander Hamilton, who backed the First Bank of the United States, would have opposed such an institution.

The court's first priority, both in terms of granting *cert* and adjudicating the law, should be to address legislation that erodes America's core values. Challenges should be mounted against anything that expands federal power at the expense of the states; anything that undermines individual initiative or personal accountability; anything that erodes the nation's moral compass. She referenced this re-balancing doctrine in her written opinions, and promoted it further in public speeches and in informal talks at law schools.

The computer finished booting itself, and the sniffer software was active and flashing green. No one was listening in on the local side of the connection. She clicked the VPN folder on the desktop, which automatically tunneled through to a proxy server in Mexico, and from there to a second server in the Cayman Islands, whence she connected to the World Wide Web. This was all made necessary by the hubbub that arose after the most recent leaked video, which she knew was a fake because she never had a working camera on her home computer. But when the video surfaced, Walter urged her to work only from his home computer until she could get a safer connection set up in her study.

Walter also set up an account for her at DeepSpaceEleven, the anonymous chat service, and gave her instructions and credentials for accessing the Action Committee's forum. She navigated to the site, logged in, and clicked the Flash Forum tab. Her avatar, *FelixTheDog*, displayed on the screen, and she confirmed her identity by entering a second password that DS11 had just texted to her. She glanced at the digital clock in the lower right corner of the screen—only a couple of minutes late.

Moments later Pendergast logged in and the session began; she watched as the conversation scrolled down the screen.

BillyBoyVero: Good evening. Thank you for your time.

FelixTheDog: Will help if I can. You know my ground rules.

BillyBoyVero: Of course. You may have heard Chen's campaign has a citizenship issue it's dealing with.

FelixTheDog: I've read about it.

BillyBoyVero: It's become a serious problem. There's lots of chatter about it in their campaign. They're going to make a preemptive public announcement within the next 48 hours to present what they have.

FelixTheDog: I wouldn't invest too heavily in this. When documentation shows up the issue will vanish. But what do you need from me?

BillyBoyVero: We're funding a pro-life organization that is preparing a lawsuit contesting her qualification to run. Can you recommend a friendly venue? We're starting at the district level."

FelixTheDog: I'll give it some thought. If I can help I will relay via *WishingWellOne*. In the meantime I have a query for you. I'm looking for something of interest about Judge Hurtig that I could use to defend myself. Do you have resources for this kind of research?

BillyBoyVero: You're worried about impeachment? With the Republicans in control of the House? It won't happen.

FelixTheDog: A simple majority in the House is possible. In the Senate I have better odds.

BillyBoyVero: I can't imagine it getting to the Senate.

FelixTheDog: You underestimate Judge Hurtig and her allies. That's why I'm looking into opposition research.

BillyBoyVero: I will advise *WishingWellOne* if I come up with something."

*   *   *

It took less than a month for an anti-abortion group called LifeGuardians Inc. to file a lawsuit in the Georgia Middle District of the conservative 11th Circuit, challenging Rachel's citizenship and her qualification to run for president in the

Georgia Democratic primary. In short order, the district court and then the 11th Circuit Court of Appeals in Atlanta concluded that her mother's citizenship could not be definitively established, and Rachel's claim of U.S. citizenship at birth was therefore invalid. They cited in their opinions the absence of original records: no passports, voter registration cards or government records of the era were found that would corroborate her mother's citizenship. Neither court acknowledged or addressed the evidence submitted by Rachel's campaign, including a certified substitute birth record for Rachel's mother provided by Alameda County, the depositions of several of her mother's living peers, and the testimony of senior passport office officials regarding lost records.

Chief Justice Salo-Baron learned of the appeals court decision through back channels before it was made public. He called Zeke and invited him over to the Supreme Court at his convenience, which in their private code meant as soon as possible. When he arrived the chief justice suggested they go for a walk, so Zeke kept his coat on and waited for the chief justice's security team to gear up. A few minutes later they were strolling along a gravel path amid the leafless dogwoods and cherry trees of the Capitol grounds, an area already off-limits to the public. Even so, Zeke counted no fewer than five agents accompanying them.

The chief justice told him about the pending decision from the 11th Circuit.

"Professor," Zeke responded, "it's wonderful that you're keeping us in the loop like this. The campaign needs every edge it can get. But as you know, I've no reason to be shocked. We've all been following the case."

"Of course, but there is an aspect to it that we haven't really talked about," the chief justice said. He stopped walking and suggested they take a seat on a bench.

Zeke focused and realized the chief justice was looking very grave. "Sir, please take a seat. Are you feeling okay?"

"I'm feeling fine, but you might want to sit down. I'm going to recuse from *LifeGuardians*."

Zeke thrust his neck back and squinted a quizzical stare. "You're not serious. How could you even consider it?"

The chief justice's face was lined with despair, like someone who had just learned of a good friend's death. "I'm sorry to disappoint, but surely you understand?" He gestured toward the bench, but Zeke declined and kept walking.

"Professor, you know there's no merit to this case," Zeke replied. He felt his composure draining away. "This is a move by an activist court to insert itself into electoral politics. It's a gross corruption of the separation of powers. How can you stand by and let this lawsuit play out when you have the ability to stop it?"

"This is all terrible and true, but it has no bearing on my obligation. I am not going to participate in a case where a named party is the fiancée of my close professional colleague."

"Professor, might I recall the half-dozen times Justice Ross should have recused herself from cases and didn't? The *Zuckerberger* fiasco was all the result of her conflict of interest in the case. You were furious, if you remember, that she did not recuse."

The chief justice nodded his agreement. "*Ja, und was lehrt uns das*?" He gestured with open palms.

This trademark response from the professor jolted Zeke back to reality. Suddenly he understood how trapped his friend felt. "Professor, I apologize, I am so sorry. I know you're in a difficult position. You know of course if you recuse, it's going to be a partisan vote, a four-four tie, and the court of appeals ruling will stand. It will be the end of Rachel's campaign."

"Perhaps," he said. "However there is one thing I can do.

I still control the court's docket, and I might be able to delay *LifeGuardians* long enough to bring HR 226 to a vote in the House of Representatives."

"Ahhh!" Zeke nodded slowly. "Now I understand. If we can impeach Justice Ross before Rachel's citizenship case is decided, that will leave a 4-3 majority to overturn." The chief justice was not so much abandoning his political child as he was trying to find another way to save her.

"Not only impeach," the professor added, "but also convict. What are the prospects for this happening? From what I've read, Judge Hurtig has made a lot of headway with her effort."

"She has," Zeke replied. "And recently she's told me she's optimistic about getting a majority in the House. It's the two-thirds majority in the Senate, for conviction, that will be the hardest—we'll need votes from at least ten Republican senators."

"Is that possible?"

"To be honest, I don't see how. We may be able to pressure or cajole a few, but think about it. Berrigan from Montana? Korn and Auster from Utah? In the absence of some smoking gun crime, these senators are never going to betray a conservative icon like Ross."

They made a slow turn around a monument and headed back towards the court. The setting sun cast their shadows on the pathways in front of them.

"So what is the timing here?" Zeke asked. "What is the deadline for achieving this unlikely goal?"

"Let's calculate," the professor replied. "It's two weeks until the winter recess, so we can get past the first of the year for sure. That's a month right there. But we'd have to take it up within two weeks after that, so let's say mid-January. Ordinarily, as a defendant in this kind of situation you'd be arguing for expedition, because you'd want your status clarified as soon as possible. But in your situation, you understand, strategically, you're not going to want to press the court for a decision. The less you push, the longer I'll be able to delay."

"Six weeks . . ." Zeke became distracted, ticking off the names of Republican senators in the back of this mind. The agents stopped traffic on First Street for them to cross.

The chief justice continued. "I can only imagine what Rachel's reaction will be. If she wants to hear it from me directly please give her my private number."

"That's very kind, but not necessary. She has tremendous respect for you, and she's a lawyer—she knows how things work."

"I'm hoping we can solve the *LifeGuardians* problem the other way—by removing Ross. As you know this would have many ancillary benefits."

"Of course. I understand. Thanks for taking the conversation outside. Safer all the way around. Give my regards to Fran."

"And mine to Rachel." The chief justice doffed his beret in salute, and two agents moved in to escort him up the 44 front steps of the Supreme Court.

11

"The greatest dangers to liberty lurk in insidious encroachment by men of zeal, well meaning but without understanding."

—LDB, dissent in *Olmstead v. United States*, 1928

WHEN ZEKE TOLD Judge Hurtig about the new impeachment timeline set by the chief justice, she became even more energized. In her mind this meant the chief justice was now on-board with her mission— not publicly, of course, but in spirit. Now he wanted Ross out by January 15th.

In fact Hurtig had good reason to be confident about the first hurdle—a simple majority in the House. Even if the votes weren't countable yet, she saw this goal as eminently achievable, and credited the No Vote Pledge campaigns they had been running in various Republican districts with tilting momentum in their favor. Every week on *Women in Charge* she reviewed the NVP totals in each of the twenty targeted districts, and in most cases the results were encouraging and trending upward. Zeke traveled to some of the targeted districts, lecturing at area law schools and organizing students to canvas their communities in support of American Majority Party initiatives, including the impeachment of Justice Ross.

At some schools as many as fifty students responded to his appeals to go door-to-door with wireless tablets, a tactic that proved to be very effective. Early in December the first Republican congressman announced he would support HR 226 after his district registered a clear NVP majority in favor of the impeachment resolution. By the end of the year, at least half a dozen Republican representatives faced a No Vote Pledge majority in their districts: they could either vote for impeachment, or expect to lose their next election.

When the first cracks appeared, support for Justice Ross eroded quickly in mainstream conservative circles. More than one commentator pointed out that if she was impeached and removed, the seat would be filled by a nominee of the sitting Republican president, and therefore letting her go would not have the same consequences as if a Democrat were in the White House. It was also noted that she wasn't helping her own cause by making defensive comments to the press and continuing to accept high-profile speaking engagements. "She's animating her enemies' arguments," one pundit wrote.

On Monday, January 11, a week after returning from its winter break, the House of Representatives voted to impeach by a vote of 228 to 206, with 17 Republicans breaking ranks to join 211 Democrats. As rare an event as this was,* there was little celebration in the pro-impeachment camp. Attention turned to the Senate, where a trial required a two-thirds majority to convict—a seemingly impossible goal.

After three days of evidence, testimony and speechmaking, the Senate adjourned for the weekend, with closing statements

---

* In 1805 the Jefferson administration engineered the impeachment of Supreme Court Justice Samuel Chase, but he wasn't convicted by the Senate and returned to serve on the bench for eight more years.

and the final vote scheduled for Tuesday. Hurtig made great progress—far more than anyone ever thought possible—but they were still two votes short of the 67 needed to convict. She huddled with Zeke, who knew virtually every senator personally, and they concluded the two best long-shot possibilities were Max Emden of Wisconsin and Oscar Devereaux of Louisiana. They split the task: Hurtig was a native of Wisconsin and 40 years earlier had been a law professor in Madison, so she took Senator Emden; Zeke got Devereaux.

Armin learned through his senate staff connections that both senators were going to be at the Washington Algonquins football game on the Sunday before the vote, where Rachel was already planning a campaign appearance. With the Algonquins in the Eastern Conference playoffs and the Super Bowl three weeks away, it was a prime ticket for aspiring candidates and incumbents facing re-election. When Zeke phoned Rachel and explained that he planned to join her on Sunday, she was delighted. "I didn't think you liked football," she said.

"I don't," he said. "I'll be working," and he revealed his and Judge Hurtig's mission. "Any advice for me about Devereaux? Or for us in general?"

"Yes," she said, "don't be seen. Arrange to meet with them in a private suite—they have boxes on the upper level. Ask Gerry, she'll know how to set it up. I think your big donor Evan Wentworth keeps a corporate suite at FedEx Field."

*   *   *

BillyBoyVero: It was disturbing to see your prediction come true.

FelixTheDog: Worse is that my prediction about the Senate may be off. There have been some defections I would never have thought possible.

BillyBoyVero: The Committee is aware and wanted to offer its assistance. We just learned that two of your defectors may be present during operation *Aim High* on Sunday. We can arrange targeting to include them if you wish.

FelixTheDog: Negative. If I benefit too much from the attack it could raise questions about my connection to it.

BillyBoyVero: Understood.

FelixTheDog: I told *WishingWellOne* of my concerns about Sunday.

BillyBoyVero: The risks may not be as great as they appear. The blast radius for each drone is three meters.

FelixTheDog: This kind of jargon doesn't inform me, it rattles me. I'm not Air Force.

BillyBoyVero: My apologies. In plain English, the drones have been modified so that we can hit precise targets without causing a lot of collateral damage.

FelixTheDog: I don't want to know any more. If you succeed with your primary targets, that will be good enough for me.

*   *   *

Zeke left his meeting with Devereaux on Sunday afternoon feeling he had done all he could. His message had been focused and succinct: Ross was not fit for the job and was doing serious harm to the Supreme Court as an institution. "Her public profile is completely inappropriate for a justice of the Supreme Court," he argued. "We in the Senate were responsible for confirming her; we should do our job and undo a bad appointment. We were wrong, we should fix it." Devereaux promised he would take Zeke's argument to his senior staff and let him know the outcome of their discussion.

Zeke exited the skybox with phone in hand, intending to call Judge Hurtig, when he was intercepted by his Secret Service handler for the day, a so far humorless ex-Marine who asked to be called by his last name, Mullen. "Sir," he said, "you have a visitor." He handed Zeke a business card.

Zeke put away his phone and took out his reading glasses. It was Moti's law school business card. On the back he had written two words in Hebrew—*ay'shet cha'yil*—an agreed-upon emergency signal. Something was wrong. Someone—Rachel, Judge Hurtig, the chief justice—was in danger.

"He's here now?" Zeke asked.

"Not right here. He saw you arrive in the Dream Seats with Carolina Leader and gave his card to an agent at the perimeter." Carolina Leader was the current Secret Service code name for Rachel. "He said he's your cousin and just wants to say hello. I can radio the field agents and have him brought up here if you want."

"No, that's okay," Zeke said. "Let's head down and I'll connect with him there." If Moti said he was going to meet him somewhere, it was probably all part of a *plan*.

Mullen escorted him out to the public ramps where they were joined by two additional agents. Zeke buttoned up his coat, pulled up his collar and put his gloves on. It was 28 degrees and everyone's breath was marked with wisps of vapor. They descended three levels and he spotted Moti waiting at the top of the long concrete staircase leading down to the field-level Dream Seats. "That's my cousin," Zeke said to Mullen. "I'd like to invite him to join us. Is that okay?"

"Sir, that's fine. Just let him know he'll need to be screened to get into the secure area."

Moti approached with his traditional bear hug and beaming smile. "*Mazal Tov!* Congratulations on your engagement! I've always liked Rachel. You'll be a great couple and I hope great parents."

Zeke processed as fast as he could. Nothing too urgent so far; this was a conversation they'd already had. "I'm headed down to the field to see Rachel now. Would you like to join us?" he offered, gesturing for his cousin to follow. "You'd have to go through security, but we could arrange it."

"No, I don't want to make trouble for anyone. I have good seats in the 200 section. But if it's okay I'll walk with you down to the gate. I have something I want to give you."

Zeke nodded at Mullen, who was within earshot of the conversation, and they proceeded down the aisle: Mullen in front, Zeke and Moti in the middle, and two agents trailing. The aisles were packed and they moved slowly, pausing to let people in and out of rows.

Moti looped his arm over his cousin's shoulder and held onto him as they picked their way down the steps. "Cousin, if I speak in Hebrew," he asked in Hebrew, "will you understand?"

Zeke was flustered, but recovered quickly. At one time, when he and Moti first met, he had been conversationally fluent; now he was very rusty. "I can understand more than to speak," he replied in his own halting, heavily accented Hebrew. "But it's okay, I will try. Speak slowly."

"Good," Moti continued in Hebrew, in a slightly lower voice. "We are being watched, and there could be lip reading. Hebrew might throw them off."

"What's the situation?" Zeke asked.

"Moti withdrew his arm from Zeke as they moved down the aisle, reached inside his coat and pulled out a book. "I read this recently, and thought you would find it interesting," he said, handing Zeke yet another copy of *The Wanting of Levine*.

"How could you know about this?" Zeke was borderline alarmed. This was far too coincidental to be a coincidence. Did his cousin have a spy, or a bug, in his office? Could Mossad be following his *mother*?

"Please try to look more surprised than shocked," Moti said, still smiling broadly. "Don't react to my next comment. You and Rachel and everyone you're with are in immediate danger. You must take this book back with you to your seat now, and you must take it with you when you leave. Your lives depend on doing that. Stop by for a bridge lesson and I'll explain everything."

Zeke forced a smile as he examined the book, opening it and looking at the spine. It appeared to be the same soft cover edition that had been sent to him by his Wheeling constituent. They were approaching the end of the aisle, where the Secret Service had set up a checkpoint.

"Did you understand everything I said?" Moti asked.

"Yes," Zeke said. "The dangerous situation," he struggled with his limited vocabulary, "can you tell me more details?"

Moti suddenly switched back to English. "This is a fiction book about a Jewish presidential candidate. It reminded me so much of your situation I wanted to share it with you."

"Well at this point," Zeke responded, also in English, "considering how you're the third person who's mentioned it, I guess I better read it."

Moti leaned in to give him a parting hug and whispered in his ear: "drone attack ETA twelve minutes. If the Secret Service hasn't pulled you out in five, leave the field with Rachel on your own. Get sick, use an excuse, whatever you need to do. Five minutes. *Hay'van-ta?*" He gave Zeke a final slap on the back, and stepped away.

Zeke nodded, looking stunned.

"Don't look so sad!" Moti called out. "He grasped his cousin by the shoulders. "Marriage isn't a death sentence; I would love to meet a woman like Rachel." He turned to join the line of spectators trekking back up the steps. "If you get a chance to read the book," he called out, "let me know what you think." He nodded to Mullen and the other agents who had accompanied them, and melted into the upstream crowd.

Zeke continued through the security checkpoint. His heart rate, already elevated, shot up when an agent asked to examine the book. He handed it over as casually as he could. The agent fanned the pages briefly and gave it back, but by then the adrenalin had done its work and Zeke barely maintained his composure. His thoughts raced as Mullen escorted him toward midfield where Rachel and her campaign entourage were seated. What time was it? The scoreboard clock read eight minutes, 34 seconds left in the second quarter. The drone attack was timed to hit during half-time, when all the politicians would be out in the open stands hoping to be picked up by network cameras panning for public figures. That was the whole point of coming to these events: free advertising in a key demographic. That was certainly why Rachel was here.

The decibel level ratcheted up even further as they approached the field and he could barely hear himself think. What should he do? He couldn't reveal his source to anyone. He could do what his cousin suggested, which was to get sick. Why wait five minutes? That's something he could do right now. A heart attack! He could pretend he was having a heart attack . . . he certainly had the pulse for it. Or, maybe he was really having a heart attack, and he wouldn't need to fake anything. Wouldn't that be convenient.

He tried focusing on his breathing, counting each inhale

and exhale. A sudden roar from the crowd distracted him, and another question popped open in his mind: how was this book going to stop a drone attack? As they walked he unbuttoned his overcoat and stashed the book inside the sleeveless down parka he always wore to outdoor winter events.

Mullen began talking into his collar microphone and the solid line of Secret Service agents protecting their seats cleaved open to admit them. Rachel jumped up and planted a kiss on his cheek. A roar went up from the surrounding stands and moments later the tender moment was replayed to the entire stadium on the scoreboard video-stream. This produced an even wilder, feminine-sounding shriek. Zeke rolled his eyes, and returned the kiss. At field level the background noise was deafening, and for a few moments he forgot completely about the threat. Then he realized that Judge Hurtig was standing next to Rachel; she must have finished her meeting with Emden. He leaned in, shook her hand, and she shouted a query about the meeting with Devereaux.

"It was good," Zeke called back to her, giving a thumbs-up. "I think it's possible. Will talk later, too loud here," and he put his hands over his ears.

He suddenly remembered everything, and looked at the scoreboard clock: 06:42. Almost three minutes had passed.

Rachel, who had flown more than 50,000 miles in the last thirty days, reached into her coat pocket, retrieved a pair of airline earplugs in a small cardboard packet, and offered them to Zeke. He took them from her and smiled appreciatively as he worked them into his ears.

"I'm actually not feeling very well," he shouted to her. "My heart's racing. I don't know if it's the crowds or what."

Rachel's public smile faded instantly. "You should sit down," she said, "let's sit down. We don't have to be standing the whole time. Do you want some water?"

"Good idea," Zeke gave a thumbs-up as he dropped into his seat. He looked at his wristwatch.

Rachel signaled to someone and a bottle of water was passed down. She also sat down, opened the bottle and handed it to him. Suddenly, right in front of them, one of the sideline photographers bellowed out, "Holy shit, what is that?" He was pointing at something in the sky that neither Zeke nor Rachel could see at first, but then players and coaches and soon spectators were shouting and pointing. A circular drone the size of a bicycle wheel was hovering mid-field about 50 feet in air, powered by four propellers. Almost instantly it lost half its altitude and approached the sideline seats where Rachel's entourage was seated. It then tilted downward as if looking directly at Zeke and began spitting out flashes of strobe light.

Zeke and Rachel were too startled to register fear or react, but the Secret Service treated it as an attack. Within moments several agents drew their weapons and started firing at the drone. The bullets bounced off a plastic undershield and the drone wobbled briefly, but then zipped away. It returned to where it had been high over the fifty yard line, hovered for several moments, and exploded. Debris rained down on the playing field.

Before Rachel and Zeke knew what was happening their whole party was hustled onto the field in the middle of a phalanx of Secret Service agents. They made a hairpin turn into one of the player tunnels, and in less than a minute arrived at the stadium's underground service garage, where a platoon of flak-jacketed agents guarded them with automatic weapons while they waited for their motorcade to arrive.

An electronic tenor voice, laced with static, drizzled down from hidden speakers. "Ladies and gentlemen, for security reasons the game has been suspended. Everyone is asked to leave the facility calmly and quickly. Please leave coolers, chairs and other bulky items behind for now. Take with you only personal items and valuables that you can easily carry. Please remain calm and make your way to the exits. All ramps, all gates are open."

"How are you feeling?" Rachel asked Zeke.

"Better, actually. My heart rate has gone down, even with all the excitement. I feel safer down here than I did out on the field."

There was a squealing of tires as a trio of black sedans barreled down the last ramp and screeched to a stop in front of them. Doors flew open and Mullen guided Zeke into the back of the second car. He left the door ajar for Rachel, who had stopped to huddle briefly with an aide. Then a sudden booming explosion, somewhere high above them, produced a shivering effect in the concrete walls and floor, followed by a rapid popping sound, like distant fireworks.

Mullen pushed Rachel into the car. "Buckle up!" he shouted as he slammed the door and then pounded on the roof. "Go, go, go!" As the car sped up the spiral exit ramp, two additional explosions, much bigger and louder, rattled the entire stadium, and the roadway began shifting beneath them. Shards of concrete and metal bounced off the bulletproof windshield. The car, moving considerably slower, finally made it to the top and shot out of the garage onto FedEx Way. Zeke and Rachel, belted into their corners, held hands and looked at each other with wide eyes.

"At least we're together this time," Zeke said.

*   *   *

President Burton Grove, who had been watching the game on television along with 37 million other Americans, witnessed in real time the damage and havoc caused by the three drones. No phone call was needed: he headed immediately from the second floor residence to the situation room in the White House basement. On all channels there was an endless stream of gruesome images: strewn body parts; screaming children covered in blood; slow-motion replays of the impacts, explosions and ensuing panic. Soon it was reported that at least one of the bombs had dispersed low-level radioactive waste. Within an hour three Air Force helicopters landed in Fedex Field and delivered a swarm of space-suited first responders—EMT's, firefighters, radiation specialists, forensic investigators—to take over rescue and recovery operations. More helicopters hovered over the site and high overhead fighter jets crisscrossed the sky.

At seven o'clock, five hours after the attack, the president addressed the nation from the Oval Office, confirming that at least 300 people had died and a similar number hospitalized with injuries. It was the third most deadly attack on American civilians in the nation's history. He mourned the loss of Representative Wyatt Runninghorse of Arizona and Undersecretary of Defense Elizabeth Ellison, as well as dozens of other federal employees and armed forces personnel who had been in attendance at the game. To the families and loved ones of all those affected he offered the nation's condolences, and promised that those responsible for this crime against humanity would see swift retribution.

Drones and other technology-based weapons, he cautioned, might ultimately force Americans to sacrifice some of their most cherished liberties. In the meantime, he was ordering the cancellation of all large outdoor public events for at least two weeks, or until better security measures could be devised. He concluded by calling on Congress to immediately take up legislation to regulate the manufacture and sale of drones and drone components, and to require outdoor arenas seating more than 5,000 people to install netting or other anti-drone defenses.

12

"At the foundation of our civil liberty lies the principle which denies to government officials an exceptional position before the law and which subjects them to the same rules of conduct that are commands to the citizen."

—LDB, dissent in *Burdeau v. McDowell,* 1921

MONDAY MORNING JUSTICE Ross sent an e-mail to her eight judicial colleagues, informing them that she wouldn't be joining them for their usual communal lunch in the justices' dining room. When her chief clerk, who had been copied on the message, asked if everything was okay, Ross thought for a few moments before responding. "Everything's fine. I'm on a crash diet, and I don't feel like sitting for an hour watching a bunch of other people eat." She also knew what would be on everyone's mind at lunch: would the United States Senate, the very next day, vote to remove her from the court? The attack at FedEx Field did nothing to delay the proceedings, Capitol Hill being six miles from the edge of the exclusion zone around the stadium.

At noon her driver pulled over to the curb near the Chinatown Metro station on 7th Street. Before exiting the car, Justice Ross donned a wide-brimmed hat and sunglasses, and tried dismissing the deputy marshal who'd been riding shotgun in the front. "I'm visiting the new Jefferson exhibit at the National Portrait Gallery, by myself. It's not on my schedule, and no one knows I'm here. If you must follow me, please do so at a distance; I'm trying to escape attention, not attract it. I'll be back here in 45 minutes."

She walked the half-block to the museum entrance on G Street and headed straight to the Atrium Café, where she purchased a roast beef sandwich, a diet Pepsi, and a slice of pound cake sealed in cellophane. The canned soda she slid into a coat pocket, the cake went into her purse. She opened the sandwich and began to consume it as she walked. At the edge of the fountain, before turning into the galleries, she passed Deputy Secretary Pendergast who was seated on a bench reading his tablet. Without breaking stride or making eye contact, she said in a low monotone as she walked past him, "third floor, twentieth century Americans."

Five minutes later they were standing next to each other, staring up at a Warhol print of Marilyn Monroe. The third-floor mezzanine was far removed from the popular Jefferson exhibit, and there were few other visitors. After a group of Japanese tourists passed behind them and turned the corner at the end of the balcony, Pendergast spoke up. He whispered sideways, in a hoarse baritone, as they both looked up at the iridescent pink and orange Marilyn.

"As I'm sure you understand," he said, "we can't meet like this on a regular basis."

Ross worked to modulate the anger that underlay her response. "I'm not concerned about that. You missed again."

"We didn't miss; they were moved off the field less than four minutes before impact."

"Because someone else's drone beat you to them. What was that about? Where did that come from?"

"We're working on it. We have leads."

"That's encouraging," Ross replied, rolling her eyes. "You assured us there was abort capability. Someone must have seen Hurtig and Chen leaving the field. Why didn't you abort?"

"It was the last-minute and only Captain DeMolay's transmitter was in range. For whatever reason he was not able to retake control in time. It could have been a software issue, or a disruption in the radio frequency from solar flares. Right now I can't say for sure."

Ross didn't respond.

"It's been less than 24 hours since the attack," Pendergast continued. We'll have answers to many of these questions very soon."

"What happened to the three meter blast radius?"

"That was accurate, but our modeling didn't include casualties from stampedes on the upper deck. The targets were all on the lower levels."

"That's your answer?" Ross worked to control herself. "You're telling me that not a single person in your group anticipated that a drone attack on a stadium might cause a panic?"

"Not that I know of."

Ross's jaw dropped. She glanced at him briefly in disbelief, then returned her gaze to the artwork.

"For a deputy secretary of Homeland Security," she said, her voice now down to a compressed hiss, "it is astonishing how little you know."

"We made an error, I admit," Pendergast continued, sounding contrite. "A serious error; we are not pleased about the casualty outcome. But we did reach two key targets, and the Air Force Nuclear Recovery Teams made a big impression on the fifty yard line. It was expensive, but important parts of our mission were achieved."

Pendergast moved several steps to his right and reassigned

his stare to another Warhol, *Italian Carbine 6.5*, a turquoise-saturated silkscreen of a magazine ad for the weapon that Oswald used to assassinate President Kennedy.

Justice Ross unzipped her handbag, fished out her sunglasses, put them on, and looked up at the new Warhol print. "It's interesting," she said. "Through polarized lenses the text of the ad really jumps out at you. He got it through the mail, the rifle and the scope, for $19.95 plus shipping. Your committee might take a lesson from Oswald. Talk about bang for your buck."

*   *   *

Monday evening Zeke arrived at Moti's bridge club fifteen minutes early, leaving time for the Secret Service to do their advance sweep. Despite his earlier plea for less formal procedures, the Secret Service resumed all protocols following the attack at the stadium.

After all the closets and bathrooms had been checked, the agents commandeered an elevator and delivered Zeke downstairs. One agent remained at the entrance; another shadowed him as he navigated into the busy kitchen. He filled a paper cup with peanuts, grabbed a bottle of juice and headed to the private room where he and Moti always met. As he passed through the larger playing room it was impossible to not notice all the furtive glances he attracted. That's what he disliked more than anything about the security routine—all the attention it attracted.

He made himself at home in the small room, clearing one of the card tables and setting up shop with his snack and phone. "My cousin will be joining me here," he said to his Secret Service shadow. "When he arrives, we'll be about a half-hour. Do you know how to play bridge?"

The agent looked at him with a blank expression. "No sir," he replied.

Zeke wondered, how do they recruit and train thousands of humorless people? Was there a test for this? They tell a joke, and if you laugh you're not hired? "Never mind," he said. "I'm just starting out with the game; it's hard to explain." The agent left the room, closing the door behind him.

Zeke hung his suit over the back of his chair and sat down. Another rare moment alone. He opened the bottle of juice and drank as he studied the overhead monitor. A bridge hand at some remote location was being played. He recognized the play of the queen of spades was a winning finesse, and followed along as the remaining tricks were played. He was beginning to see the attraction: each deal was a mathematical puzzle that you must try to solve on the fly, using a combination of logical inference and dynamic memory.

Moti arrived and Zeke leapt up, hugging his cousin in a long embrace. He then thanked Moti passionately for saving his and Rachel's lives—*again*.

"Your thanks are appreciated, but we are not celebrating," Moti responded. "We don't consider 309 casualties a great success." His expression was grim. He put a sandwich and cup of water on the table and sat down. "Before I gave you the book on Sunday we made three very credible threats, by phone and by e-mail, that should have shut down the event, but the officials in charge of this game were determined to keep it going. You Americans are obsessed with what you call football. To everyone else in the world football is soccer; your game looks like something from the Roman Colosseum."

"Why do you think they didn't close it down earlier?"

"Our information is that they were underinsured. Canceling the game would have cost them tens of millions of dollars in ticket refunds and advertiser rebates, and it would have disrupted the play-off schedule, costing even more. It appears someone made a bad decision, however, because the liability from lawsuits will be in the billions."

"I can't help myself... where would you get that kind of information? You have a source inside the Algonquins organization? Or the insurance industry?"

Moti shrugged his shoulders and began unwrapping his sandwich. "Do we have anything more important to talk about?" he asked, fixing his cousin with an earnest look.

"Okay," Zeke relented. "Tell me what happened on Sunday. If I understood your Hebrew, you said at our next bridge lesson you would explain everything. Enlighten me, please."

"Of course," Moti nodded, but first took a bite of his sandwich, chewed for a moment and swallowed heavily. "I'm sorry," he said. "I didn't have time for lunch, and I'm playing in the 7:30 game." He took a drink of water.

"Please, take a couple of minutes. We're not in that much of a rush." Zeke poured some peanuts onto a napkin and began eating them. From the corner of his eye he saw his cousin devouring his dinner, and the scene triggered a memory from their university days in Israel. He now remembered observing that Moti often ate meals with military precision. Once the knife and fork were raised, no words were spoken and no motion was wasted. It was simply a matter of how quickly and efficiently the meal could be conquered.

Inside of three minutes Moti was dusting his hands over the empty paper plate. He drained the water cup. "Now," he said, "I will tell you about Sunday. The same rules apply. I will deny that we ever spoke of these matters."

Zeke nodded.

"Okay, here it is *ahl reh-gel ah-khat*." Moti said, using the Hebrew expression *on one foot*. "The short version: at 08:30 hours on Friday we learned that FedEx field was the location of an Action Committee operation code-named *Aim High* that was planned for Sunday. Other than Rachel and Judge Hurtig they had three other targets, and reached two of them: Ellison and Runninghorse.

"We made anonymous threats to get them to cancel the game. When this didn't work, you were our last hope. You were Plan D. The book you carried back to your seat had a micro-transmitter that acted as a beacon for our pre-emptive drone strike. You may have read that when it detonated it scattered a thousand steel tacks over the playing field. That finally got them to call off the game."

"Ah, so that was your doing."

Moti nodded. "And your's. Where is the book I gave you? Where is it now?" he asked.

"Right here," Zeke said, "with my coat. I brought it with me."

"*Yofi!* Perfect. I will take it off your hands. Otherwise I would have asked you to destroy it."

"And why is that?"

"It contains electronics that investigators will be looking for. The drone we used was carrying a bulletproof shield, an explosive charge and ten pounds of nails, so to save weight we had to use a low-tech guidance system that relies on a beacon to find its destination. Investigators will be looking for such a homing device, and of course we don't want them to find it."

"An agent looked at the book before I went through the gate. He flipped through the pages and didn't say anything."

"That is good, but as part of the investigation they will recreate events. The three Secret Service agents who know I gave you a book might report this. So if anyone now asks you what has happened to this book, you need to be ready to answer this question."

"You have this all planned, no doubt."

"We do. If you are asked about the book by anyone, for any reason, we want you to say you threw it away. You have a reason for throwing it away."

"Yes, of course, I already have a copy. Now it's time for a question. How did you know about the book? Has Mossad bugged my office?"

"Mossad has not; the Action Committee has. But again they used surveillance equipment that we sold to them, so we can listen in. We don't listen in real time, but everything gets recorded. On very short notice we had to come up with something to give to you, something that you would then have a reason to throw away."

"Our offices were checked for bugs. They assured us everything was fine."

"We are working on this. We have been following the two technicians who did the sweep work in your office, and it appears they keep some interesting company."

"I'm not sure what that means. I have a long relationship with Deecop Inagi; I have to believe he's done proper work."

"We also are not sure what is happening. No doubt you trust your friend, but for technical work he relies on independent contractors. In this world things are not always what they seem. The government can easily manipulate these people. I will let you know if we make any progress with this. In the meantime, I want to return to the question of what to say if someone asks you about the book."

"I'm supposed to say I threw it away."

"Yes. How does trash get taken out of your apartment?"

"I have no idea. It's a hotel. Housekeeping comes in during the day and empties the trash cans."

"Is there a place for trash in your kitchen area?"

"Under the sink."

"That's where you put the book."

"Understood. It was just a coincidence that you gave me another copy."

"Bingo. Is this correct here, this expression?"

"Bingo is fine. You said we were being watched as we walked down the steps. Who would have been watching us in a crowd like that?" Zeke finished up his juice and peanuts.

"From the opposite side of the field, anyone in one of the upper level suites could zoom in on us with a video camera, record our encounter, and then replay it to read our lips. In the surveillance world this is common practice."

"My question is not how, it's *who*. Who would be watching us like this?"

"No one would be watching you; someone might be watching me."

"I see. Meaning someone might suspect you're more than a law professor?"

"That is why I tried so hard to make our meeting look like a family interaction. This protects you also."

"Of course," Zeke said. "Please understand, I am grateful for all you've done."

"I assume your fiancée and Judge Hurtig still know nothing about me?" Moti queried.

"No. Not a word."

"Good. Please keep it this way. This has become a very dangerous situation for me. Every time a new person learns about my second job, it increases my risk exponentially."

"I'm being very careful," Zeke assured him. "But shouldn't I do something about the bugs in my office? Should I hire your Israeli company to come in and find them?"

"You could," Moti said. "You could call CL Associates and

say you were referred by Rachel, who met them through her work. We are requesting, however, that you do nothing right away."

"Why is that?"

"Two reasons. First, if you look for bugs again in your office and now they are found, it could easily raise the question 'why did you check a second time?' The question implies you knew there was a reason to check again. How did you know? This is a question you don't want to be asked, and don't want to answer. Indirectly this question leads back to me, to this conversation."

Moti paused for Zeke to think about it.

"Second," Moti said, "if the bugs are uncovered immediately by a private company, the people who planted the bugs will know, and they will race to cover their tracks. This will make it more difficult to find them when the authorities are ready to act."

"Alright, what do you recommend?" Zeke asked. You always have a plan. What's the plan now?"

"We suggest you wait ten days and then ask the U.S. Capitol Police to do a counter-surveillance sweep of your Senate offices. They'll find the bugs, and if the investigation that follows is proper, it should lead back to the Action Committee and its online forum. This would be the best outcome; it would expose everything without involving us at all—you or Mossad."

"Sounds good to me, except why wait ten days?"

"The Action Committee has an asset in the Capitol Police, which is not a big organization. We are concerned about this asset learning in advance about your request and warning the Committee. He is due to leave for vacation eight days from today, so any time after that is good."

Zeke squinted at Moti. "How do you know this stuff? No, never mind. I can train myself not to ask."

"But you agree to wait ten days?"

"Yes, I will do nothing about the bugs for ten days. I'll just watch what I say."

"That's fine, but be careful not to alter your behavior so much that the people listening in will realize you're concerned about a bug. Try to carry on a normal routine."

"Normal routine?" Zeke pressed his palms to his temples. "The new normal for me is narrowly escaping death by drone."

"We must all continue to be on guard. They still have two Vultures left, and they have other means as well. But between our intelligence and your Secret Service protection, you should be safe."

"I don't know why I'm not comforted by that statement."

Moti's phone beeped. He stared at it for a few moments, tapped something, and then looked up, smiling at Zeke. "It's almost 7:20; I'm going to head out to the game soon. Want to spend a few minutes on bridge?"

"Sure, but I have just one more question. Why has the Action Committee bugged my office?"

Moti was astonished. He imitated Zeke's head-between-his-hands gesture. "How is it possible you don't see this? You talk on a regular basis with Rachel and the chief justice and Judge Hurtig—three people at the top of the Action Committee's hit list. You're about to marry one of them, and you're a confidential advisor to the other two. Why would they *not* bug your office?"

Zeke stood up and jump-shot the crumpled paper cup toward a trash can against the far wall, missing badly. He retrieved his drink bottle, picked up the wad of paper, and dropped them both into the can. "It's surreal. It's just hard to believe." He returned to the table and adjusted his seat so he could better see the monitor. "I'm ready for bridge. I've played online a few times since we last met—not real games, but the tutorials. I recognize now when to finesse—I know what to do. It was fun. I got the hang of it, I think."

"I'll show you something I've been reading about," Moti said as he opened his tablet and connected it to the overhead monitor. "Squeeze plays. This is a more advanced technique, but it's among the sexier moves you can make in bridge."

Moti concentrated on finding a bridge deal where the declarer had a long suit to run. He found the example he was looking for—a hand with seven spades to the ace-king-queen in the dummy. "So a squeeze is a situation in which the opponents have to throw away winning cards in their hands because they have to play a card to every trick the declarer plays from his long suit—in this case the run of spades. Since they don't have spades, they must throw other cards. What cards are they going to pitch? This is called a squeeze."

He demonstrated by playing all the spades, forcing East and West to throw away hearts, clubs and diamonds. "Squeezes operate in a lot of different situations, so there's a whole *kama sutra* of different squeeze plays. There are simple squeezes," he said, "like the one at work here," and he concentrated momentarily on coaching the computer through the play of the hand. "But you also have strip squeezes, single-suit squeezes, and double and triple squeezes. There's even something called a backwash squeeze—let your imagination run wild with that."

Zeke was concentrating hard, trying to follow the cards that the East and West hands were throwing away. "I see it. I see what's happening. If they throw away their clubs, the clubs in the declarer's hand will become winners. I get it." He smiled, pleased with his grasp of the concept.

"Anyhow"—Moti hesitated as the computer finished playing out the hand—"as I said, this is an advanced topic. You don't have to learn this technique in advance. It just happens, and you'll start to recognize it when you see it."

"So there are finesses and squeezes. Other types of plays also, I assume?"

"Oh, many. We haven't discussed end-plays. If you think foreplay is fun, you should try scoring an end-play in a bridge game sometime. It will knock off your socks!"

13

"If you would only recognize that life is hard, things would be so much easier for you."

—LDB, *to his daughter Susan, as reported by a family friend.*

❧

ON TUESDAY, EVEN though both Emden and Devereaux ended up voting to convict, at roll call only 65 votes materialized, and Justice Ross retained her seat on the Supreme Court. Senator William Bosch of New Hampshire, a moderate Republican who had joined the impeachment effort early on, reneged at the last moment. When pounced upon afterward by his shaken colleagues, the senator revealed that his 30-year-old second wife threatened to leave him if he voted to convict. The inevitable tabloid headline: *Senator Screws Entire Country So He Can Get Laid*.

Rachel's citizenship case, in the form of *LifeGuardians Inc. v. Chen*, was to be decided on Friday. Zeke didn't think the chief justice would change his mind about recusal, but he also thought he should at least try to persuade him. He called and texted the professor on his private line but did not hear back. He called again on Wednesday, leaving a message that he had information related to the nation's vital interests that the chief justice should know about.

The chief justice returned his call and agreed to meet, but refused to do so in a public place, or in either of their offices.

"Professor," Zeke advised his friend, "you should learn how to play bridge. It will serve you well in your retirement."

"I beg your pardon?" the chief justice replied.

"I've started to play bridge. It's very interesting, actually. I'm taking lessons at a bridge club on Fifteenth Street. They have private instruction rooms. We could meet there for a lesson. Arrive separately."

"Oh, I see. You mean tonight? Let me think for a second. This is a location you recommend?"

"It is." Zeke gave him the address and they agreed on a time. After they hung up, Zeke called Moti and pressed him into meeting that evening for another bridge lesson, for himself and a friend.

*   *   *

Zeke and Moti were already seated at a card table when the chief justice was escorted into the room. They both stood up to greet him.

"I'd like you to meet my cousin, Moti Rivlin" Zeke said. "Moti knows our trade, he's a law professor at GW, but he's also, as it turns out, a terrific bridge teacher. I've learned a lot from him in a very short time." Handshakes were exchanged, and the chief justice dismissed the deputy marshal holding open the door. "I expect to be about fifteen minutes," he said. "No calls or interruptions please." The agent nodded, glanced around the room one more time, and closed the door.

"Professor," Zeke picked up immediately, "Moti is the relative I mentioned who was responsible for your early departure from my house last year, the night of the attack."

"Oh!" The chief justice reached out for Moti's hand again, this time clasping it with both of his, and holding on. "My dear friend, my wife and I are forever in your debt."

"Sir, you understand this was not my personal action," Moti protested. "I am part of a team of people that has been working to protect you. I was chosen to be the contact person because I happen to be a cousin of your good friend, but there are many other people involved—dozens."

"The experience has turned me into a student of Zionism. I've become fascinated with some of the early writers, Ahad Ha'am and others. But aside from that, please convey our most sincere thanks to your team. We are very moved by the efforts that have been made on our behalf."

"I will relay your message to my colleagues." Moti motioned for them all to take a seat at the table, where the bridge paraphernalia had been removed to make room for a pitcher of water and an inverted stack of plastic cups.

"Professor," Zeke joined in, "it's not been reported, it *cannot* be reported, but I want you to know that the attack at FedEx Field last Sunday, where I was sitting with Rachel and Judge Hurtig—we were saved again by Moti and his team. Without his intervention, we could easily have been killed."

"My god!" the chief justice blurted out. "I've been reading every detail of the attack. Nothing like that has been in the news. What did you do?" he asked, turning to Moti.

"The first drone to arrive at the stadium, the one that exploded over the field, was a Mossad action," Moti said. "It was a pre-emptive effort to get them to stop the game."

"Ahhh . . ." the chief justice exhaled, nodding slowly. "That's when they moved you off the field. And right after that is when they suspended the game. I'm very impressed."

"It is good that you are impressed," Moti said, "but as I have explained to Zeke, I will deny any knowledge of these events, and also this conversation. Nothing we say here can be discussed outside this room."

"I've addressed this with the chief justice," Zeke said, looking first at the professor and then at Moti. "I believe we're all on the same page."

"We are," the chief justice said, "and I want to reiterate my appreciation for all you've done. At the same time, you'll understand I can't help but ask the obvious question: why these threats are not being addressed by American agencies? The last I checked Israel and the U.S. were allies, on very good terms, especially in the area of security cooperation. This is all taking place on American soil. What am I missing here?"

"Mr. Chief Justice," Moti replied, "the U.S. and Israel continue to be close allies, and on most security matters we share intelligence. But last year we shared some information that ended up in the hands of a U.S. domestic terrorist group called the Action Committee. When we tried to resolve this through normal channels, we discovered that certain individuals in the U.S. security establishment were protecting the Committee and apparently working with it. That is when we started to be more cautious about sharing information, and that's why we decided to approach you directly to warn you about the attack at Senator Sherman's home. It is this group that has been targeting you and Ms. Chen, and also Judge Hurtig."

"Zeke has explained this to me. But if you know of this Committee and have evidence of its illegal activities, why not take this information to the proper authorities?"

"Most of our information," Moti said, "has been obtained illegally as part of a foreign espionage operation. The number of American laws we have broken is too many to count, so we cannot just hand everything over. My superior, who reports to a cabinet minister every day, is working hard to find a way to close down our operation here in D.C., and give you some limited information you can use to build your own case. This is easier to say than to do. Can you imagine the political scandal there would be in both of our countries if this all came out in the open right now?"

Zeke and the chief justice nodded their agreement, and Zeke poured water into plastic cups for all three of them.

"I'm part of a team of 40 people," Moti continued. "We have been working seven days a week for over eight months. We've had some good results so far, but now we must close it down. While we do that, we plead with you to keep your silence. Those who benefited from this operation must do their job, and your job is to never say anything to anyone."

"Mr. Rivlin," the chief justice said, "we are agreed on that point. You don't need to be concerned. Zeke has also told me you believe Associate Justice Ross of my court is involved in this Committee. That is something you are sure of?"

"Our latest information, Mr. Chief Justice, confirms that Walter Ross, Justice Ross's husband, is a member of this Committee. It now appears that Justice Ross agreed to participate in the Committee's on-line forums on certain occasions, as a guest of her husband. She has perhaps lent them advice, or encouragement. We are still trying to analyze data that may reveal more about the relationship there, but we don't currently believe she's a regular participant in the Committee's affairs."

"Moti," Zeke interrupted, "I thought Justice Ross was directly involved in the timing of the drone attack at my house. Has that changed?"

"No. She was involved, but we don't know to what extent. She participated in numerous sessions around the time of the attack. Our best guess now is that the attack on your home was a test. It was the first of six stolen Vulture drones, and they were trying it out to see what it could do. It's possible Justice Ross suggested the target, perhaps informally through her husband, or during one of the forum sessions she joined as a guest."

The chief justice sat quietly for some moments. Zeke refilled everyone's water cups.

"Shall I assume, then, that this is the matter of vital national interest that you wanted to speak to me about?" the chief justice asked Zeke.

"It is."

"And what are you advising that I do? What action shall I take? We can't talk to anyone about this. As far as I can tell this is a fantastic story that appears to be true, but there's nothing we can do about it."

"You can start by not recusing yourself," Zeke replied, "and voting tomorrow to affirm Rachel's citizenship."

"And how would that remedy any of the problems you've just described? How will involving myself in *LifeGuardians* do anything other than make the court look more partisan than it already does?"

Zeke lowered his voice, trying to mask the tremble that was starting to emerge. "Sir, a member of your court is engaged in a criminal conspiracy to murder a presidential candidate, and failing that, to prevent her from running through an abuse of judicial power. By recusing yourself you are abetting her acts."

"I ask again, how will my participation in tomorrow's vote do anything to address Justice Ross's criminal actions?"

"It will deprive her of a victory."

"That sounds like a political motivation."

"When you follow the rules, and the opposition doesn't, who do you think is going to win?"

"Zeke, I am not a politician. I am not trying to win anything, and there is no contest going on. I'm a judge. I'm doing my job as best as I can under trying circumstances. No one wants Ross gone more than I, but surely you can see tomorrow's vote will have no impact on whether she remains on the court. The two matters are unrelated."

"So you're prepared to let Rachel's candidacy go?"

"I am. I remind you it was my idea to begin with. I am no less disturbed at this turn of events than you are. Yet you seem convinced that I am the only one who can fix the problem here. What about you? Can't you step up to the plate?"

Zeke gulped hard. He had a flash memory of Professor Salo-Baron asking him a question in his constitutional law class at Columbia twenty-three years earlier. Then, as now, he had no idea what the *question* was, much less the answer.

He turned to look at Moti, and then back to the chief justice. "Maybe if you identify the plate, I'll let you know whether or not I can step up to it."

"You see no alternate path for yourself in this situation? You could be a hero here, to Rachel and to the nation, but I can see it's the farthest thing from your mind."

Zeke summoned his most puzzled and helpless look, and threw up his hands.

"Run for president! Get in the race! Pick up her delegates and beat them at their own game! If you're elected, she'll be your chief of staff, she'll be running it all anyhow. She can keep up the campaigning just as she's doing now; you can be a figurehead candidate."

Zeke felt dizzy. Heat began to rise through his collar. His powers of rational thought and analysis, usually abundant, now seemed to be hovering in a nearby imaginary cloud that he stared at with a kind of disembodied horror.

The chief justice persisted. "You've not considered this at all, have you?"

"Professor, I have never given serious thought to running for president. Why would I consider it now?"

"Because now the circumstances are different."

"How is that?"

"You're engaged! Your future wife is running for president and is being treated very unjustly in a system being manipulated by partisan zealots. You're in a position to support her, to turn the tables on her enemies, to regain control for the good guys! Why are you so reluctant to do what so obviously needs to be done?"

"Professor, I'm listening to you. I hear you." He stared his friend down. "I want you to know that. Now, I ask you the same courtesy: listen closely. I've *never* had an interest in electoral politics. The Senate thing was a fluke, I never should have agreed to it. You know who I am," he gestured with open hands to demonstrate he was hiding nothing. "I'm not a politician. This is not me."

"That's why this situation is perfect for you. Your fiancée already has everything set up. All the groundwork—the organization, the fundraising—has already been done. You could just pick up her campaign where she leaves off and continue with the same staff, the same scheduling, everything. All you need to do is change out the candidate."

Zeke was close to meltdown. Was it not the Professor who was responsible for precipitating his fiancée's presidential ambitions? Shouldn't he be the one doing everything possible to make it right? He clenched his jaw and focused on restraining himself . . . there was nothing to be gained by going down that path. These may have been the professor's ideas, but he and Rachel were still responsible for their own decisions. He also had asked the chief justice to be counsel to the situation, which is what he was doing.

"Professor," Zeke said, "as always, I am grateful to have your advice." He turned to Moti, who had been watching their exchange like a tennis match. "So, cousin, what do you think?"

Moti grinned and surrendered, holding his hands above the table. "Forgive me, if possible I want to refrain—or abstain, if that is correct to say. I am not a U.S. citizen. I have no standing—except that I have had a very high regard for Professor Salo-Baron, for many years." He turned to the chief justice. "At one point or another I've read all of your major works, in constitutional law and the evolution of equity courts in common law jurisprudence. Some of your books are still part of the curriculum at GW."

"That was a long time ago," the chief justice said, staring into a distant nowhere. "It was such a serene business, writing those books. By comparison with the court, I mean. But," he slapped his thigh and stood up, "that was then, and this is now."

Zeke and Moti followed suit. The chief justice again reached out and held Moti's hand. "I want to repeat our thanks, our appreciation for all that you've done. My wife and I have started to travel recently, and we plan to make a trip to Israel at our next opportunity."

He then turned to Zeke. "And now you, my dear friend, have some thinking to do. I will leave you to it. I'm available to talk if you want, but not about *LifeGuardians*."

"Why am I suddenly feeling trapped?" Zeke looked pained, and tried covering it with a forced smile.

"Oh, my friend," said the professor, "you're not trapped. Trapped is when you've run out of money, or you're completely alone, or your health is shot. You're not trapped—you're unhappy. You want things to be different than they are. But what you're looking for doesn't exist. There's no such thing as an easy path or an ideal job. It all requires sacrifice, it's all about compromise."

After the chief justice left, Moti looked sympathetically at his cousin and shrugged. "I don't know what to say." He sat down while Zeke started pacing.

"Believe me," Zeke said, "this is not the outcome I expected when I arranged this meeting."

Moti kept his silence. He could sense his cousin was trying to concentrate, to comprehend, to regain control of events.

"The professor says I'm not trapped," Zeke said out loud, "so why am I thinking I've got no choice in the matter? Was there any way I could ever have gotten off this train? Am I doomed to run for president?" He turned and faced Moti. "Mossad does all this planning and calculation. Would you take my problem to your team and see if they can figure a way out for me?"

Moti laughed. "Are you serious?"

"No. But I am desperate. Do you have *anything* for me? You're always pulling solutions out of thin air." Zeke refilled his cup from the pitcher and took some sips.

Moti accepted the challenge. He shifted in his chair, folded his arms, and sat thinking. After some moments a slim smile emerged. "Please, could you pass to me one of those teaching tablets," Moti asked, pointing to a docking station on a side table. Zeke complied.

Moti booted the tablet and toggled his screen to the overhead monitor. He then began flipping through a series of bridge deals.

"I must have missed something," Zeke said. "Did I somehow trigger a bridge lesson?"

"*Reh-ga!*" Moti gestured with an upturned bouquet of fingertips, the standard Israeli gesture for *wait a moment*. "I will explain." He finally found what he was looking for and pointed to the monitor. "I don't see a way out for you. I'm sorry, the situation is what it is. But I can illustrate with this bridge hand what your tactical position is. You've been end-played by the chief justice."

"What do you mean?"

"Watch this. This is a deal where south is the declarer, playing in four spades, and they've already progressed through nine tricks. There are four tricks left to play. Good bridge players remember what cards have already been played in each deal, and with other clues they get from the bidding they come up with a mental picture of which four cards each opponent is likely to have in his hand."

"Jesus, how do they do that?"

"By counting, cousin; a combination of counting and memory. Bridge is push-ups for the brain. Anyhow, in an end-play the declarer—the person playing the hand—at some point gives the opponents a trick that they are entitled to win. Here North leads a spade, giving East the king of spades he was always going to win. But now East is on lead and is trapped. He has to lead away from his ace-queen of clubs, allowing North to win the king of clubs. Do you see that?

Zeke was able to follow Moti's narration and remained focused on the deal for a few more moments.

"Do you see the parallel?" Moti asked. "The chief justice has put you on lead and you have no winning play. I know this is not a solution, but this describes your position."

"No fucking kidding," Zeke replied.

Moti shrugged his shoulders, swiped the tablet off and handed it to Zeke, who returned it to its slot in the docking station.

"For what it's worth," Moti said, "in bridge you often don't know an end-play is coming until . . . well, the end, when suddenly you realize you are cornered. My point is that it may have been difficult for you to see this coming."

Zeke's phone began chirping. "That's my emergency ring," he said, patting down his pockets to locate the device. He found it, pushed back from the table and excused himself with a raised index finger. After a whispered, pacing conversation he put the phone away and announced his departure. "There's an emergency committee meeting back on the Hill. My car is waiting." Zeke gathered up his coat and briefcase. "Thanks as always for saving my life."

Moti stood up to accept Zeke's embrace. "Thank you for introducing me to your chief justice. I've been studying his *dossier* for years, but in person it is different. It was an honor to meet him."

"I keep thinking if I hadn't arranged this meeting, I wouldn't be in the position I'm in now."

"There is no profit in the pursuit of history," Moti replied. "My only advice to you is to stay in the present. Stay loose and concentrate." He snatched a canvas backpack from under a side chair. "I'll walk out with you. Tonight is a gym night."

It was dark outside when they emerged from the lobby of the CL Associates building on Fifteenth Street. Zeke was immediately corralled by his Secret Service handlers and hustled into a waiting car.

Moti walked north for two blocks and then turned left onto M street. In the middle of the block he was confronted by two business-suited men, one of whom flashed a U.S. Marshals badge. "Professor Matthew Rivlin?" he asked.

"Perhaps. Who is asking?" Moti shifted his backpack to his left shoulder.

"I am Deputy Marshal Dellacorte, this is Agent Demolay. We're investigating the drone attack at FedEx Field and want you to come with us to answer some questions." He motioned toward a gray government sedan that was double parked at the curb with its rear door ajar.

Moti glanced at Dellacorte's ID. "Vincent Dellacorte," he said, raising his voice a notch, "and Agent Demolay—I know you as Captain Demolay. I am not available to go with you, but I can save us all a lot of time. I know who you are, and you know who I am. You are Action Committee; I am Israeli Mossad. Who has more resources do you think? The vehicle directly across the street that is flashing its lights, this is one of four units that is backing me up. Do you think if you kidnap or kill me you won't personally meet a similar fate within hours, if not minutes? You may know the unofficial slogan of Mossad: *eye for an eye, tooth for a tooth.*"

Dellacorte drew his gun and hustled Moti into the back of the sedan. Demolay ran to the front passenger side, doors slammed and the car sped off, making a screeching fishtail turn onto Sixteenth Street northbound.

*   *   *

When Zeke first arrived at the Senate as a mid-session appointee he started at ground zero in terms of seniority, but an unusual confluence of promotions resulted in his early assignment to the powerful Armed Services Committee, and thence to its Subcommittee on Emerging Threats and Capabilities.

Of all his committee responsibilities ASSETC was his favorite because its oversight portfolio included things he knew about—domestic terrorism, weapons of mass destruction, any large-scale threat to domestic tranquility. In these areas Zeke had extensive practical experience and his legal expertise was on a par with the subcommittee's counsel, a former Justice Department lawyer who made a regular practice of consulting with Zeke before issuing his own opinions.

At one point Zeke was so confident of his ASSETC authority he exceeded it. The subcommittee was holding a public hearing on the terrorist attack at the Boston Pops and Zeke chose the occasion—with no forewarning—to argue that machine guns were weapons of mass destruction that should be regulated under the Patriot Act. "If a radical Islamist detonates a homemade bomb at an outdoor concert and kills three people," Zeke had argued, "that person is labeled a terrorist and is prosecuted under the Patriot Act for using a weapon of mass destruction. Yet when a fourth generation American walks into a Colorado football stadium with a pair of assault rifles and kills 39 people, he not only is *not* prosecuted as a terrorist, but his access to these weapons is defended as a constitutional right. Shouldn't the definition of a weapon of mass destruction be related *in some way* to the number of people it kills?"

This unscheduled riff generated a minor publicity coup for Zeke through two news cycles, but his colleagues on the subcommittee—both Democrat and Republican—were not amused. He had violated the leadership's prerogative to control the agenda of public hearings, and generated substantial pushback from the NRA. If things got out of hand it could affect the senators' fundraising—a cardinal sin. Zeke found himself in the doghouse for many months afterward.

He had participated in perhaps a dozen ASSETC meetings, the majority of which were closed to the public and off-limits to most staffers because of security clearance requirements. Agendas were always developed weeks or even months in advance. This was the first time an emergency session had been called. According to Armin, the president's national security advisor requested it to discuss options currently under review by the president for lifting the ban on massive outdoor public events, which she referred to as MOPES. There would be top-secret testimony from two different Air Force commands.

Since the attack at FedEx Field three days earlier, the entire D.C. Metro area remained under lockdown. Zeke's Secret Service sedan, traveling 25 blocks from Moti's club on Fifteenth Street to the Senate, had to clear multiple checkpoints before being granted access to the Capitol grounds. Once inside the building he was directed to one of the "quiet" meeting rooms on the lower level, which was closed to the press and equipped with counter-surveillance equipment to prevent eavesdropping.

Although his own national security aide, a former Navy captain, had the required clearance to attend, Zeke decided it wasn't necessary. Upon arrival he was pleased to see that most of his peers had also come alone. He counted 22 people in the room: seven senators plus two staff; the subcommittee's counsel and his JAG liaison; the national security advisor and her entourage, plus two Pentagon suits and their aides.

In her opening statement the national security advisor made the administration's case: in the 72 hours since the president announced his two-week ban on MOPES, pressure to rescind it had already been applied *ad summum* by lobbyists for professional and amateur sports, representatives of academia and the NCAA, stadium and arena operators, broadcasters and advertisers, civil liberties advocates, and at least a half-dozen other interest groups. The Super Bowl was in limbo, and the NFL had retained Jones Day's appellate practice to seek a stay of the order from the Supreme Court. It was clear that the ban would not be extended, and may not even survive the full two weeks.

President Grove, however, was not prepared to have another major drone attack reported on his watch, so he asked the Joint Chiefs if the military had any technologies or capabilities not otherwise available on the open market that could be quickly deployed to help defend upcoming MOPES against such attacks. Their answer was yes, and two Air Force officers were on hand to brief the subcommittee on what those capabilities were. The substantive question before the subcommittee boiled down to this: if the president deployed military resources to protect civilian MOPES from terrorist threats, would Congress view this as an infringement of the Posse Comitatus Act,* and if it did, would the subcommittee be willing to draft and sponsor any needed amendments?

Zeke pretended to be listening attentively to the Air Force officers' presentation, but his mind was at least half-occupied by the question of whether or not he should be running for president. He could think of nothing less appealing than spending days on end making the same speeches and responding with packaged phrases to every question at every town hall. In his youth, he had seen an old Robert Redford movie, "The Candidate," in which an aspiring senator is driven to babbling insanity by the relentless grind of the campaign. It was easy to imagine a similar fate for him.

Leaving aside the fundraising, could he really allow himself to be packaged and promoted like a consumer product? He began to feel queasy—the whole notion was repulsive. While his mind might conclude this is what he should do, he could feel his emotional core resisting.

The Air Force presentation concluded. The chairman of the subcommittee, Howell Mosely of Arkansas, thanked the officers and invited questions from his colleagues.

Mosely, in his second Senate term, seemed to Zeke a decent enough public servant. A balding former Walmart executive in his mid-60s, he took the job seriously and worked hard to get it right. In his role as chairman of ASSETC he was always

---

* Posse Comitatus is a Reconstruction era (1878) federal law, updated in 1981, that prohibits the federal government from deploying U.S. military personnel domestically to enforce state laws. Exceptions to the act were made during the modern civil rights era under the authority of the Enforcement Act of 1870, which permits the dispatch of federal troops to quell unchecked violence that prevents citizens from exercising their constitutional rights.

prepared, thorough, usually direct and to-the-point. Zeke knew, however, that Mosely had never quite forgiven him for the machine gun stunt. Because Zeke wasn't running for reelection, his motivations were different from those of most senators. He might veer off at any moment and blow a wide hole in almost anything.

Zeke's peers had several questions, but because there were no reporters present their questions were actual interrogatives; the speechmaking and preening that was standard operating procedure for public hearings was absent. Again Zeke feigned close attention, craning left and right to look at the senators as they asked their questions, and nodding at the NSA and her military colleagues as they gave their answers.

In his mind he returned to his election dilemma. It shouldn't be too hard to analyze. There were only two possible outcomes. If he lost, the whole thing would be over in eleven months or less and he could move on with his life. If he won, where did that path lead? At least four years of nonstop responsibilities: speeches, meetings, crises, decisions, and more speeches. He'd be on the hook 24/7 for 10,000 plutonium warheads. But easy was not what he was looking for. The real question was, if he won, could he do things differently? In order to win you have to play the game, but after you've already won, can't you *then* change the rules?

Could he get rid of the nuclear warheads, or reduce them to some non-insane number?

His reverie was broken by Chairman Mosely. "Senator Sherman," he said, "in light of your personal experience with drones, I'm surprised we've not heard from you. Would you care to add anything?" He gave Zeke an encouraging nod.

Zeke shifted his attention to the chairman and summoned a more genuine-looking smile, pausing several seconds for effect. If he became president, he thought to himself, one thing he would *not* do would be to shovel this kind of political bullshit off to a Senate subcommittee on a Wednesday night at nine o'clock.

"Thank you for your consideration, Mr. Chairman," Zeke finally replied. "I have had my fair share of run-ins with drones over the past year. I have one comment and one question. My comment is that this meeting cannot be about seeking relief from Posse Comitatus. Two years ago in the National Defense Authorization Act, at the administration's request, Congress restored exceptions to Posse Comitatus for acts of terrorism and for immigration enforcement. I know this because I was on the dissenting side of the committee that approved it. The language of the amendment is broad enough for the proverbial truck to drive through. So the administration needs no sanction from ASSETC or anyone else for its proposed actions. That's my comment.

"My question, Madame Advisor, is what is the administration's real reason for bringing us together? Posse Comitatus is a cover story; what's really going on here? *You're among friends; you can tell us.*" Suddenly Zeke was now focused and alert. This was a courtroom tactic he had honed over the years—de-cloaking from nowhere, armed and ready for battle.

The NSA, a stern, petite woman named Roglyn Sunstein whom one would not ordinarily want to cross in a global conflict, sat motionless, her jaw visibly dropped. Zeke could practically hear her inner voice: *things were going so well; who is this asshole?*

Zeke turned to Chairman Mosely, looking for support. The chairman shifted his attention back to Sunstein. "Madame Advisor? Do you have an answer for the senator?"

"Senator Sherman, I'm not aware of any cover story or hidden agenda. My understanding of the reason we're here is that the administration recognizes Congress's sensitivity on the subject of Posse Comitatus and is making a proactive effort to keep you informed, at the earliest stages, when a potential conflict with the act appears on the horizon."

"Madame Advisor, there is no conflict on the horizon. The administration has all the authority it needs under current amendments. I happen to be expert in the field, but this is not a fine legal distinction; any intern in the White House counsel's office would come to the same conclusion. What's your *real* reason for being here?"

"Senator Sherman," Sunstein said, "you seem to be accusing us of ulterior motives. If we have another agenda—other than trying to protect the 22 million Americans who want to attend MOPES events every year—what do you think it is? What do you think it could possibly be?"

Zeke leaned into his microphone and lowered his voice. "Madame Adviser, ordinarily in congressional hearings the committee members ask the questions and the witnesses respond. But I'll check with the chairman." Zeke eyed Mosely with a mischievous grin. "If you want me to answer her question, I will."

"Senator Sherman, please tell me you're not going to relate this somehow to your obsession with assault weapons."

"With machine guns . . . no Mr. Chairman, this has nothing to do with machine guns, but as I said, it also has nothing to do with Posse Comitatus. I think the real reason the administration is here is because they're trying to help out their friends at NASCAR, who will lose hundreds of millions of dollars if they can't find a way to reopen their speedways. Drones could put them out of business for good."

The low-grade chatter that had been buzzing in the background suddenly dissipated, and the room fell silent. Everyone's eyes settled on Zeke.

"Senator Sherman," Mosely said with some caution, "you're

going to need to explain yourself further. Do you have some basis for making this claim?"

"I'm not suggesting there's a *quid pro quo* or anything improper. My only claim is that I have a reasonable explanation for why we're here—something the administration has failed to provide, even though they summoned us. If no one else is curious to know why we're here, I'm happy to stand down."

Mosely leaned forward in his chair to survey his colleagues' reaction. "Your questions will be limited in scope to this inquiry? This isn't leading anywhere else?"

"Mr. Chairman, I assure you my questions will relate only to the subject at hand."

Mosely paused, lifted his eyebrows, and nodded his go-ahead. He then scanned the room and whispered into his microphone, "as a precautionary measure, we recommend you keep your seat belts fastened in case of unexpected turbulence." A chuckle rolled through the room, though Sunstein was not amused. Her glare at Zeke had frozen over.

"Madame Advisor," Zeke began, "you're aware President Grove is a NASCAR fan?"

"Everyone knows the president is a NASCAR fan."

"You're aware that both Admiral Lynch and General Hollingsworth of the Joint Chiefs are NASCAR fans?"

"I know they've attended NASCAR events with the president."

"As have you, Madame Advisor?"

"On two occasions, yes. I'm not a personal devotee, but I was invited by the president so I joined him."

"You've referenced a meeting that took place between the president and the Joint Chiefs on Monday evening, the day after the attack at FedEx Field, to discuss possible deployment of the Air Force at MOPES events. Did you attend this meeting?"

"I did."

"How long did the meeting last?"

"Approximately 25 minutes."

"Was there any discussion or acknowledgment by any participant in that meeting that NASCAR would be a beneficiary of this initiative?"

The NSA covered her microphone with her hand and leaned aside to consult her counsel. After several seconds she returned to provide her response. "I'm going to decline to answer that on grounds of Executive Privilege."

"I'll take that as a yes."

"You may not interpret it as a 'yes,' senator. It's a 'no comment.' It's a privileged conversation."

"I'll move on," Zeke said, making eye contact with Chairman Mosely, who since his successful seat belt quip seemed to be enjoying himself immensely. "Madame Advisor," Zeke continued, "you just mentioned, and I saw it in one of the presentation slides, that public events designated as MOPES will attract upwards of 22 million people next year?"

"That's our estimate, that's correct." One of the NSA's assistants began flipping through a copy of the "TOP SECRET" briefing book that had been distributed, and handed it to her with the relevant page tagged.

"The slide showed, if I'm not mistaken," Zeke said, "that almost a quarter of it is NASCAR attendance: 5.2 million people."

"Yes, I see that."

"So would you agree that if the Administration proceeds with its plan to assign the Air Force to protect MOPES events, about a quarter of the benefit so bestowed would accrue to NASCAR?"

"That is another way of saying the same thing."

"Is that a 'yes,' Madame Advisor?"

"Yes."

"For the record, Mr. Chairman, here's a *third* way to say it. The administration has presented an operating budget of $2.4 billion for this program over three years. If this amount is apportioned per capita to MOPES attendees, we learn that the value of the service the military will be providing at NASCAR events is $200 million per year.

"Madame Advisor, in all your budgeting and planning I don't see any revenue. You're apparently not planning to charge the private sector sponsors of the events that are being protected for either all or a portion of the projected cost. Was this option ever discussed or considered?"

"It was discussed, Senator. The president doesn't view this program as a giveaway to NASCAR or NCAA or the NFL or any other organization that is benefiting from this initiative. He believes it is a legitimate government function to protect the public and its right to assemble peaceably for any reason. Unfortunately the threat from drones can't be effectively met by traditional, state-based law enforcement, or even federal law enforcement. The best technologies available to protect the public from drone attacks happen to be in the hands of the Air Force's Domestic Airspace Command, and the president, in cooperation with Congress, wants to make this happen."

"Madame Advisor, I have only one further question. If I recall correctly, in your opening remarks you stated the president asked the Joint Chiefs if the military had drone protection capabilities not otherwise available on the open market. The presentation you've put together, as far as I've seen, doesn't address this at all. What is available on the open market?"

"Senator, we're planning to deploy modified AWACS aircraft over MOPES events. The software to be used is highly proprietary. We included no information because there is nothing comparable in the open market."

"And you're certain there's no other way to effectively

protect MOPES events from drone attacks—AWACS is the only way?"

"The Joint Chiefs are recommending it because they see it as the best, most reliable solution, and the only one that can be deployed in an immediate time frame. We're dealing with tens of thousands of lives at each event; we're not looking for half-measures."

"We should all, then," Zeke looked to the left and right, to include his colleagues, "take this as an object lesson in how isolating a job it must be for the Joint Chiefs, how sheltered and cut off they are from the real world." He returned his attention to Sunstein. "Madame Advisor, if you would be so good as to inform the Joint Chiefs about a company in Israel called Rafael Advanced Defense Systems—they go by the acronym RADS. They manufacture the Iron Dome antimissile system, and they just announced a scaled-down version intended for rapid deployment at temporary venues. It's been modified to track drones and aircraft flying as low as 800 feet off the ground."

After many seconds of silence, the room began to stir. Several of his peers were staring at him, their eyebrows up. Sunstein became a study in contained steam. Zeke felt sorry for her staff; when it was all over they would surely be eviscerated. One of them was already online, trying to find out what he was talking about. "Senator," she finally replied, "I'm not sure at all what you're describing would provide the same protection as our AWACS umbrella, or even that it would be less expensive."

"My point precisely, Madame Advisor. You don't know. Because you've not really investigated the open market, have you?"

Sunstein looked beaten. Her back was bowed slightly; her energy gone. "Senator, I will relay this information to the Joint Chiefs. May I tell them how you came to be aware of it? Do you happen to subscribe to Jane's *Land Warfare Platforms*?

"I read it in *The Economist*."

This produced general merriment around the room. Chairman Mosely winked at him. Even Sunstein seemed relieved at the break in tempo.

"Senator Sherman, do you have more questions?" Mosely asked.

"No, Mr. Chairman. I'd like to conclude, if I may, by summarizing for the record why I think the administration called us here. I'm not asserting proof of anything. I'd just like to lay out the most likely explanation for all the known facts. May I proceed?"

"Please do, Senator," Mosely replied. "By all means."

"I'm guessing that Monday morning, the day after the FedEx Field attack, NASCAR officials learned that even if they got the president, or the Supreme Court, to rescind the MOPES ban, insurance for unprotected MOPES events would no longer be available at any price. NASCAR is a privately held company; the liability would be too great to go uninsured.

So they called their friend the president to see if there was anything he could do. He spoke to the Joint Chiefs Monday evening, and over the next two days Operation MOPES was hatched. In the process they realized if they took this action unilaterally, they might well be accused of giving special treatment to NASCAR—as the NSA pointed out, everyone knows the president's a NASCAR fan. So they looked for some way to get Congress's imprimatur added, and that's why we were called here tonight. The issue with Posse Comitatus is a pretext; the administration wants Congress on board with this program for political cover."

There were sighs and nods of understanding up and down the dais. Senators began packing their briefcases and checking their phones.

"Madame Advisor," Senator Mosely addressed Sunstein,

"if this in any way relates to why we are here, please inform the president that ASSETC is not available to provide political cover for his proposal. If this is not why we were called into emergency session, if the administration's real goal is to devise a way to protect the 22 million Americans who attend MOPES every year, we invite you back to consult with us—preferably during regular business hours—when you have complete information about available options and costs. This meeting is adjourned."

14

"A man who practices law—who aspires to the higher places of his profession—must keep his mind fresh. It must be alert and he must be capable of meeting emergencies—must be capable of the tour de force."

—LDB, Letter to William Harrison Dunbar,
February 2, 1893.

~

FRIDAY AT NOON the Supreme Court announced its decision. In a four-four tie, it left standing the 11th Circuit Appeals Court ruling that Rachel Chen was not a "natural born citizen" as required by Article II of the Constitution, and therefore she could not run for president.

By two o'clock the small crowd that had started out the day protesting in front of the Supreme Court building swelled to over 5,000 people. At 3 p.m., following the Twitter lead of Judge Hurtig, tens of thousands of women left work and began streaming towards the east end of the National Mall. The Capitol Police were caught off guard. There had been no advance notice, there were no barriers or personnel in place, and traffic around Capitol Hill came to a standstill. The Democratic leadership granted interviews on the Capitol steps with the massive protest as a backdrop, denouncing the court's decision as a stepchild of

Bush v. Gore—an unsolicited and unjustified judicial intrusion into presidential politics. Marina O'Leary, the House Minority leader, made a public plea to restaurants in the downtown area to open their bathrooms to the protesters.

There was no podium, no public address system and no program of speakers, yet the crowd—which had swelled to an estimated 90,000—responded pretty much as a cohesive group to cues and instructions from Judge Hurtig's Twitter feed. At dusk the temperature sank into the high 20s, snow flurries appeared, and Hurtig called it off. She Tweeted her thanks to all who joined in, asked everyone to "stand by for future action," and put in a plug for her upcoming appearance on *Women in Charge*, which she was hosting that evening at 8 p.m.

The Court's decision and the spontaneous protest were the lead stories on the evening news. Several Democratic pundits framed the outcome as a consequence of the failure to convict Ross in the Senate the previous week; others simply lamented that the Court had bankrupted itself with the ruling. Some Republicans supported the ruling, but not all. Senator Eleanor Dottin, the Chairwoman of the Senate Judiciary Committee, was scathing in her condemnation. "When a court ignores facts and common sense," she said, "in order to produce a patently partisan ruling, it loses all credibility as an impartial institution."

The press clamored for a reaction from Rachel's campaign. She drafted a statement she planned to read at a 9 p.m. press conference, and e-mailed it to her senior staff and Zeke for comments. In his office at the Hart Building, Zeke read it and immediately called her on her private line.

"I got the e-mail," he said. "I don't think you should make a public statement right away. I would give it another day—wait at least until tomorrow morning."

"Why?"

"The protest, the public response, is a good thing. Let it run its course. If you get in the picture now it will divert attention away from the protests. We want the court to reap the full measure of what it has sown. There's no law that says you must respond tonight."

"Okay. That's thoughtful. I'll consider it. Anything else?"

"Yes. When you do speak, I think it would be a good idea to acknowledge the chief justice's recusal, and educate the public about the need for all justices to adhere to these same standards of impartiality. It's a teachable moment if ever there was one. At the same time it would show support for the chief justice, which is what he needs right now."

"Zeke, this is all very good. Suddenly you take an interest in my campaign. It's a wonderful gesture, but your timing is a bit off—it being over and all."

"I've been thinking about that also."

"What do you mean?" Rachel asked.

"What if I joined your campaign as the candidate? I'm a U.S. citizen. I've got my birth certificate—I was born in West Virginia."

There was a long pause and then nervous laughter. "Did you just say what I think you said?"

"We could get married and run as a couple. It would be romantic."

More silence, but this time no laughter. "You're serious?" she finally asked.

"You'll be the chief of staff. You'll run the country while I smile and wave to the people."

"I can't believe it," Rachel said, her tone one of utter disbelief. "After running away from it as hard as you can, for as long as you have, suddenly you're going to change course. Why?"

"This is the professor at work again. I know that takes away all the gallantry, but this is not a scheme that could ever have arisen spontaneously in my own mind."

Rachel didn't respond, but Zeke could practically hear her cogitation through the phone. He held back.

"It might be his suggestion," she finally replied, "but you're the one who has to do the job. You're sure this is the way you want to go?"

"I've come to terms, in my own mind, with the campaign. It's a finite period of time—I can keep my sights set on that and I'll get through it. If we win, though, I'll be counting on you to do the heavy lifting. Think of Eisenhower—I want to be like President Eisenhower. I want to play golf in the afternoon. Is it a deal?"

"Zeke, you hate golf!"

"I know, but I've been learning to play bridge. My Israeli cousin introduced me to it. Fascinating game. I'll teach you how to play."

"Why don't you meet me in my hotel room," Rachel replied, her voice now a rasping whisper, "and give me my first lesson. After that we have a lot to talk about."

"Grrr . . ." Zeke growled quietly into the phone. "Give me a few minutes to finish up here and I'll be on my way."

"I'm on the top floor. The Secret Service will direct you."

He hung up and buzzed Armin on the intercom. "Cancel the rest of my day. I'm going to head over to the Hilton to help Rachel with her statement."

"You want to leave now? Should I notify the Secret Service?"

"I'll be ready to go in five minutes."

"No problem. We'll handle the appointments." After Armin clicked off Zeke retrieved an away bag and his overcoat from a closet. He returned to his desk to find his phone chirping and dancing on the glass tabletop. It was Moti.

Zeke reminded himself before answering: *no details over the phone.* "Good evening, cousin," he said. Good to hear from you as always."

"I'm leaving for Israel tonight and I wanted to say good-bye in person," Moti said, his voice sounding tense. "Can we meet as soon as possible? It's important."

"Right now's not good," Zeke answered. "I'm leaving for Rachel's campaign hotel in a few minutes, where among other things I hope to bid and make a grand slam."

"*Mazal Tov.* Congratulations. Enjoy. I'm on my way to the airport. If you tell me what location this is, which hotel, I can meet you in the lobby for a few minutes. Let me buy you a drink."

"Okay, it sounds like you have a plan. Rachel's campaign is at the Washington Hilton on Connecticut Avenue, north of DuPont Circle. There's a lobby bar next to the concierge desk. I can be there in a half hour."

"Thank you. I know this is a busy time for you. I'll only keep you for a few minutes."

*　*　*

When Zeke arrived at the hotel he found Moti already seated in a lobby armchair holding a glass of wine. As he approached he realized his cousin was wearing a grim look he had never seen before. Something was different—something was wrong.

"Senator," Moti called out, remaining seated. "Thank you for meeting me here for a few minutes." He raised his glass at Zeke and gestured for him to sit in an adjacent chair. The area was low-lit and piano music filtered down from overhead speakers.

Zeke lowered himself into the overstuffed chair, noticing only now that Moti's left arm was in a sling, and his glass-bearing right hand was wrapped in a bandage. He had small cuts on his face and a suture strip on his forehead. "My god, what has happened?!" Zeke asked. "Were you mugged?"

"More or less. After I left you last night, on my way to the gym, I was approached by representatives of the Action Committee. Fortunately they were thinking clearly and things did not escalate." He flapped his damaged left arm. "I suspect two of them are less mobile than I am right now."

His eyes adjusted to the dim light, Zeke could now see his cousin's movements were stiff and tentative. "You're in pain—I am so sorry. What happened?"

"This is again a situation where it would be best if you do not hear details. All you need to know is that there was a standoff, and they decided not to call Mossad's bluff. I was the only casualty on our side, and I'm feeling much better already with this glass of wine. As you know I never drink, so this makes it almost fun for me."

"Have you seen a doctor?"

Moti gestured at his bandaged hand. "Of course. I'm fine. This could have been much worse. Some Mossad enemies don't care if they die and a threat of mutually assured destruction is like an invitation to a party. Americans tend to be more rational."

"Of course I understand now why you're leaving," Zeke said, "but we are very sorry to see you go. We've benefited so much from your presence—Rachel and I, not to mention the chief justice. When will we see you again?"

"Unfortunately, never. If things go according to plan, I will be dead in a few days."

"What?!" Zeke blurted out. "What are you saying?"

"It's okay," Moti said in a lowered, calming tone. "It's not exactly that, but not so different either. I will explain."

"Please do. This can't be good."

Moti cleared his throat. "You know for twenty years I have been making my career as a law professor. About three years ago I started to spend more time with Mossad, and this last operation with you and the chief justice has pushed me out into the open. My academic cover is in serious jeopardy. The bottom line is that my double life is no longer viable. It's too risky. I'm going to officially 'die' in an accident that Mossad will arrange, and after some plastic surgery I will come back with a new identity."

"I'll never see you again as my cousin?"

"My life as *Matityahu Ephraim Rivlin* is coming to an end in a few days. Even if our paths cross you will not recognize me, and I won't approach you. The risks are too many."

Zeke splayed back in his chair, limp and speechless.

"Part of the reason we are doing this," Moti continued, "involves you. Remember on the phone I said it was important for us to meet before I left?"

Zeke nodded.

"This is the reason. I must ask you now to pay close attention. This is important."

"Uh-oh." Zeke moaned.

"Have you decided if you are going to run for president?" Moti asked.

"Not finally. I raised the idea with Rachel on the phone. I'm headed upstairs to talk to her about it after we finish here."

"The point I want to make is that if you run for president and it's reported that your Israeli cousin who you meet at football games is a Mossad agent posing as an academic at a U.S. law school, your campaign is toast. Israel's relationship with America is toast. My career is toast." He made an exploding gesture with his hands. "Everything will be toasted."

"No kidding," Zeke said quietly. "That would not be good."

"No it would not," Moti agreed.

"What are the chances this could happen?" Zeke asked.

"The technical answer to your question is 25 percent. Part

of our team does risk assessment, and that's their current estimate."

"Wow." Zeke shifted in his seat and ran his fingers through his hair a couple of times. "Well, I could also see this as good news. This may be the excuse I need to *not* run."

"Don't make your conclusion so fast," Moti said. "We've planned things so that if the story does come out, you'll look like a hero. You'll be protected. You won't have to lie about anything."

Zeke was lost. "I'm not following you," he said.

"If my cover gets exposed and your association with me is questioned, we want you to respond in a specific way. Describe me as your cousin and close friend from university days who called out of nowhere, revealed his connection to Mossad, and warned you about the attack on the chief justice at your house. You'd known me for twenty years, we're blood relatives, so you trusted me—and I turned out to be right. After that, when I came to you with the warning about the football game, you had every reason to believe me. Are you following so far?"

"I think so," Zeke said.

"Israel will claim that I acted on my own, outside of the chain of command, and that I was motivated by loyalty to my family. Very conveniently, by the time this all comes out, I'll be dead, so there will be no way to refute the story."

"Okay, I think I see it. Now I'm getting it."

"In order for this to work, all you have to do is tell the truth. The only thing that needs to be finessed is my acting alone; but who else on my team have you met? As far you know I *am* working alone."

"In order for this to work, you have to be dead?" Zeke asked.

"If I was alive I would have to be prosecuted. I broke dozens of laws. I'd be in jail for the rest of my life."

"So you're going to be fake-killed and then come back as a different person?"

Moti nodded, looking rueful. "If you think you were end-played, look at my situation—this is the ultimate end-play."

"But you'll still be alive. Who will you be? And why can't we stay in touch?"

"It's not a good idea. This has been done before. Trust me. We need to say our good-bye's now."

Zeke's breath went away. His heart pounded and tears began to well up. "I'm not *part* of the reason you're losing your identity, I'm the *entire* reason you're losing it. I do not accept this . . . this is not something I want to be responsible for. What if I don't run for president? Will that change anything?"

"No. There are other factors here that I can't begin to describe. In any scenario, my identity must come to an end."

"So this is it?" Zeke asked. "I'm just going to say good-bye to you now and it's all over? I'll never see you again?"

"I'm afraid so. However I have for you this going-away gift." He opened his palm on the table to reveal a small key-chain flash drive, which he then dangled between two fingers. "This is the backup plan. It contains technical proof that links Walter Ross's home computer to the Action Committee's phantom cloud forum."

"The backup plan? You need to help me out here . . . the primary plan being . . . ?"

"Plan A we discussed Monday night. You're going to invite the Capitol Police into your senate office. They're going to find bugs that should lead them to the Action Committee and its forum participants, including Walter Ross. If that plan doesn't work for any reason, if after a month nothing has happened, this digital file will do the same thing." Moti handed the flash drive to Zeke. "Get it to a news source—anonymously is okay, but best to hand it over in person if there's a reporter you trust."

Zeke drew back in his chair. His eyes were wide. "Moti, I am in awe. And again in your debt. Whoa!" His jaw dropped.

"I suggest you to make a copy as soon as you can," Moti continued. "There's no password. Keep a back-up in a safe place. These things are so easy to lose."

"A reporter will know what to do with this?"

"It's not all technical; there's a narrative also. Once they've verified everything with experts they will publish it, and this will draw the attention of authorities."

A waitress approached. "Sorry, nothing for me," Zeke said. "I'm leaving in a couple of minutes." She asked Moti if he wanted anything else.

"Nothing more for me," Moti said. "Does this cover it?" He brandished a $20 bill, and declined her offer to bring change.

"Moti, I'm still having a lot of trouble with this," Zeke said as he stowed the tiny device in his billfold. "I don't want to be responsible for even your faked death. God forbid your family should think you've died! Will your family know you're alive?"

"What I'm supposed to say now is that I am not allowed to discuss it, and you are to assume that everyone, including my family, will think I have died in an accident. But on my own—I am *not* authorized to say this—I'm telling you that my immediate family will know I'm okay. Like you, however, they will deny any knowledge of my second life, and I'll never be able to come home or be seen in public with them. You must never acknowledge to anyone at all—including your mother— that you know."

"So there's going to be a funeral?"

"I've already said too much. Leave it at that. You can't discuss this with anyone." He lifted his eyebrow. "*Hay-vanta?*"

"Yes, I understand," Zeke replied. "Still, I'm very opposed to this. There's no other way?"

"Cousin, think about what's been accomplished. It's not been a total success, but we've saved a lot of lives. Some sacrifices have to be made. I'm making mine, and we are asking you now to do your part to help close up this operation with no loose ends. Will you help us?"

"Of course. Of course I will."

"Then the plan requires that you not reveal to anyone, for any reason, that you know that I'm still alive. You'll do that? I'm asking you to do that."

"Yes."

"Good. You also will never acknowledge that I was acting under orders from Mossad?"

"Yes. I understand. I will remember that."

"Excellent."

"Explain again," Zeke persisted, "why you can't be in touch with me after the dust has settled. I can handle the new identity thing. It's weird, but I could handle it. You can't tell me where you're going to be?"

"I don't know myself. I'll probably end up with a desk job somewhere overseas. I'm going to miss the academic life. I was very happy as a law professor. But not all is lost—I have ten months of vacation to start! I've not taken time off for four years."

"What are you going to do, travel?"

"My first business is to find a steady girlfriend or maybe, if I'm lucky like you, a wife. I haven't dated for several years because I didn't want to expose anyone to my work."

"I noticed. I'm sure that wasn't easy."

"I played bridge instead. But now I can play bridge during the day, play with my girlfriend at night—*I'll be having sex all the time!*"

"I'm happy for you, cousin," Zeke replied with faux enthusiasm. "But I can't help but wonder . . . if you're not around, who's going to save our lives?"

Moti's smartphone chimed. He swiped it open, consulted it briefly, and returned it to his pocket. "My team is leaving now," he said. "You will need to look elsewhere for security. Even if I wasn't going to be dead, I couldn't be your protector forever."

"I understand that. But if you were alive I could at least consult with you. After what we've been through, I don't trust anyone else."

"I can offer you one last consultation. My ride to the airport will be here in five minutes."

"This is like a bad dream." Zeke said. "How can this be happening?"

Moti remained impassive. "It is what it is. I can imagine far worse outcomes for everyone involved."

"That is very true." Zeke paused, thinking of the attack on his home. "We will not forget what you've done for us—me, Rachel, the chief justice, Judge Hurtig. We are all in your debt."

"Again, this was not just me—there is my team. But that's our little secret. The official story is that I acted alone, outside the chain of command." Moti drained his wine glass and stood up, brushing off the front of his slacks.

"Of course," Zeke said as he rose from his chair to say goodbye—forever—to the man who had been keeping him alive for the past five months. One last consultation: what question should he ask? It was a classic case of *you do not know what you do not know.* "Since you're leaving, and I'll never see or speak to you again, do you have any general advice for Rachel and me, about our security? *Ahl regel ah-chat*—on one foot, as you say?"

"Hmmm." Moti weighed the question with a brief nod and an analytical frown. "If you left the presidential race I assume Rachel would return to her television show? She would continue to be a public figure?"

"Oh, I think that's a safe assumption. She's not suddenly going to become a wallflower."

"Well then, cousin, I know this is not what you want to hear, but my advice to you is to run for president. I can think of no safer place for you and your family than the White House."

- End -